The Fatal First Edition

Meadowfield Mysteries
Book 3

Agatha Frost

Pink Tree Publishing LTD

WANT TO BE KEPT UP TO DATE WITH AGATHA FROST RELEASES? *SIGN UP THE FREE NEWSLETTER!*

www.AgathaFrost.com

You can also follow **Agatha Frost** across social media. Search 'Agatha Frost' on:

Facebook
Twitter
Goodreads
Instagram

Also by Agatha Frost

1. **Pancakes and Corpses**

<u>Claire's Candles</u>

Head to Northash to join Claire as she solves mysteries from her candle shop…

Chapter 1
The First Page

Ellie Swan stepped back from the column she'd just finished papering in Meadowfield Books, tilting her head to study the fragments of text now permanently fixed to the surface. The pages for the wallpaper had come from books too damaged to save. Spines cracked beyond repair, pages water-stained and wrinkled, but she couldn't bear to simply throw them away. Now, upcycled snippets of adventures and romances wound their way up the column like ivy, giving new life to old stories.

"Is that what I think it is?" Granny Maggie peered at the column, adjusting the reading glasses that hung perpetually on a chain around her neck. "That particular shade of heartbreak could only be Jane Austen."

"*Pride and Prejudice*," Ellie confirmed, brushing paste from her hands and wincing as a glob threatened her clean jumper; a rare sight, given her usual uniform of paint-splattered hoodies. The 'scruffy decorating clothes' section of her wardrobe now took up three drawers and an overflowing washing basket. "The copy was falling apart, but I couldn't bear to bin it. That's the scene where Sallybeth reads Darcy's letter. My favourite part."

"Mine too," Maggie said, running her fingers over the words. "Though the real romance has always been in the margins. All those pencilled notes from readers over the years, each finding their own Darcy between the lines."

Oliver appeared from behind the newly installed coffee station by the till, arranging his famous sweet loaves on a wallpaper-pasting table by the window. The Giggling Goat's owner—and Ellie's half-brother—had outdone himself with the spread: lemon drizzle, chocolate marble, and his new lavender-and-honey loaf, arranged like delicate treasures on vintage cake stands.

"If anyone asks," he announced, adjusting a slice of banana bread that dared to be slightly askew, "I absolutely did not stress-bake three extra loaves at four this morning, so, you're welcome."

"Only three?" Joey, the handyman, teased from where he was scribbling book quotes from a long list Ellie had put together on paper coffee cups. "Losing your touch, babe."

"Stress-baking is a *precise* science," Oliver shot back with a grin. "Though I notice you didn't complain when I brought the test batches to your building site yesterday."

Maggie beamed at her grandson. "The village would riot if we didn't have your baking at the launch."

"That's assuming I'll have any customers left by the end of the week with these prices," Oliver said, squinting at the little chalkboard menu perched atop the new bean-to-cup coffee machine. "You're practically poaching my regulars with these bargains."

"I doubt we'll be matching your quality," Ellie replied, patting him on the back. "Coffee's just a side thing for us. You're welcome to start selling books if you want to even the playing field."

"I'll overlook it, this once, but any cheaper and you'll be giving them away for free." He planted the menu back and gave the machine a fond pat. "I opened my shop with this beauty five years ago. She's served me well, and she'll do the same for you, if you treat her right." He pointed an accusatory finger at Ellie. "And I'll be checking your latte art to make sure you're not copying my designs. It's bad enough you've ordered your beans from the same supplier."

"I don't think we could achieve your barista heights even if we tried," Maggie replied, peering over her glasses at the coffee machine as if it might leap off the counter and bite her. "Does it come with instructions?"

"No," Oliver replied, and that was that.

With minutes to go until the shop opened and nothing left to do, Ellie leaned against the counter, marvelling as morning light streamed through the freshly cleaned windows of Meadowfield Books. The sunlight caught the stubborn glitterdust that still danced in the air, defying their best efforts to banish it. They'd waited so long for this morning, but so far, everything felt ordinary. Yet it wasn't. How could it be? The building work was done, and today was *the* day.

The old shop was almost unrecognisable from the near-derelict shell it had been just months ago. The peeling wallpaper and rotting floorboards were gone, replaced by warm wooden shelves and inviting reading nooks nestled between the stacks. The musty scent of neglect had vanished, replaced by the comforting aromas of coffee, old paper, and fresh paint. Armchairs were dotted around the room, and a snug attic hideaway waited upstairs, promising quiet escapes for eager bookworms.

Ellie's heart fluttered as she glanced through the window at the small crowd gathering outside. This was it—the moment they'd been racing towards since the first wallpaper scraper had hit the wall. Yet, despite the anticipation, it all felt strangely surreal. She pinched her wrist lightly, half-expecting to wake up from yet another stress dream. She'd had so many lately. Visions of empty shelves ablaze or, worse, her hands inexplicably turned into paintbrushes, smearing globs of colour across pristine pages. But no, the sharp press of her nails into her wrist confirmed it: she was wide awake.

"I can't believe we actually did it," she murmured, more to herself than anyone else.

"Believe it," Maggie said, fussing with a stack of vintage Agatha Christies in the window display. The well-worn books, their spines softened by time, sat alongside brass candlesticks and a pair of Victorian reading glasses they'd picked up from the antique shop down the street. "Did you ever doubt we would?"

"About twelve times a day," Ellie admitted, her hand hovering over the door handle. She turned to her grandmother, suddenly overwhelmed. "Is there really nothing left to do?"

Maggie stepped closer, adjusting Ellie's collar poking out of her khaki jumper with gentle hands. "Remember what you'd say as a girl, curled up in that window seat?"

"That one day I'd live in a bookshop?"

"That one day you'd help people find their next favourite story." Maggie's eyes glistened as she tucked a stray strand of Ellie's chestnut hair behind her ear. Her touch was warm, familiar, and for a moment, Ellie felt like that little girl again, curled up in the window seat with a book and a dream. "Took the scenic route, but here we are. So, shall we get this show on the road?"

"Shouldn't there be a ribbon to cut?" Oliver called, leaning against the counter with his arms crossed, a smirk playing on his lips. "This is the grand re-opening of a beloved local institution, not a *Slimming World* meeting at the village hall. Where are the fireworks and fire-breathing jugglers? Where's the pizzazz?"

Maggie rolled her eyes but couldn't suppress a grin. "Surviving the makeover was ceremony enough, don't you think? Besides, we've got books, coffee, and good company. What more could anyone want?"

Ellie's stomach churned as she glanced at the door holding back the small crowd of familiar locals. "I thought you never doubted it?" she asked, her voice wavering slightly.

Maggie's expression softened, and she reached out to squeeze Ellie's shoulder. "Touché, dear. But doubting and doing aren't mutually exclusive, are they? We doubted, we did, and here we are." She placed the key firmly in Ellie's palm and curled her fingers around it. "Your turn, Manager."

Gulping down her nerves, Ellie turned the key. The lock clicked, smooth and satisfying, and she pulled the door open. The new bell chimed, a soft, melodic sound that seemed to sing out their triumph, as the first customers flooded in.

"About time!" Sylvia from the cheese shop next door exclaimed, barging in with her usual gusto. She thrust a wheel of Brie at Ellie. "For the occasion, naturally. Now, let's see this marvel of yours!"

Ellie laughed, the tension in her chest easing as Sylvia barrelled past, her floral scarf trailing behind her like a banner.

Zara from the gift shop stepped in next, her rainbow layers brightening the room like a burst of sunlight. She paused just inside the doorway, her eyes widening as she took in the transformed space. "You have done a remarkable job, ladies," she said, her voice tinged with awe. "It is unrecognisable."

"And yet it *feels* the same," Ellie's Auntie Penny

chimed in, twirling on the spot as she took in the shelves. "Oh, it's lovely. Wouldn't you agree, Carolyn?"

Carolyn, Penny's sister and Ellie's mother—and Maggie's least favourite relation—grumbled her agreement as she stepped inside, her downcast gaze sweeping the room. She lingered near the doorway, her arms crossed tightly over her chest, as if unsure whether to fully commit to the moment.

"Shabby chic," she said finally, and Ellie decided to take the observation as a compliment despite her mother's clenched jaw.

But Granny Maggie refused to react to her never-was daughter-in-law. As more villagers stepped inside, filling the once-silent shop with chatter, she transformed into her element, weaving between the shelves like she was slipping into a comfortable story she knew back to front, sharing tales about the shop's history with anyone who'd listen.

As more customers flooded in, Joey helped Ellie build a fire in the restored fireplace at the back of the shop, the crackling logs scenting the air. Though it was a warm spring morning, the fireplace was the soul of the shop. Meadowfield Books wouldn't be Meadowfield Books without its beating heart.

"Good things come to those who wait," Oliver said, leaning down to kiss her on the cheek. "All those meltdowns in my café... worth it?"

"We'll see," Ellie said.

Oliver laughed, ruffling her hair. "Own it, sis. You've nailed it. You filled this place up."

"We've only just begun," Ellie said, looking around the bustling shop. "And I'd still be staring at damp walls without you, Joey."

"Anytime," Joey said, flashing his trademark grin and a wink. "Crack or creak, call and I'll have you back in shape in no time." He pushed up from the fireplace, patting a polished timber beam overhead. "These old buildings don't like to stay pristine for long."

"If we had any sense we'd knock the whole village down and start again," Oliver exclaimed. "Who wants to live in centuries old houses, anyway?"

"Me?" Ellie replied.

"Yes, well, you've always been the *kooky* sibling. Now, if you'll excuse me." He peeled back his sleeve to squint at his watch. "I have a café to run, and this lot'll be raiding the buffet soon, and when they want a second helping, you send them my way." They glanced at the table, where Auntie Penny was building a mountain of each sample on her straining paper plate. "Joey, free lunch if you're keen. And Ellie," he paused, turning her around, "Smile. You've earned it."

Oliver and Joey slipped out the back as a camera flash blinded her. The local press had captured the moment—Meadowfield Books, reborn like a phoenix from the ashes of a medieval story as old as the building surrounding her. It may have been crumbling and centuries old as her brother pointed out, but now that the old place was singing again, Ellie wouldn't trade it for anything. The photographer paused to check his shot, and Ellie seized the chance to escape to the counter, where Maggie was glowering at the coffee machine.

"You said this contraption was idiot-proof," Maggie muttered, pressing a button that released a hiss of steam. She jumped back, nearly decapitating a bookstack. "My kettle at home has one button, Ellie. *One!*"

"It's simple, really," Ellie insisted, gently nudging her aside. "On, water, grounds. And you steam the milk here. Three steps."

"Three steps closer to madness." Maggie's eyes danced over the dials and knobs. "What's wrong with a simple cuppa?"

"You can still make a cup of tea." Ellie pointed to the hot water button, still coming to grips with the thing herself. "But coffee and books go together." She poured more beans into the compartment at the top, deeply inhaling. "Don't you smell that? It's perfect. Like cream and jam or—"

"*Tea* and reading," Maggie interrupted. "I get your point, and I will admit, it does smell delicious in here. But I'm never going to figure this thing out."

"Where's that woman who used to teach history to hundreds of teenagers everyday?" Ellie nudged her lightly in the ribs with her elbow. "You're not going to be defeated by this caffeine contraption. You'll master it by Friday."

Maggie chuckled. "Reckon there's a *For Dummies* guide in the food section?"

Before Maggie could retreat to the safer territory of

the shadowy book aisles, the doorbell jangled violently. Benjamin Brown bustled through, clutching a leather satchel to his chest like it held government secrets. His round glasses sat askew, and his usually pristine jacket looked slept-in.

"Maggie," he barked, ignoring the festivities. "A word. *Now*."

Maggie's eyebrows shot up, but she nodded, gesturing towards the back room. "I was expecting you earlier."

"There's been a hiccup with the books," Benjamin replied tersely, already striding towards the back. "We must talk now."

Ellie had forgotten all about their launch day event, though she'd never wanted to have Benjamin's romance book launch on the day they opened. Granny Maggie had planned the signing as a surprise and Ellie hadn't been able to pluck up the guts to talk her into arranging it for another day. Manager in name, but the bookshop would always be her gran's.

Ellie moved to follow, but a customer thrust a leather-bound Jane Eyre at her.

"Latte with this? And one of those quote cups for my daughter? I saw some girls carrying them around and they look so cute."

Ellie forced a smile, tracking Maggie's exit over the woman's shoulder. "Thank you. Of course. Latte coming up."

As she fumbled with the coffee beans, Ellie caught

Sylvia's eye. The cheese shop owner was hovering by the cookbooks, ears pricked.

"Sylvia," Ellie whispered, beckoning her over. "Could you…?"

Sylvia didn't even wait for her to finish. "Say no more," she murmured, sidling towards the back room. "I'll be your ears."

"Lifesaver," Ellie said gratefully, turning back to the queue.

Ten minutes later, the back room door burst open. Benjamin stormed out, his cheeks flushed the colour of a prune. "Move!" he snapped at a faraway teen browsing the poetry section.

The door slammed, leaving a startled silence. It didn't last. The buzz resumed, peppered with exchanged glances and raised brows.

Seconds later, Sylvia materialised, quivering with gossip.

"What was that about?" Ellie asked, keeping her voice low.

"He was in quite a state. Something about his books being lost in the post or possibly *stolen*. He's convinced someone's trying to stop 'the truth' from getting out."

Ellie arched a brow. "What truth?"

"He didn't seem to want to say," Sylvia said, leaning closer. "But he mentioned someone called Peter—"

Ellie almost scalded herself with the boiling milk as she made another latte. "My father?"

"I'm not sure," Sylvia admitted, "but he said

something about how 'he's hiding,' and you haven't seen your father in a while, have you?"

Ellie's stomach twisted. "I—I don't technically know where he is. I think he's off on some birdwatching adventure, but he's not one for keeping in touch."

"Well, your grandmother told Benjamin 'all was forgiven', and—"

"Enjoying the show, are we?"

Ellie and Sylvia turned to see Maggie standing behind them, arms folded.

"Spying on your old gran, Ellie?" Maggie asked, usurping the coffee machine.

"I was curious," Ellie admitted. "He seemed furious."

"Benjamin's a walking daytime soap," Maggie said dismissively. "He ordered his books too late and he's throwing a tantrum that they haven't arrived in time for the signing. He thinks the postman stole them, but why would anyone want to do such a thing? He stormed out instead of thinking critically about it."

"To stop 'the truth'?" Ellie pressed. "That's what Benjamin thinks. And what's Dad got to do with it?"

"Ancient history," Maggie said firmly, seizing a cup. "Let's just focus on today. We've earned it."

"Gran—"

"Later," Maggie said, her voice softening. "Look around. We're thriving without the most unromantic man in Meadowfield's big debut. I know you didn't want him here anyway, but I felt like we had an old score to settle."

"And I suppose you're not going to tell me what that score was either?"

Maggie turned away, her customer-service smile sliding into place as she took her natural place behind the counter.

"Sounds like there's a conspiracy afoot!" Sylvia whispered to Ellie after blending in with the books. "Though if your gran says it's ancient history, perhaps it's best left alone." Brightening up, she added, "Did I ever tell you I went on a date with Benjamin Brown when I first moved to the village?"

Ellie shook her head, surprised by the admission. "How did it go?"

"Well, I didn't get engaged to him, if that's what you mean. You know he's been engaged *six* times?" Sylvia leaned in closer. "He took me to a lovely Italian restaurant in Oxford and spent the entire time berating the waiters and droning on about spreadsheets and inheritance tax brackets." She shuddered. "Painfully dry, even for an accountant, but I hear he never got over his first love leaving him. Maybe that's what he's written about?"

"Maybe," Ellie agreed, but her mind was somewhere else.

Ellie wanted to believe whatever Sylvia had overheard was ancient history. But as she watched Benjamin Brown through the window, now confronting the postman who was attempting to deliver mail at the soap shop across the street, she couldn't shake the feeling that something was very wrong—and that her father was somehow involved, wherever he was hiding.

Chapter 2
An Unexpected Return

The afternoon air in Meadowfield Books smelled of possibilities. Fresh paint mingling with old paper, brewing coffee competing with the sharp tang of wood polish. Ellie had gone over every surface with such dedication Joey had started calling it her 'polishing pilgrimage.'

"You're going to wear the wood away before we even open," he'd teased, but she couldn't help herself. The shelves deserved it.

She'd fought hard to keep the original Victorian bookshelves, despite Joey's warnings about the extra work. Three broken drill bits and one bandaged finger later, he'd looked up from where he was anchoring the final shelf to the wall and grudgingly nodded.

"Fine, you were right. They've got character. Can't buy that new."

Ellie restocked those hard-won shelves with secondhand *Sherlock Holmes* novels, the editions spanning from weathered 1920s hardbacks to dog-eared 90s paperbacks. As she worked, she couldn't help stealing glances through gaps in the books at the customers browsing the shop. There was Auntie Penny, predictably still hovering near Oliver's buffet table, but so many others too, heads bent over open pages, fingers trailing delicately along spines, faces lit with that unmistakable reader's glow as they discovered new worlds. For someone who usually preferred books to people, seeing the shop this full filled her with a feeling of pride she didn't want to fade.

Despite losing her so-called 'dream job', Ellie had managed to translate her TV studio experience into project-managing the bookshop. Years spent scrutinising scripts for historical accuracy while juggling tight production schedules and tighter budgets had sharpened her eye for detail far more than six miserable months serving overpriced coffees to Cardiff commuters ever could.

She'd kept the best of her grandmother's old ways: Maggie's leather-bound inventory ledger still sat proudly in the back room, and her genre-arranging system—designed for maximum 'flow'—remained, in Ellie's opinion, flawless. But she'd also nudged the business into the modern age where it counted.

Restocking complete, Ellie joined her gran behind the counter. Maggie was battling the espresso machine, muttering encouragement as though it were a stubborn pet.

"Come on, you beauty," Maggie whispered, giving

the machine a gentle pat. "Work with me now! We were just starting to get along."

Ellie smiled as she tapped at the new tablet till to check their takings for the day so far, still getting accustomed to its twitchy sensitivity. The digital till had been a hard-won compromise with her grandmother, who hadn't seen 'the big fuss' about being able to take card and contactless payments.

The bell above the door jingled, and Ellie looked up, her heart skipping a beat when she spotted Daniel Clark. His dark hair was windswept, his glasses sliding down his nose as always, and he clutched a small gift bag in one hand. Their eyes met across the shop, and his face lit up with that smile that still made her stomach flutter, even after as many months as she'd been home.

"Busy?" he asked, weaving between browsing customers to reach the counter.

"Wonderfully so," Ellie replied, leaning forward for the quick kiss he planted on her cheek. "I thought you had lunch duty today?"

"Swapped with Penelope from Year One," Daniel said, adjusting his glasses. "Told her I couldn't miss today for anything. Not even for her homemade shepherd's pie."

"That's serious dedication," Ellie teased, touched by the gesture.

"If anyone's dedicated, it's you." Daniel gestured around the transformed space. "Look at this place, Ellie.

It's incredible what you've done in such a short space of time."

"It felt anything but short."

"Rome wasn't built in a day," he reminded her. "And you've built something special here."

Ellie felt a flush of pride warm her cheeks, but before she could respond, she noticed a woman hovering behind Daniel. There was something familiar about her poised stance, hands neatly clasped, watching the scene with quiet, critical approval. She looked to be in her late sixties, silver hair in a tidy bob, dressed in a stiff skirt and a dark cardigan that all but shouted 'teacher', even without the ID badge hanging from the lanyard around her neck.

Daniel followed Ellie's gaze. "Oh! Ellie, you remember—"

"Miss Mills," Ellie said, recognition dawning as she extended her hand. "Our Year Six teacher. Of course!"

The woman's grip was just as firm as it had been when Ellie was eleven.

"Now Year Six teacher *and* deputy head," she said, patting Ellie's hand as she looked her over. "It's been years, but you still look like the same little Eleanor Swan." Her eyes crinkled with warmth. "Still surrounded by books, and still tagging along with shy little Daniel. What was that sweet nickname your father used to call you?"

"Sparrow," Ellie replied, her smile turning bittersweet at the mention of her father, a face she'd hoped to see in the crowds—but hadn't.

"That's it. Now, please, call me Sarah," Miss Mills said, releasing her hand. "I couldn't resist tagging along after Daniel's little speech in the staffroom this morning."

Ellie raised an eyebrow. "Speech?"

Daniel's face turned the colour of the red leather bookmarks stacked beside the till. "I-I was j-just letting people know the bookshop was reopening," he stammered. "Thought they could spread the word to the kids, who'd then tell their parents."

"He also mentioned how *proud* he was of his girlfriend for working so hard to get it ready," Sarah added with a conspiratorial wink at Ellie. "Quite the glowing review."

It was Ellie's turn to blush as she pictured Daniel in the staffroom, stuttering through his announcement, earnest and sweet. She slid her hand across his lower back. "Meadowfield Books thanks you for the promotion."

Daniel smiled, peering over his glasses, cheeks still flaming. "Anytime."

Sarah craned her neck, scanning the shop. "I heard Benjamin Brown was launching that romance book he's been talking about all year."

"Sarah was once engaged to Benjamin," Daniel explained, his eyes widening slightly as he realised what he'd revealed.

"Oh, please!" Sarah waved a dismissive hand. "I was *very* young, and we were both *very* different people. I just thought I'd pop along to support an old friend, that's all."

"The book launch has been pushed back," Ellie said. "Benjamin's books didn't arrive and he's convinced the postman has stolen them."

Sarah's eyebrows shot up. "Is that so? Why would the postman want to do that?"

"I don't know," Ellie admitted. "I haven't had a chance to read the book yet. He gave an early copy to my gran so she could approve it for the launch."

"And?" Sarah moved closer, suddenly interested. "What did she say? Was it good? Nobody was more surprised than me when I heard he's written a *romance* novel. The man is the driest accountant in the whole of Wiltshire."

"She said it was... serviceable." Ellie decided to leave it there, unwilling to repeat Gran's actual assessment, which had involved the phrases 'as romantic as a tax return,' and 'about as steamy as a tepid bath.'

"Well," Sarah checked her watch, "I'll just have to pop by tomorrow to show my support. I should leave you lovebirds alone. Want to have a browse before I head back to school."

As Sarah wandered towards the fiction section, Daniel and Ellie lingered in the middle of the shop. Ellie felt her grandmother watching them from behind the counter, her keen eyes missing nothing.

"Thanks again for the staffroom shoutout," Ellie said. "That was really sweet of you."

"No big deal." Daniel shrugged, but his pleased expression gave him away.

"No, really, I appreciate it." She squeezed his hand. "How about a drink tonight to celebrate?"

"Well, it's karaoke at The Old Bell."

"The Drowsy Duck it is," Ellie said with a decisive nod. "After work?"

"Sounds good to me." Daniel thrust the small gift bag forward. "Also, I got you a little something to mark the occasion. I know you love your 'I Love Meadowfield' pen, but I couldn't help noticing how scratchy it is, and I'm a bit of a stationery nerd, so..."

Ellie opened the box to reveal a gold pen resting in a plush black velvet box with 'I Love Meadowfield' engraved along the side. The original had been bought from Zara's gift shop as an ironic joke when she'd first moved back, but the irony had since been lost.

"Smoothest writing experience around," he promised, his cheeks flushing again. "There are some extra cartridges in the bag."

"Daniel..." Ellie ran her finger over the smooth metal. "This is also really, really sweet."

She thanked him with a kiss, and just for a moment, everything stopped. The customers, the coffee machine, and even the afternoon light seemed to stand still.

"Go have a wander around before you need to get back," she told him, reluctantly pulling away as the tablet till pinged with a new sale. "I'll see you tonight."

Ellie joined her grandmother at the counter. She

greeted Ellie with a knowing smile that suggested she'd witnessed every moment of the exchange.

"I think I've got the hang of these lattes," Maggie revealed, consulting a book splayed open beside the espresso machine. She tapped a finger on a detailed diagram of milk-to-espresso ratios. "Found this in the cooking aisle. Everything good with Daniel?"

"Very good," Ellie replied, unable to keep the smile from her face. "We're going to The Drowsy Duck for a drink later."

"Oh, good idea!" Maggie banged the metal milk jug on the counter with a decisive snap. "We'll need something to cap off the day. I feel like celebrating."

Ellie didn't point out that her grandmother had just invited herself along. "The more the merrier," she said instead, eyeing the bulky coffee manual. "The book is taking up a lot of space, but these picture guides are helpful..."

She pulled out her phone, lined up the camera, and snapped photos of the most crucial pages. "I'll go and print these out for you to tape by the machine."

"Look at you go," Maggie said, watching with genuine awe. "You make me feel like a Luddite sometimes, dear."

Ellie chuckled to herself as she headed towards the back office. As she approached the door, she noticed it was ajar, and through the gap, she spotted movement inside.

"Oh, excuse me, you can't be in—" The words died

on her lips as Sarah Mills turned around, Benjamin's manuscript clutched in her hands.

"Sorry, Ellie," Sarah said, her expression genuinely apologetic. "I couldn't resist a sneak peek. It's just... Benjamin Brown, writing a romance? It makes no sense."

She placed the book back on the desk with careful precision, as if afraid of disturbing its pages. Stepping closer, her voice dropped to a conspiratorial whisper.

"You know he's been engaged six times? I was the first. But there was always something between us that never quite fitted." She gave a small shrug, a flicker of wistfulness passing across her face. "You'd never believe it now, but he was young and exciting once. Before he became an accountant. Before—" She paused, holding a finger beneath her nose as though fighting back tears. "Before Sally died. That changed him. He never really came back from it. And we… we didn't survive the change."

Ellie reached out gently. "I'm… I'm sorry to hear that."

"Oh, ancient history!" Sarah said with a hollow little laugh, waving away the emotion. "Hold on to that spark with Daniel while you have it. One day it's there, the next…"

Before Ellie could respond, Sarah slipped past her and out of the office, leaving behind a cloud of subtle perfume and unanswered questions.

Ellie tried not to overthink the encounter as she crossed to the printer, transferring the coffee diagrams from her phone. While the machine hummed and warmed up, her eyes kept drifting back to Benjamin's manuscript.

The printer whirred into life, but Ellie found herself drawn to the desk. She flicked through the first few pages of the manuscript before returning to the beginning. The title page caught her eye: *The Last Love Letter* by Benjamin Brown.

"Sentimental for an accountant," she murmured, turning the pages with growing curiosity.

"'The final letter of importance came on the tenth day of the tenth month'," she read aloud, her voice barely a whisper in the quiet office.

The story continued, describing a love letter in such flowery language that it made Jane Austen and her contemporaries seem subtle. The style seemed at odds with everything she knew about Benjamin. The perturbed and always serious accountant, who had never been anything other than absolutely robotic. Until today. As she flipped through more pages, she noticed something strange.

"No chapter numbers," she whispered, flipping back and forth between pages with a frown. "Or titles." The text flowed on with only little squiggly symbols breaking it up. Benjamin seemed like the type who had a spreadsheet to keep track of his tie collection, so this sprawling, unstructured approach felt off.

The printer beeped its completion, jolting her back to the present. Through the office doorway, she noticed her grandmother craning her neck towards the back office, curiosity getting the better of her.

Ellie set down the manuscript and collected the printouts, hurrying back to the main shop floor. She handed the pages to Maggie, who immediately began taping them to the side of the coffee machine.

"Weren't having a sneak peek, were you?" Maggie asked, her tone light but her eyes shrewd.

"No," Ellie said, the lie small but uncomfortable. She busied herself straightening a stack of bookmarks. "What's the big secret about that book?"

Maggie exhaled through her nostrils, and Ellie thought she was about to clam up again. Instead, Maggie leaned in, glanced around the bookshop, and said, "Maybe it went over my head, but nothing jumped out. Like I told you, it's *fine*, but it's nothing worth the postman losing his job over."

After a while at the counter with Benjamin Brown and his strange romance book on her mind, Ellie climbed the narrow staircase to the cosy reading area they'd created in the loft space. Once relegated to nothing more than a storeroom, cushions lay scattered across the floor, and a few abandoned teacups perched on the small tables. As she began to tidy up, she spotted a lone figure sitting in the corner, gazing out of the circular window that overlooked the cobbles of South Sreet.

"Mum?" Ellie couldn't keep the surprise from her voice. "I didn't know you were up here."

Carolyn Swan didn't turn from the window. "I

never used to understand why you'd come and hide up here whenever you'd had enough of me." A wistful smile played at her lips. "Remember that time you ran away from home when you were ten and I found you up here in your sleeping bag?"

They both laughed, though the memory wasn't entirely a happy one. Ellie had been devastated when her mother sold the rare set of Charles Dickens books her dad had bought her. The money had funded Carolyn's latest set of headshots that were supposed to be 'the ones' to catapult her back onto the small screen in the New Millennium. Ellie had forgiven her, eventually, but this was as close to an apology as her mother had ever come.

And Ellie knew that meant one thing. Carolyn Swan wasn't trying to act her way through.

"It's quiet up here," Ellie said, settling onto the window seat beside her mother. "A peaceful little hideaway from the rest of the world."

Carolyn nodded, her fingers absently tracing patterns on the wooden windowsill. Something was definitely off-kilter about her today. There was a tightness in her jaw that Ellie recognised from childhood. How her mother looked when she was holding back disappointment for yet another failed audition.

"Is there something on your mind?" Ellie asked gently.

Carolyn opened her mouth, closed it again, then finally spoke. "Have you..." she started, her voice unusually tentative. "Have you heard from your father yet?"

The question took Ellie by surprise. "Yet?" she echoed, but her mother didn't respond. "Not since that postcard before Christmas." The one promising he'd be back in the new year. "Why... have you?"

The silence that followed spoke volumes, filling the tiny space like fog.

"Mum?"

Carolyn turned away from the window, her face pale and her lips pressed into a thin line. She hesitated, as if weighing her words carefully, before finally speaking. "Ellie, there's something I need to tell you. Something about your father—and about Benjamin's book." Her voice wavered, and she glanced towards the stairs, as if willing someone to interrupt at any moment. "It's not just a story he's written. It's... it's tied to something that happened a long time ago. Something that involves all of us."

Ellie's stomach knotted. Was this about the 'ancient history' Granny Maggie had hinted at? She perched in the armchair across from her mother. "What do you mean? What are you talking about?"

"I've heard rumours," Carolyn whispered, leaning closer. "People are saying Benjamin's book explains what really happened to his sister, Sally."

"Who?" Ellie asked, the unfamiliar name hanging between them.

"Sally Brown." Carolyn's voice was barely audible now. "She drowned in the pond in the middle of the village fifty years ago. And your father, he... he got wrapped up in it somehow."

Ellie's mind raced, connecting dots she hadn't even known were there.

"Are you saying Benjamin Brown thinks my father drowned his sister?"

Carolyn looked away, reluctance etched into every line of her face. After what felt like an eternity, she gave a small, tight nod.

"You're not denying it," Ellie whispered, the weight of it hitting her like a hardback she hadn't yet dared to open. "Is that why Dad's been gone all this time? Because he's hardly been in contact with anyone, and—"

Heavy footsteps thudded on the stairs. Carolyn recoiled, folding in on herself as she turned to stare out the window, the conversation vanishing from her face as though it had never happened.

"There you are!" Auntie Penny announced with a laugh as she lumbered into the room, slightly out of breath from the climb. "I've just been in every shop on South Street looking for you."

"I needed a moment to sit down," Carolyn said, her voice suddenly light and airy, the serious woman of moments ago completely vanished.

"Have you told Ellie the good news yet?" Penny asked, her round face beaming with pride for her sister.

"Good news?" Ellie looked between them.

"Oh," Carolyn waved a dismissive hand, "just some catalogue modelling job."

Coming from a woman who usually boasted about every minor acting gig, her indifference was jarring.

"Not just any catalogue," Penny chimed in. "One of those posh ones where a nightie costs £89.99. This could be regular work, and all part of the big comeback!"

Carolyn's smile was brittle as glass. Ellie could see her heart wasn't fully in it.

"Mum?" she asked softly, trying to steer them back to the conversation that had been so abruptly cut off. "Do you know where Dad is?"

But Carolyn was already on her feet, hurrying towards the stairs, her voice bright and distant.

"We need to restock my highlighter while we're out. And I'm nearly out of that under-eye concealer with the seaweed in it…"

Just like that, she was gone. The secret she'd been about to share vanished with her.

Alone in the snug upstairs, Ellie reached into her bag and pulled out the postcard she'd received months ago. Her father's scruffy handwriting shimmered in the light as she turned it over in her hands. The Scottish Highlands scene on the front felt a world away from Meadowfield's spring warmth. He'd promised to be home for Christmas. Now it was May.

What had happened? And what was the connection to this village that everyone seemed so determined to keep from her?

Whatever the link between her father, Benjamin's

book, and Meadowfield, it seemed everyone knew—except her.

* * *

As the final customers trickled out, Maggie stood behind the counter with a triumphant grin, piping frothy milk onto a perfectly poured espresso. The machine hissed and steamed, no longer an adversary but a conquered foe.

"Look at this masterpiece," she announced, turning the cup to display an approximation of a leaf pattern on the surface. "Not bad for a first day, eh? As long as I keep this little cheat sheet." She tapped the diagram—now laminated—taped to the machine.

Ellie offered a bow of congratulations. "You've picked it up faster than I did."

Maggie slid the cappuccino across the counter and took a tentative sip, her eyebrows raising in surprise. "Not half bad, if I do say so myself." She studied Ellie over the rim of the cup. "Do you ever miss it?"

"The coffee shop?" Ellie laughed, gathering stray cups from the nearby table. "Faking my way through small talk while I make bad coffee for people with worse attitudes?"

"I meant the studio," Maggie corrected, wiping foam from her upper lip. "All that film glamour and excitement?"

Ellie paused, considering the question properly. "Sometimes," she admitted. "But this, today..." She gestured around the shop, taking in the bookshelves, the armchairs with their cushions deflated, the remnants of their buffet table picked back to the bones. "I've never had a feeling like this at work. Never. It was nice directing for once."

For all the warmth she felt after the day's success, the same questions kept nagging at her thoughts like stinging papercuts.

"Gran..." Ellie started, her tone weighted with purpose.

"I know that voice," Maggie interrupted, suddenly very interested in the clock on the wall. "Well, would you look at that. Closing time!" She clapped her hands together with exaggerated enthusiasm. "Would you do the honours and flip the sign?"

Ellie sighed, recognising the evasion for what it was. Her grandmother might have accepted her changes for the shop—coffee machine and all—but she could still be stubbornly tight-lipped when she wanted to be. Whatever connection existed between her father, Benjamin's book, and the village would remain a mystery for now.

Her feet aching and spirit yearning for that promised drink with Daniel, Ellie plodded to the front door to lock up. Through the glass, a lone figure stood on the pavement, peering in with the nervous expression of someone afraid to enter. The fading daylight cast hazy shadows across his weathered face, but Ellie would have known him anywhere.

Her heart stopped, then raced, as she ripped the door open.

"Dad?" The word came out as little more than a whisper.

Peter Cookson stood frozen, his tired eyes crinkling at the corners as they always did when he smiled, though the smile itself was hesitant, uncertain.

"Hello, Sparrow," he said softly. "I couldn't miss your big reopening, could I?"

Ellie flung herself forward, wrapping her arms around him before he could retreat. He was thinner than she remembered, his frame almost frail beneath his bulky anorak and brown flat cap, but his familiar pine and dirt scent brought back memories of bright spring days birdwatching in the countryside. She had so many questions, so many things to say, but at that moment, she was simply glad to see him.

"Come inside," she managed, pulling back to look at him properly. "Please."

Peter followed hesitantly, carrying an oversized camping backpack that had seen better days. His shoulders hunched as if bracing for impact.

"I didn't want to cause a scene earlier," he explained, his voice low and uncertain. "I waited and waited, and then I got nervous, and I thought I'd be too late, and…" He trailed off, his eyes darting around the shop before landing on Maggie.

"Come here, son," Maggie commanded, crossing the room with outstretched arms. She enveloped him in a hug that belied her small stature. "You're too thin. Haven't you been eating?"

"I have, Mum," he insisted, his voice muffled against her shoulder. He pulled back, his eyes downcast. "I'm... sorry. For everything."

"There's time for all that," Maggie dismissed, though her tone was gentler than her words. "I'm happy to see you, really, I am."

"Me too," Ellie added, studying the new lines carved by time into her father's face. "But Dad... where have you been?"

Peter set his backpack down. "Scotland, mostly. Wild camping. It's been... an interesting experience."

Even for a man of few words, he was being unusually vague. Ellie had grown up deciphering her father's silences, and something about this one felt wrong. Strained, like a taut wire ready to snap.

"Look at this place," he said, clearly changing the subject as his gaze travelled around the shop. "You've really turned it around."

"It was Ellie, mostly," Maggie said. "She steered the ship, and I never would have navigated the storms without her."

Peter nodded, his smile genuine—but distracted. His gaze kept drifting across the shelves, scanning, searching.

"I hope you're proud of yourself, Sparrow," he said at last. Then, almost too quickly: "Do you have a copy of the book that launched today?"

Ellie and Maggie exchanged a glance.

"Benjamin Brown's?" Maggie asked carefully. "He delayed the launch until tomorrow. The stock was lost in transit."

Peter exhaled, some invisible weight lifting a little.

"I see," he murmured.

Ellie stepped closer, her unease growing. "Why do you need it so badly?"

He didn't answer. Instead, he shifted his backpack as if preparing to leave.

"How about you leave that here," Ellie offered gently, "and come to The Drowsy Duck? We're celebrating."

"Oh no, I can't," Peter said, too fast, reaching for the bag again.

"Yes, you can," Maggie said, brooking no argument. "You've been gone more than a year. The least you can do is share a drink with your daughter."

Peter hesitated, eyes flicking to the door, haunted. Then, with effort, he straightened.

"Of course I'll come," he said, taking Ellie's hand and pressing a kiss to her knuckles. "There's nowhere I'd rather be. I just… wish I'd come sooner."

Looking into his pale, wounded eyes, Ellie believed him. He seemed older, wearier, than when she'd last seen him. The last time had been when he'd visited her in Cardiff for the day while she was still working at the studio; they'd gone out to lunch and mostly talked about the weather. Now, she had so many questions burning inside her, but knowing her father, she understood he would only open up when he felt ready. And right now, he couldn't have looked more uncomfortable if he'd tried.

They locked up the shop and stepped out into the cool evening air. They walked to the top of South Street, and across the small central car park, the village pond lay unnaturally still, its surface black and mirror-like beneath the darkening sky.

Peter froze mid-step, the blood draining from his face. A visible tremor ran through him as his gaze fixed on a lone figure sitting on a bench by the water's edge.

Benjamin Brown sat hunched over, not moving a muscle, just staring into the dark water like he was waiting for something to stare back. In the half-light, he looked more like part of the landscape than a person. Another shadow among shadows.

"Dad?" Ellie whispered, feeling an inexplicable chill that had nothing to do with the evening air.

Peter swallowed hard, unable to tear his gaze away from the pond. "I... I've never liked that water," he managed, his voice hoarse. "Never trusted it."

Maggie, who hadn't noticed the exchange, was already at the pub door, rubbing her hands together in anticipation.

"I don't think any glass of wine has ever been more earned," she declared. "In fact, forget that. We need champagne. Harold's finest!"

She threw open the doors with a flourish, and warm golden light spilled out onto the street. Through the doorway, Ellie spotted Daniel in the corner, raising a hand in greeting. His cantankerous nan sat beside him, nursing what looked like a gin and tonic. Daniel mouthed 'sorry' across the room, and Ellie nodded that it was okay.

"I don't think I can do this," her father whispered, stepping back through the door before it closed behind him. His eyes kept darting back to the pond, towards Benjamin.

Ellie grabbed his hand before he could retreat further. "I'll be right here," she promised, squeezing his fingers reassuringly. "The whole time."

Peter glanced down at their joined hands, then back at Ellie's face. His smile was tinged with sadness, but sincere.

"I've missed you, Sparrow. So much."

"I've missed you too, Dad." The words caught in her throat. "And I know this won't be easy, but by the end of tonight, I need the truth. All of it."

She drew a steadying breath. What came next weighed heavy on her, but it had to be said.

"I need to know why you really left Meadowfield. Why you took money from Gran before you went. And why you didn't come back when she broke her hip."

His eyes widened slightly as he nodded, saying nothing, letting her lead him into the pub.

Behind them, by the water's edge, the silent figure of Benjamin Brown stood motionless—a shadow in the twilight. Ellie couldn't shake the feeling that whatever secret bound the two men was stirring from the depths like something long buried, ready to breach the surface after fifty years submerged in the village's memory.

Chapter 3
A Toast to The Truth

With their first round of drinks, Ellie eased into her seat opposite Daniel's nan. She held her gin and tonic like a conductor's baton, guiding the conversation with crisp authority. Though she lived next door to Ellie's mother, a connection that seemed to taint her view of anyone linked to Carolyn Swan, Ellie included, she appeared genuinely intrigued by Peter's birdwatching tales. For now, curiosity trumped her usual disdain.

"You mentioned seeing a white-tailed eagle in the Highlands," she cut in, halting Ellie's third attempt to steer the talk back to her father.

Peter brightened, the years peeling back as he leaned forward, enthusiasm bubbling.

"Oh, absolutely spectacular," he said. "The wingspan alone—" He flung his arms wide, nearly toppling Daniel's pint. "—must've been enormous. And the way the light caught its feathers... breathtaking. He patted his pockets, hopeful. "I've got photos... somewhere," he added, as if half-expecting a stack of snapshots to appear from his weathered anorak.

Ellie suppressed a sigh, watching her father drain his glass in three swift gulps. His eyes flicked to the bar, clearly weighing up a second. His knuckles tightened around the empty glass, and a sheen of sweat glistened on his brow, despite the cool draught rising from the open cellar door.

"Another?" Daniel nodded to Peter's empty glass. The simple question seemed to startle him.

"Please," Peter said, his voice cracking. "A whisky chaser wouldn't go amiss, either."

Granny Maggie stood at the bar, deep in conversation with Benjamin Brown, who had left the pond not long after they'd settled. His animated gestures jarred against her composed stance, but Ellie caught the tension in her grandmother's shoulders. Every few sentences, Benjamin glanced at their table. His gaze would land on Peter before he looked away.

Peter hadn't acknowledged him, but Ellie had noticed the shift the moment Benjamin walked in. Her father angled his back towards the bar, feigning indifference, yet he flinched at the sound of Benjamin's voice and tapped his foot, agitation building with each tick of time.

"The gannets were rather spectacular too," Peter said suddenly, his voice pitched a little too high. "Diving from incredible heights with such precision. They hardly make a splash, even at that speed."

Daniel's nan leaned in with exaggerated interest. "My sister, Pat, went on one of those boat tours to Bass Rock. Said the noise was deafening. And the smell! She had to wash her coat twice."

Ellie took a small sip of cider. The sweetness now sat sour on her tongue. She'd barely touched it, too focused on her father as he waited for his refill. This wasn't the reunion she'd imagined.

"Did you make it to The Isle of Skye?" Daniel asked, returning with Peter's fresh pint. Ellie sent him a silent thank-you. He might not know the full story, but his gentle questions kept things ticking along.

"For a few weeks," Peter replied, his eyes finally sparking with genuine enthusiasm. "The puffins were just—"

"I think I need the loo," Daniel's nan cut in, setting down her glass with a decisive clink. "Daniel, be a dear and help your old nan to the ladies', would you? These boots weren't made for wobbly pub floors."

Daniel stood with an apologetic glance at Ellie, offering an arm his nan clearly didn't need. "Back in a tick."

As they shuffled off, Ellie seized her chance. She dragged her chair closer to her father's, its legs scraping against the floorboards. Peter flinched, eyes wide like a startled animal.

"Dad," she said quickly, voice low and urgent. "I know about Sally Brown."

The colour drained from his face. His hand shook as he set down his empty glass. "What?" he whispered.

"I know she drowned in the village pond fifty years ago," Ellie pressed on, the words tumbling out. "I know you found her. I know Benjamin blamed you. And now he's written some book that supposedly reveals 'the truth'. Is that why you ran? I mean, that's what I've pieced together from the scraps people are giving me. Judging by your face, I think I'm right." She paused. He didn't even open his eyes. "Is that why you stole from Gran's biscuit tin and vanished for a year?"

Peter's gaze swept the pub, searching for eavesdroppers. When he spoke, his voice barely rose above a whisper. "I didn't kill her, Ellie. I just found her."

"And Benjamin's book?" she prompted, remembering what Sylvia had overheard at the bookshop. "He's written something that's going to expose everything, hasn't he?"

Peter swallowed hard, his Adam's apple bobbing. He gave a single, tight nod. "*His* version of the truth."

"Please, Dad." Ellie reached across the table, covering his trembling hand with hers. His skin felt papery and cold. "Talk to me. I need to understand. You're scaring me."

For a moment, she thought he might. His expression shifted—a flicker of vulnerability, the beginning of confession—but the pub door creaked open, letting in a gust of evening air and two familiar silhouettes.

Oliver froze in the doorway, jaw dropping at the sight of his father. Joey hovered just behind, a steadying hand on Oliver's elbow.

"Dad?" Oliver's voice cut through the pub, turning heads. He walked over, his expression a muddle of shock, disbelief, and tentative joy. "You're back? And you weren't going to call me?"

"It wasn't like that," Ellie jumped in. "He just turned up at the bookshop after closing and—"

But Oliver wasn't listening. He pulled his father into a tight hug unlike any they'd shared while Ellie was growing up. Her father had always kept a cautious distance from Oliver, as if unsure of his role, especially after Angela Cookson—Oliver's mother and a no-nonsense detective—made no secret of her loathing for Peter. And all because Ellie had been born to the local actress.

Now, Peter returned the embrace stiffly, his body tense as iron.

"It's good to see you, son," he said at last, the words sounding rehearsed.

"This," Oliver said, stepping back and gesturing to the handsome man beside him, "is Joey. We're seeing each other." His chin tilted in subtle defiance.

Peter nodded distractedly, barely touching Joey's offered hand. "Yes, right, of course. Joey. Good to meet you."

"Not this again. 'You'll grow out of it, just a phase,'" Oliver muttered, shooting Ellie a look.

"No, no," Peter said quickly, realising. He clasped Joey's hand more firmly. "Sorry. It's great to meet you, I just…" His gaze flicked to the bar, where Benjamin still chatted with Maggie. "I need to grab drinks. Beers all round?"

He didn't wait for a response.

Turning away, he bolted for the door.

The silence that followed hung awkwardly in the air.

"Well," Joey said, breaking it with a wry smile, "not quite the meet-the-parents moment I pictured."

Oliver slid into Daniel's nan's empty seat, eyes on his father downing a pint at the bar in three quick gulps. "He's jumpier than usual," he said. "And since when does he drink like that?"

"There's something off," Ellie murmured. "And I'm sure it's tied to Benjamin's book. That's why he ran, why he stole from Gran, why he's barely contacted us. He's been hiding from Benjamin, and whatever's in that book."

"And he picks today to come back? On the day of the book's launch?" Oliver frowned. "Why now?"

Their attention shifted to the bar, where Peter wiped his mouth with the back of his hand, leaving a foam moustache on his weathered skin. He lingered, fingers tapping a nervous rhythm on the polished wood. His eyes strayed repeatedly to Benjamin, still deep in conversation with Maggie. Every few seconds, Peter shifted his weight, stepped forward, then back again, like a sparrow too cautious to take the crumbs.

"…and Mrs Henderson says my lavender loaf should be declared a village treasure," Oliver continued, trying to preserve some sense of normality. "She's starting a petition to have it protected by the parish council."

"That's nice," Ellie murmured, her gaze locked on her father. Benjamin had finally noticed Peter's presence. Their eyes met across the bar, and tension sparked like static. Benjamin's mouth flattened into a thin line.

Maggie gestured placatingly, but Benjamin shook his head, muttered something, and strode towards the gents, deliberately veering away from their table.

"Did you see that?" Ellie whispered to Oliver. "They can't even stand to be near each other."

"I still can't believe that bloke wrote a romance novel," Oliver said. "He's an accountant. I expected something like *How To Easily File Your Taxes*. I'd actually read that."

At the bar, Maggie now spoke to Peter alone, her face serious. He stood hunched, head bowed as he listened. Then he shook his head sharply and waved down Harold behind the bar.

Maggie returned, pausing when she noticed Daniel and his nan had been replaced by Oliver and Joey.

"I see the cavalry's arrived," she said, lowering herself into her seat with a sigh. "Your father's in quite a state."

"What were you talking about?" Ellie asked, nodding towards Peter, who stared into his pint like it might explain his past. "I was trying to get him to open up. Then you and Benjamin were whispering, and now this...?"

"I was trying to get Benjamin to clear the air," Maggie said, taking a long sip of wine.

"You mean about his book?" Ellie pressed. "The one he supposedly wrote about Dad?"

"Well, according to him now," Maggie said cautiously, "it's not about your father." She glanced at Peter, who was ordering another drink with a trembling hand. "He won't say more, but he's convinced he knows the truth about what happened."

"The truth about *what*?" Ellie demanded, frustration bubbling. "Why haven't I heard any of this before? A drowning, accusations… why has everyone kept me in the dark?"

Maggie opened her mouth to reply, but her eyes widened, fixed on something beyond Ellie. "Oh heavens, not now…"

Ellie turned to see her father bump into a broad man in a high-vis jacket, splashing the man's pint over his boots. The man, built like a rugby player, grabbed Peter by the collar.

"Watch where you're going, mate!" he bellowed, drawing curious looks from nearby tables.

Ellie leapt to her feet, Oliver close behind. Peter looked terrified, pale as milk as he tried to wriggle free.

"I-I'm sorry," he stammered. "I tripped—"

"You're wearing steel-toes," Oliver cut in smoothly, stepping in beside him. "Surely not in *that* much pain? No need to kick off over a pint, is there?"

The man squinted at Oliver, clearly weighing his

options. Joey appeared at his shoulder, silent but imposing, his builder's frame speaking volumes.

After a tense pause, the man let go with a grunt. "Keep your old man on a tighter lead, yeah?" he muttered, retrieving his pint and stomping off to the pool table.

"Thanks," Peter whispered, still shaking as he straightened his coat. He looked utterly drained.

"What would you do without us, eh?" Oliver said, brushing his father's jacket with a half-smile that didn't quite hide the concern. "I'm glad you're home, but what's going on?"

Peter's eyes flicked toward the gents' loo, where the door had just swung open. "I... I think I should go," he said, reaching for his coat. "This was a mistake."

"Please, Dad," Ellie said, taking his clammy hand in hers. "You can't keep running."

Benjamin emerged, halting when he saw the Swan family gathered at the bar. His face shut down, and he moved towards the door, clearly aiming to avoid them.

Something shifted in Peter. "You're right," he murmured. "I can't keep running."

Before she could speak, Peter moved, stepping straight into Benjamin's path. Benjamin tried to sidestep, but Peter blocked him, his jaw set, hands visibly shaking.

He cleared his throat, voice cutting through the lull in conversation. "Benjamin. I... I won't be accused of something I didn't do. I've said for fifty years I wasn't involved. If your book suggests otherwise, you'll be hearing from my solicitor."

Benjamin leaned in, voice too low for Ellie to catch. Whatever he'd said made Peter's face twist with fury.

"Just leave me alone!" Peter roared, slamming his glass down. Beer splashed over the rim, silencing the room.

Every conversation ceased mid-sentence. Even Harold froze behind the bar, cloth suspended over a half-dried pint glass. Peter looked around, suddenly aware of the dozens of eyes fixed on him. His face flushed crimson, embarrassment edged with fear.

Without another word, he turned and fled, the door banging against the wall in his haste to escape.

"*Dad*!" Ellie was ready to follow, but Maggie's firm grip stopped her.

"Let him go," her grandmother said gently. "He needs space."

"Space?" Ellie tried to pull free. "He needs *help*, Gran. What's going on? Why is he so afraid of Benjamin's book? What happened fifty years ago?"

The silence thickened. The room seemed to hold its breath, the whole village suddenly very invested in their drinks, pretending not to listen.

Benjamin cleared his throat, loud and theatrical. All eyes turned to him as he stepped into the centre of the room, eyes glittering with something between mischief and mania.

"It's true," he said, voice carrying. "I've written a romance novel. Shocking, isn't it?"

A few titters. He smiled, thin-lipped and wry.

"I know what you're all thinking. 'The man couldn't get down the aisle if his life depended on it.' And you'd be right."

He paused, letting the silence stretch.

"But I've got your attention now, haven't I?" Benjamin raised his glass, amber liquid sloshing close to the rim. "Tomorrow. Come to my book launch at the bookshop on the corner. Read it. Find what I've hidden in the pages. The truth about what happened to my sister fifty years ago." His voice hardened. "Maybe if enough of you figure it out and go to the police, they'll finally care."

Near the bar, Sarah Mills stepped away from a group of teachers Ellie recognised from visits to Daniel's school. Her elegant frame moved with quiet purpose.

"Come on, Benjamin," she said softly. "I think you've had one too many."

His eyes narrowed as he stared at her, something unreadable passing between them. Then he raised his glass higher, the toast now clearly aimed at her.

"Tomorrow," he repeated, his voice dropping to a near-whisper that still carried. "You'll all find out…"

"Alright, Benjamin," Harold called from behind the bar. "That's enough. You've had your say."

Maggie took Ellie's elbow and gently guided her away from the scene. At their table, bizarrely, Daniel's nan was chatting to Oliver, apparently unaware he wasn't Peter.

"…and that's why curlews return to the same

nesting grounds," she was saying. "Fascinating creatures, really."

"Mmhmm." Oliver caught Ellie's eye, his expression one of bemused disbelief. "Are you going after him?"

"He's used to running," Maggie said, her voice heavy.

"But shouldn't we?" Ellie asked, unable to shake the image of Peter's stricken face. "This is different. He's not chasing some bird; he's *running* from something."

"Hasn't he always?" Oliver muttered, bitterness edging into his tone.

"*Excuse* me," Daniel's nan cut in, sharp as a pin. "We were having a conversation."

"Actually," Oliver said, seizing the exit, "it was lovely chatting about birds. Pigeons rock, but I have to leave."

"Pigeons are *vermin!*" she cried, visibly affronted.

Daniel appeared beside Ellie, slipping an arm around her waist. "Everything alright?" he asked quietly.

"Not really," she said, leaning into him. "My father came back, and now he's vanished again. And I think he might be in trouble."

"He's not in danger," Maggie said quickly, but her eyes betrayed doubt. "I'll tell you everything, but not here. Let's go home."

Ellie turned to Daniel, guilt creeping in. "Sorry our drinks didn't exactly go to plan."

"Don't be," he said, giving her hand a gentle squeeze. "Family comes first. Always." His brown eyes scanned her face, the smile behind them soft and sincere. "I'll see you tomorrow? Lunch at the café?"

"It's a date," she promised, a flicker of calm in the chaos. She leaned in for a quick kiss, resting her forehead against his. The moment anchored her.

Daniel's nan gave a loud huff, muttering about 'public displays' as she turned away in theatrical disgust.

Outside, the night air had a spring bite. Maggie stood beneath the pub sign, her gaze fixed on the black-glass surface of the pond, stars scattered above it.

"Let's walk," she said, linking her arm through Ellie's. "We might bump into your father."

They walked in step, their pace matching the distant toll of the church bell striking ten.

"It's turned into one of those days," Ellie murmured.

"And it's not over yet," Maggie replied softly.

The cottage welcomed them with the familiar creak of its old door, like a yawning stretch after a midday nap. The sound slipped around Ellie, soft as sunshine. Maggie swept past her with a theatrical shiver, muttering about 'spring damp being worse than winter,' as she shrugged off her coat and made a beeline for the fireplace. She knelt on the faded hearth rug, poking at the embers.

"Pop the kettle on, love, would you?" she called over her shoulder, already stacking kindling into a neat pyramid. "Nothing sets the world to rights like a proper cuppa."

Ellie filled the dented old copper kettle and set it on the stove. The clink of mugs and rattle of the tea spoons offered a small comfort amid the whirlwind in her head. She reached for Maggie's favourite—the chipped one with the faded Penguin Books logo—and her own, the chunky robin mug that always fitted just right in her hands.

"I can't make heads or tails of it, Gran," she said, leaning in the sitting room doorway while the kettle boiled on the stove behind her. "Dad turns up out of nowhere, Benjamin's dropping cryptic hints about his book, and everyone is acting like they're in some second-rate whodunnit. It's just… too much."

Maggie didn't answer straight away. She struck a match, its sudden flare throwing sharp shadows across her face, deepening the lines carved by time and laughter. She held the flame to the kindling. The fire caught quickly, its glow spilling into the room like a deep, contented sigh.

"Your father turned up like this once before," Maggie said at last, easing into her chair with a soft groan. "Soaked through, shaking like a leaf. June 1975, it was. A wild storm raged outside, the wind howling and rain battering the windows, the kind of storm that made you wonder if the world was about to split in two."

The kettle's whistle sliced through the quiet. Ellie returned to pour the water, steam curling into the air as she stirred in milk. By the fire, she handed Maggie her mug, then curled into the chair opposite, pulling her knees up and wrapping her hands around her own. The logs crackled gently. For a moment, the outside world felt miles away.

"He couldn't get the words out properly," Maggie said, eyes on the fire. "I sat him right where you are now and made him cocoa. He was sixteen. Still figuring himself out." She paused, a small smile tugging at her lips. "Lanky as a pine tree, quiet as a shadow, but so bright at school. That was the year I bought him his first pair of *proper* binoculars. He kept borrowing your grandfather's, but he was never much for sharing." She chuckled softly. "Peter would sit for hours at the window, eyes to the sky. Watching the swifts, the sparrowhawks—anything with wings. Never seen a person more content doing something."

She took a sip of tea. The smile faded.

"When he finally spoke, he said he'd been walking in the rain when he saw someone in the pond. Sally Brown, floating. He pulled her out, but..." Maggie shook her head. "It was too late."

Ellie held her mug close like it was holding her together as the details emerged from the blur of confusion.

"And that's what he told the police?" she asked.

"His story never changed," Maggie said with a slow nod. "Your father was never arrested, never charged. He was only questioned. They had no reason to doubt him, despite how things looked. No evidence he'd done anything wrong." Maggie's eyes hardened. "But Benjamin wouldn't let it go. He claimed your father had a teenage crush on Sally."

"Did he?"

Maggie snorted. "He didn't care about relationships back then. Still waking up at four to log birds in the garden. But Benjamin needed someone to blame. For years, he pointed the finger at Peter."

The fire popped, sparks tapping the grate. Outside, the wind picked up, moaning through the eaves like a low wail.

"Is that why Dad ran off last year?" Ellie asked, setting her mug on the side table. "Because of Benjamin's book?"

"I don't know," Maggie admitted, her shoulders drooping. "The irony is, Benjamin doesn't think Peter's guilty anymore. That's what I tried to explain before your father stormed out. Benjamin asked me to host the launch. He said he'd discovered the truth—that Peter didn't cause Sally's death. I thought it might finally mend things, after all these years."

"That was the 'old score' you were settling?"

She exhaled. "A fresh page in a new story, but your father wasn't around and I've had no way to get in touch with him. If Benjamin's book is why he left, I never connected the dots. How would he even know about it? Benjamin, at least with me, made it seem like nobody could know anything until the book was released."

Ellie frowned, thinking back to her conversation

with Sarah Mills. "Sarah's a teacher who works with Daniel and had heard rumours. She said he's been working on the book all year. Maybe Dad heard something too?"

"Rumours are all well and good," Maggie said, rising from her chair with sudden purpose, "but facts are better."

She disappeared into the hall and returned moments later with a yellowed newspaper, its edges brittle with age. She placed the issue of the long-defunct *Meadowfield Gazette* in Ellie's lap. The headline, stark against the faded page, read: 'Village in Shock: Drowned Teacher's Missing Locket Sparks Murder Probe.'

Ellie's breath caught at the photograph below. A young woman with bright eyes and a gentle smile stared out at her, yellowed and frozen in time. "She was so young," she whispered, tracing the outline of Sally's face.

"Just twenty-two," Maggie said, settling back into her seat. "I couldn't throw it away. It felt… important."

Ellie scanned the article. Her father was named as the one who found the body. But as she turned the page, another headline grabbed her: 'Jewel Heist at Meadowfield Manor: Thousands in Family Heirlooms Stolen.'

"What's this?" she asked, holding it up for Maggie.

Maggie squinted through her glasses. "The robbery? I'd nearly forgotten. All I remember from that time is

Sally and the pond… and having to defend Peter at every turn."

"The same night," Ellie murmured, eyes skimming the details. "Meredith and Jonathan Winchester refused to comment, but their daughter was said to be at the house during the heist." She looked up. "Could they be connected?"

"I couldn't say," Maggie said, thumb circling her mug's rim. "But if Benjamin has found the truth and left clues in his book, why didn't I see anything in the manuscript?"

"Maybe it wasn't the final version?" Ellie suggested, heart racing. She folded the paper with care. "So what do we do now?"

"Nothing," Maggie said firmly. "We eat dinner, curl up with our books, and get some sleep. Tomorrow's the book launch, so we need to be sharp. Let's hope Benjamin sleeps off the beer and shows up in a better mood."

"I hope so," Ellie murmured, stifling a yawn. "And I hope his book clears something up, because I'm more confused than ever." She gave a quiet laugh. "Funny. I spent weeks fretting about the bookshop opening. Turns out that was the easiest part of the day."

Maggie chuckled, though without much humour. "That's life, love. You can plan all you like, but it still throws in a plot twist or two."

Ellie looked down at the newspaper again, at Sally's soft face frozen between the headlines about her death and the manor heist.

"And what about when life throws two plot twists… on the same night?"

"Maybe the police looked into a connection?"

"And if they didn't?"

"We could always invite Angela round," Maggie said dryly. "See if your father's ex-wife fancies sharing classified police files over a cuppa."

Ellie caught the note of sarcasm and raised an eyebrow. They both laughed, the kind that creaks out when your heart's too tired to do more.

"Enough doom and gloom," Maggie said, folding the newspaper and tossing it onto the coffee table. "What if we dared to imagine that tomorrow goes off without a hitch? Benjamin launches his book, clears the air with your father, and everyone gets their happy ending."

"That sounds like a perfect day," Ellie said. But as she followed her gran into the kitchen to start dinner, she couldn't shake the feeling that, after the day they'd had, tomorrow had other plans.

Chapter 4

Bump in the Night

E llie jolted awake, blinking at the luminous numbers on her bedside clock. *1:47 AM.* The house creaked around her as she sat up against the headboard, rubbing her eyes. Sleep had come in fits, her mind too restless despite her aching limbs and the bone-deep fatigue of the day.

Her notepad lay open on the floor, the gold pen Daniel had given her glinting in a shaft of moonlight. In cramped handwriting, she'd scrawled names and dates tied to Sally's death, arrows criss-crossing the page. 'Meadowfield Manor Jewel Heist' had been circled several times, the pen pressing so hard it nearly tore the paper.

Two events, one night. A drowning and a theft in a village you could walk end to end in twenty minutes. Coincidence?

Tap.

Ellie froze. That's what had woken her.

Tap. Tap.

Pebbles at the window.

"Ellie." Her name floated up from the garden, barely a whisper.

Heart racing, she slipped from bed and moved to the window, easing back the curtain. Below, a shadow shifted in the moonlight—her father, hunched and fidgeting.

"*Dad?*" she whispered, pushing the window open. The spring air rolled in, cool and damp, laced with the sharp tang of whisky rising from below.

"Come down," he called softly, his voice frayed at the edges.

Ellie grabbed her dressing gown and didn't bother with slippers. She padded barefoot down the stairs and through the darkened kitchen. The flagstones chilled her feet as she turned the key in the back door lock, the scrape of metal sounding far too loud in the sleeping house.

Her father stood on the path, swaying slightly. He looked worse than he had at the pub: shirt buttoned wrong, hair wild, eyes glassy and unfocused. Ellie couldn't remember ever seeing him drunk.

"Dad, where have you been?" she asked, stepping onto the cold stone step. "We've been worried sick."

"I'm sorry," he said, words tumbling out. "So sorry, Sparrow. For everything. For leaving you. For leaving your gran."

"Come inside," she urged, reaching for his arm. "You're freezing."

He jerked back, nearly toppling. "No, no. Can't stay. Just had to tell you—whatever they're saying, whatever they think I did—it's not true." His voice cracked. "None of it's true."

"Dad, no one's saying—"

"I know how it looks," he cut in, his hands fluttering like frightened birds. "It always looks bad for me. Wrong place, wrong time. Always the *wrong* place." He jabbed a finger into his chest. "Do you think I killed her? Is that what you think? Your own father?"

"Of course not," Ellie said quickly, stepping closer. "Why would I think that?"

"Benjamin knew. He knew I didn't do it. But it's too late." Peter's eyes darted past her, scanning the back of the house like he hardly recognised it. "Too many years wasted. And it's happening again…"

A siren wailed faintly in the distance. Peter's head snapped up, eyes wide with terror.

"They're coming," he whispered. "I knew they would."

"Dad, that's just the bypass. Probably an ambulance," Ellie said, reaching for him. "Please, come inside. We can talk—"

"I can't stay," he repeated, spinning with a sudden burst of energy. "They'll find me here."

He bolted for the garden gate, his movements clumsy but driven.

"Dad!" Ellie cried, chasing after him. "*Stop!*"

She grabbed at his coat, but her dressing gown snagged on the pergola. The cotton tore with a soft rip, yanking her back. By the time she freed herself, Peter had already flung the gate open and vanished into the dark.

"Stop this!" she shouted, her bare feet slipping on the dew-wet grass as she reached the gate. "Dad!"

But the lane was empty, the night silent save for the echo of footsteps, fading into shadow.

"What in heaven's name—" Maggie appeared in the doorway, wrapped in her ancient tartan dressing gown. Her silver hair stuck out at odd angles, but her eyes were sharp, alert—like she hadn't slept at all.

"It was Dad," Ellie said, backing towards the house, toes numb with cold. "He was just here, and he's not okay, Gran." She gestured helplessly at the empty lane. "He's drunk, rambling about Sally, saying people think he killed her. And that it's happening again. We need to do something."

Maggie's face tightened. "Come inside first," she said, pulling the door open wider. "You're barefoot."

"But Dad—"

"Your father knows this village better than anyone," Maggie said firmly. "He won't have gone far, not in that state." She guided Ellie back into the kitchen. "Put the kettle on. I'll make us some cocoa."

Ellie clutched her mug, seeking warmth that felt absent from the world. A steady tapping filled the kitchen, her foot against the tiles, too restless to keep still. Across from her, Maggie scrubbed at a dinner plate that had already been clean for at least two minutes.

"Going after him won't help," Ellie said at last, watching her grandmother scrub with needless vigour. "He's too quick, knows too many hidey-holes. We'd just be wandering in the dark."

Maggie set the plate down with a firm clink. "Why did he come here? And why in the middle of the night?"

"I've never seen him like that," Ellie says. "He was drunk."

"Even at Christmas, he'd nurse one sherry all night. Normally I wouldn't believe it," Maggie admitted, shoulders drooping as she stared out into the dark. "But now? I don't know. It almost felt easier not knowing where he was."

Ellie leaned against the counter, watching her. "What was he like, just before he left? I was in Cardiff, completely cut off from Meadowfield."

"He was himself," Maggie said slowly, as if testing the shape of the words. "Birdwatching. Reading. Quiet, but he was *always* quiet." A small smile flickered across her face. "I had a hunch he might've been seeing someone. Now and then he'd come home smelling of perfume, and he'd always seem... cheered up."

"Really?" Ellie straightened, surprised.

"I was glad," Maggie said, wringing out the dishcloth harder than necessary. "He's always been so lonely. Watching him age... I wondered if I'd prepared him properly for life."

"He's got survival skills," Ellie offered. "Camping. Fishing. He could live off the land if he had to."

"That was your grandfather. All those camping trips, the long silences. The fishing." Maggie's voice caught. "I could've done more. Taken fewer classes, fewer afternoon clubs." She turned to Ellie, her eyes shining in the low light. "Oh, love, I think I've been a better gran than I ever was a mum."

"Don't say that," Ellie said gently, placing a hand on her grandmother's arm. "Dad's just… Dad. Things will settle down."

"And if they don't?" Maggie's voice held a rawness that hit Ellie like a blow.

"Then we'll make them," Ellie replied, trying to sound confident. "Let's leave the washing up for the morning and get some sleep. We've got the shop to open. That's what this week was meant to be about, right? Finding our rhythm."

"We've found it, all right," Maggie said with a dry laugh, grabbing a wooden spoon and tapping it against a pot. "Rhythm of free-form experimental jazz." She gave a few more pots a discordant whack before letting her arm fall. "There's nothing funny about any of this."

"Better than crying," Ellie said with a small smile, linking her arm through Maggie's.

Together, they made their way down the hallway to their bedrooms, leaving the kitchen behind in rare disarray.

* * *

Ellie's eyes snapped open, her body recognising what her brain hadn't: she hadn't had nearly enough sleep. The first grey light of dawn seeped through the curtains. Too early. A second later, she sensed it—someone in the room.

Her pulse spiked as she fumbled for her phone, its glow revealing Maggie's face, drawn and anxious in the cold blue light.

"Sorry, love," Maggie whispered. "Didn't know how else to wake you without giving you a fright."

"So you thought standing at the end of my bed like Marley's ghost was the subtle option?" Ellie croaked, her throat dry. "Did I miss my alarm?"

"No, love." Maggie twisted her fingers, something she only did when nerves got the better of her. "You should come down. Angela's here."

The quiet weight in her voice swept away the last of Ellie's sleep. She pulled on yesterday's clothes from the floor beside her laundry basket and followed Maggie downstairs, heart thudding.

The cottage's sitting room was caught in half-light, neither night nor morning. DS Angela Cookson stood by the fireplace, studying a photo frame with an unreadable focus. It was her wedding photo with Peter, both of them stiff in formal wear, too young, too awkward.

Ellie cleared her throat. Angela turned, setting the frame down carefully.

"I don't know why she keeps that thing out," Angela said without looking at her. "We only married because I was pregnant with Oliver. It seemed like the right thing to do."

The old guilt stirred in Ellie's chest. She knew her birth had splintered that marriage beyond repair. Still, she'd never understood what those two had seen in each other to begin with.

"I'd ask if everything's alright," Ellie said, stepping into the room and glancing at the mantel clock. Just past six. "But seeing as you're here at this hour, I'm guessing it's not?"

"Is he here?" Angela asked, her tone brisk, professional despite the hour and history.

"Who?" Ellie replied automatically.

Angela's jaw tightened. "I don't need your smart mouth right now. Your father. Is he here?"

Ellie shook her head, heart pounding. If Angela was looking for him, he was at least alive. But why was she searching at six in the morning? Last night's strange visit flashed through her mind, and she hesitated, unsure whether to mention it.

Maggie entered with a tray, thrusting tea at Ellie and coffee at Angela. The detective accepted it with a reluctant nod, something that might've passed for a smile. She didn't drink.

"What's happened?" Ellie asked, her voice steadier than she felt.

Angela studied them both, her expression unreadable. "A man was found in the pond a few hours ago," she said at last. "Drowned."

"Benjamin Brown," Maggie breathed, the name

hitting the room like a dropped stone.

Angela's eyes narrowed. "Yes."

"He's dead?" Ellie said, the words absurd even as she said them. Of course he was dead. People pulled from ponds in the early hours weren't enjoying a swim.

The floor seemed to shift beneath her. Hours ago, Benjamin had been alive, raising a glass, making cryptic remarks about his book, staring out at that same pond. And now…

"Why are you looking for my father?" she asked, her voice distant in her own ears.

"Because a man matching his description was seen fleeing the scene at around half past midnight."

Ellie's thoughts spun. Her father had appeared at the cottage around quarter to two. If he'd walked the long way around and paced outside the gate for as long as he probably did, he might have come straight to see her, if she was to believe Angela's mystery witness.

"That's absurd," Maggie said sharply. "Peter would never—"

"These are serious allegations," Angela cut in, professional mask firmly back in place. "Especially after the confrontation at The Drowsy Duck."

"That was hardly a confrontation," Maggie snapped. "Benjamin was drunk, putting on a show—"

"So was Peter," Angela said coldly.

"You don't think Peter…" Maggie trailed off, unable to finish the thought.

"I'm not here to speculate."

"This isn't just some case," Maggie said, voice

cracking. "This is your ex-husband. The father of your child. You *know* he didn't do this."

"I'll know what I know when I have the facts," Angela replied. She took a deep swallow of coffee, as if bracing herself, then set the mug down. "If you hear from him, call me first. For his sake."

After she left, silence clamped down like a lid. Benjamin Brown had died in the same pond where his sister had drowned fifty years before. And Peter, who had once pulled Sally from those waters, was now a suspect in her brother's death.

"I can't search all of Meadowfield," Ellie said, her mind racing. "But I can start somewhere."

"Where?" Maggie asked, sinking into her armchair.

"My mother's."

"Your father wouldn't go *there*."

"He might've." Ellie thought back to her mother's odd behaviour in the bookshop. "Yesterday, she asked if I'd heard from him 'yet.' She said something about dark family secrets. It was like she was trying to warn me. She knows *something*."

The first true light of morning crept across the floor, cold and grey despite promises of sunshine. In a few hours, they were meant to open the bookshop for Benjamin's launch.

Instead, he was dead.

And her father—wherever he was—stood accused.

Chapter 5
Drowning in the Past

As the rising sun nudged grey into blue, Ellie hurried through the quiet streets of Meadowfield, heading for her mother's terraced cottage in the heart of the village. On the village green near the war memorial, she spotted Auntie Penny with Duchess the Third trotting beside her on a rhinestone-studded lead. Ellie ducked behind a row of parked cars before the little dog, who adored her far too loudly, could spot her and start yapping. She'd get more out of her mother without her most enthusiastic cheerleader getting in the way.

The front door, as expected, was locked. Ellie gave the handle a few hopeful rattles before knocking, but knew full well her mother wasn't the type to answer the door for anyone, least of all at this hour. She darted down the alley that ran behind the row of terraces, and using Daniel's nan's bin as a makeshift step, hoisted herself up and over the garden wall.

"Oi! What d'you think you're doing?" came a voice from above.

Ellie looked up just in time to see Daniel's nan leaning out of her upstairs bathroom window, still in her rollers and nightie, toothbrush in hand.

"Get off my wall, you little vagabond!"

Ellie gave her a sheepish wave and mouthed an apology before she slipped past the greenhouse and through the unlocked back door of the cottage.

"That you again, Penny?" Carolyn's voice called from the sitting room. "First, you forget your keys, then the doggy bags…"

She stepped into the kitchen looking like something out of a low-budget horror flick. Her usually sleek hair was stiff with gloopy dye, and a green clay mask froze her face into a wide-eyed stare.

"Oh—Ellie," she blinked, her features cracking slightly. "Bit early, isn't it? I'm just doing some photoshoot… maintenance."

"Have you heard?" Ellie asked, skipping past small talk.

"Heard what?" Carolyn's frown made her mask flake at the edges.

Ellie hesitated. The truth about Benjamin's death weighed heavy on her tongue, but something about her mother's too-casual tone, the way she fluttered about in her silk robe and pretended not to notice the strain in Ellie's voice, made her hold it back. Better to test the waters first. See what floated up.

"That my father's back."

Carolyn's eyes flicked away. That was all Ellie needed.

"You knew," she said, circling the gleaming marble island as her mother walked around the other way, putting a safe distance between them. "He came to you before the bookshop, didn't he? That's why you asked if I'd heard from him 'yet', isn't it? Because *you* already had."

Carolyn sighed, a dusting of clay falling onto her silk dressing gown and onto the marble. She dusted it off with the back of her hand. "Yes. It took all afternoon to convince him to show his face at the launch. He'd come all this way, and I knew you'd want to see him, so—"

"But why come to you first?" Ellie asked. "No offence, Mum, but you and Dad have barely spoken two words to each other since I was born. You've used Gran as a go-between for as long as I can remember."

"We've said more than *two* words," Carolyn replied, rolling her eyes, more flakes of clay mask tumbling onto her dressing gown. "And you've been away a long time. Your father and I... we've been on better terms."

"Why?" Ellie asked, genuinely baffled.

"Because we never really had a problem," Carolyn said with a dismissive wave. "And anyway, I don't want to get into that. It's ancient history."

"Just another dark family secret?" Ellie snapped, her palms slapping against the cold marble. "That's what you meant at the bookshop. Dad and Benjamin tied to something buried. It's about people thinking he drowned Sally Brown, isn't it?"

Carolyn's eyes widened, the mask cracking like old plaster. "We always agreed that if you ever found out, we'd explain. But we wouldn't volunteer it unless we had to." She shook her head slowly. "I'm just surprised it took this long."

She sighed and reached for the glossy catalogue spread open on the kitchen island. An array of overpriced, silky nightwear stared up at them. She pulled it close, flicking the page as if it offered sanctuary, not even pretending she wanted to have this conversation. Not after thirty years of keeping it sealed.

"He didn't do it," she said at last, flipping to the next page with a snap. "I barely knew him then, truthfully. I was filming *Heatherwood Haven* the night Sally drowned. We were out on the green shooting the big reveal—my *big* stalker storyline—when the storm rolled in. The director herded us into The Old Bell to wait for it to pass. We spent hours there, drinking, learning our lines, trying to stay ready for the moment the rain passed. Gruelling schedule, but I'd go back in a heartbeat. It was the most fun I've ever had."

She smiled, and for a hint of a moment, Ellie felt a rare connection—something real, unpolished, from a woman who usually lived behind perfectly posed expressions.

Carolyn's gaze drifted, softening as memory took hold.

"Then someone burst in, shouting that a lad had

pulled a girl from the pond. That she was dead." She shook her head, voice quiet. "Total shock. But once I heard who it was, and the whispers started... I just knew. That kid always wandering with his binoculars, always polite, a little odd maybe, but kind—he didn't drown anyone. Not Peter. I never believed it for a second."

She turned on the tap, letting the water run as if it gave her something to do with her hands.

"I didn't tell him I never believed the rumours until 1993. Karaoke finale night." She paused, catching Ellie's reflection in the mirror above the sink. "Well... you know how you came to be."

Ellie said nothing, and Carolyn pressed on, her voice softer now.

"I'd been judged by my own reputation too. No work coming in, freshly divorced from David. I was still adjusting to life without his producer's salary. That was before the VHS revival, before the second wind. I was at a low point. And, well... I'd noticed your father had been at one too ever since that night in '75."

She turned off the tap and dried her hands, slowly. "We got talking. About perception, pressure, all of it. After years of being *Mrs David Swan*, your father's honesty was... refreshing."

Ellie stood frozen. She'd heard the story of her conception more times than she cared to count—but never *this* part. Never what had truly drawn her parents together: a shared understanding of what it meant to be judged in a village that never forgets.

She knew that feeling all too well.

At eighteen, she'd been quietly cruelly accused of causing her ex-fiancé's death. Three weeks after she ended the engagement, he'd taken a corner too fast on his motorbike and hadn't lived to explain himself. The whispers had chased her out of Meadowfield and across the bridge to Cardiff.

She'd run too.

Maybe she wasn't so different from her father after all.

"Do you know why he ran?" she asked, voice barely above a whisper.

Carolyn rinsed off the last of the green mask, patted her face dry, and smoothed on a creamier one. She returned to the counter, circling poses in her catalogue with a pen, as though they were discussing the weather.

"You *know* why he ran," Ellie said flatly, watching for even the slightest flicker in her mother's poised exterior.

"Yes," Carolyn admitted, setting down her pen. "It was my fault, in a way. Or Penny's, depending on how you look at it." She paused, choosing her words. "Your auntie overheard Benjamin Brown in The Drowsy Duck, talking to someone about a *new* clue in Sally's case, and he was writing a book to expose whoever did it." She absently traced a swirl on the glossy catalogue page. "Penny told me. She was worried it might drag the family into something. So I warned Peter. I didn't think he'd actually run."

Finally, the truth. "And you didn't think to tell me?"

She looked up, regret softening her features. "I

didn't want to believe it was the reason he left. I told myself it was a coincidence. But deep down, I knew. He sent me postcards here and there to let me know he was alright, but I wasn't sure if he'd ever come back."

"Why did he?" Ellie asked, hearing the demanding tone of her voice. "Why now?"

"He hasn't exactly been chatty since he's been back," Carolyn replied tersely. "He told me he's been using library computers to check local news. That's how he saw the article about the shop and the book launch. It felt like a sign that he couldn't keep running. He was ready to come home and see his family, and face the music—whatever tune Benjamin was singing."

Ellie jolted. She hadn't told her mother about Benjamin's death.

She opened her mouth, but Carolyn spoke first, nodding towards the back door.

"He's been sleeping in the greenhouse," she said, matter-of-fact. "I wanted to tell you, but he needed time to acclimatise. I offered him the guest room, but he said he… preferred being outside." Her gaze met Ellie's, calm but laced with concern. "He didn't come back last night. His bag is still out there."

Ellie paused, her thoughts a blur. He'd been *here*—sleeping just beyond the back door—and now he was gone. Again.

She didn't speak. There was nothing left to ask that Carolyn could answer.

* * *

The garden smelled of damp earth and washing powder as Ellie stepped outside. A car door slammed nearby. The shutters of a garage door clattered open. Somewhere in the back alley, milk bottles clinked in a crate.

Next door, Daniel's nan was already hanging freshly washed sheets, shaking them out like they owed her money. She spotted Ellie, her thin lips pursing in disapproval.

"I've heard what they're saying about *your* father," she called over the low stone wall, skipping any greeting. "Drowned the sister *and* the brother. Some families just can't help bringing trouble, can they?"

Ellie opened her mouth, but Daniel appeared just in time to spare her the effort of crafting a polite reply. He stepped outside in neatly pressed blue cotton pyjamas and intercepted his nan with effortless grace, gently steering her back toward the house.

"Let me take over, Nan," he said, taking the pegs from her. "You'll only aggravate your arthritis."

She let herself be steered away, but not without a final glare through the kitchen window.

Daniel turned back with an apologetic wince. "Sorry about her," he said, taking over the washing. "I was going to call, but I didn't know if you'd be up. It's a circus down at the pond. Police tape, the works."

Ellie leaned against the garden wall, sighing. "Of course it is." She pinched the bridge of her nose, eyes closed, trying to keep the emotion at bay. "I'm not sure

I'm ready for my family secrets to become village gossip."

"Pointless mudslinging," Daniel muttered, shaking out one of his nan's floral pillowcases.

"Mud sticks," Ellie said, her gaze drifting to the rooftops beyond. To the pond, where officers were searching the waters inch by inch. She hesitated, watching Daniel work. "You haven't seen my dad, have you?"

He shook his head, clipping the last corner of the pillowcase to the line.

Ellie scanned the garden. Daniel's nan was at the kitchen sink, pretending to wash a mug while watching them. But aside from her, they were alone.

"He came to see me last night," Ellie admitted, lowering her voice, moving closer to the wall. "He was rambling. Apologising. Kept saying it looked bad, that it was all 'wrong place, wrong time.' I thought he meant Sally, but he spoke about Benjamin in the past tense. I think he *knew* Benjamin was already dead."

Daniel stepped closer, his expression darkening. "When?"

"About an hour after he was supposedly seen at the pond."

The timeline settled between them like a lead balloon.

"The question is," Daniel said softly, "how likely is it that *both* times—both siblings—it was just coincidence?"

Ellie nodded, about to reply, when the back door burst open.

Auntie Penny rushed out, breathless, Duchess the Third trotting behind her.

"Ellie! There you are!" she cried as the dog yapped for her attention. "The most awful thing has happened. Benjamin Brown—"

"I know," Ellie cut in, casting a glance at the back gate. "Are we still on for lunch?"

"Absolutely," Daniel said at once. "The Giggling Goat at one?"

"Perfect." She mustered a smile. "And I promise no family drama. With luck, I'll have answers by then."

Daniel's expression softened. "You can talk to me about anything. Anytime. You know that."

"Thank you," she said, warmth blooming in her chest despite the grim start to the day.

They shared a quick kiss over the garden wall that sent Auntie Penny back into the cottage, adding another audience member through the kitchen window.

As Daniel disappeared inside with the empty basket, Ellie lingered a moment, grateful for his steady presence. Then she lifted her head and walked towards the greenhouse.

It stood at the far end of the small yard, tucked against the stone wall. Inside, the air was warm and damp, thick with the scent of soil. Most of the plants were wilting. Carolyn's gardening bursts never lasted and Auntie Penny was always left to take over.

In one corner, a rolled sleeping bag rested on a folded blanket. Beside it sat a battered rucksack Ellie recognised.

Her father's.

She paused, uneasy. Rifling through his things felt wrong, yet the need for answers pushed her past the discomfort.

The main compartment held what she expected: a change of clothes, his worn bird guide, a pair of binoculars. But tucked in a side pocket, bound with a rubber band, was a stack of envelopes.

She pulled them out, frowning. The earliest was postmarked 1975. The most recent from last year. All had been opened, then carefully resealed.

He'd kept them. For decades.

Ellie hesitated, then slid one free. It was dated three years ago. Inside was a short, typed message:

Just checking in, Peter. Good man for keeping our secret. Keep it up and nobody gets hurt. I'd hate for something to happen to your mummy in her bookshop, or your son in his café, or your little Sparrow over in Wales.

Her breath caught.

This wasn't just a letter. It was blackmail.

Someone had been threatening her father—and watching them all. Watching *her*, in Cardiff. *Sparrow.*

No signature. No return address. Just a cold, impersonal threat on plain paper.

Heart pounding, Ellie stuffed the entire stack into her coat pocket. This changed everything. Her father hadn't just run from suspicion—he'd been *protecting* them. From someone who knew where they lived. Someone who had been watching for *years*.

She glanced around, then slipped out the back gate

into the lane, avoiding Auntie Penny and her inevitable questions.

She needed to get to the bookshop.

If anyone could help make sense of those letters, it was her gran.

As Ellie crossed the village, the envelopes in her pocket felt heavier with each step. She'd meant to cut through the alleys to avoid the pond, but Old Mrs Parker and her lumbering greyhound had parked themselves squarely in the path, nudging Ellie towards the village centre.

The scene ahead matched Daniel's description. Blue-and-white tape fluttered in the breeze, cordoning off the pond. Officers moved slowly along the banks, combing the ground with methodical care. A respectful crowd had gathered, murmuring behind gloved hands.

DS Angela Cookson stood off to one side, her posture rigid as she spoke in low tones to a uniformed colleague. The moment she spotted Ellie, her expression tightened. She murmured something to the officer, then crossed the distance with purposeful steps.

They met outside The Drowsy Duck. The pub was still shut, but warm light glowed behind the frosted glass as Harold and his mother, Tilly, prepped for the day.

"Have you found him yet?" Ellie asked, skipping the niceties.

Angela shook her head. Morning light caught the

silver streaks in her dark hair. "I was about to ask you the same."

Ellie hesitated. Telling Angela her father had shown up at quarter to two in the morning might help clear his name, but something about the timing only strengthened the case against him. She needed to know what happened earlier in the evening before she added fuel to the fire of his charges.

"I haven't seen him since last night," Ellie said, and given the early hour, it was only a half-lie.

Her gaze drifted past the pond to Meadowfield Manor. Behind its ornate gates, the red-brick Victorian mansion loomed over the village, its many windows like watchful eyes. From the upper floors, you'd have a perfect view of the water.

In one of the windows, the curtain moved.

Or had it?

Was someone watching?

Or was it just her imagination?

"My father was accused in 1975—and again last night—both times because he found the body," Ellie said, thinking aloud. "Maybe people believed it so easily because there was no one else. No other suspects. No alternative."

She nodded towards the manor. "What do you know about the heist at Meadowfield Manor? The same night Sally drowned."

Angela's expression stayed neutral, but surprise flashed in her eyes that Ellie had drawn the connection.

"I've read the case notes," she admitted, folding her

arms. "It was mentioned at the time, but nothing ever stuck. No evidence. Nothing to go on." Her gaze sharpened. "But this time, there's a witness. Someone saw your father fleeing the scene."

She stepped closer, her voice low. "If you're going to do anything, Ellie—find him. Get him to turn himself in. Before this gets worse."

Then she turned, her sensible shoes crunching the gravel as she rejoined her team.

Ellie stayed where she was. The pond lay still, mirroring the clear spring sky, as if it hadn't claimed two lives from the same family, fifty years apart.

She tried to picture Benjamin's final moments: his head forced under, lungs burning, realising he would die exactly as his sister had. Had he fought? Shouted? Or simply surrendered to the symmetry?

She thought of her father. The same hands that steadied her binoculars, bandaged her knees, trembled with joy at the sight of a kestrel—*those* hands, murderous?

She couldn't believe it.

Ellie reached the bookshop as the bright sunlight caught the gilt lettering above the door, making *Meadowfield Books* gleam against the freshly painted green-and-cream façade. Through the window, she spotted her grandmother at the counter, head bent over what looked like Benjamin's manuscript. Oliver lounged nearby in one of the new armchairs, buried in a hefty Princess Diana biography.

The bell jangled as she stepped inside. Both heads snapped up, and their matching expressions of relief tugged at Ellie's chest. They'd been worried.

"Any luck?" Maggie called, setting the manuscript aside.

Oliver unfolded himself from the chair and crossed the room, pressing a takeaway cup into her hands. The scent of English breakfast tea, just the way she liked it, rose from the lid.

"Did you find him?" Maggie asked, coming around the counter. "Was he at your mother's?"

"No," Ellie said, accepting the tea gratefully. "Not anymore."

"I *knew* he wouldn't be," Oliver muttered, leaning against a bookshelf.

"But he *was*," Ellie said, watching their faces shift. "Since Thursday, apparently."

"He's been here since Thursday?" Oliver's eyebrows shot up. "And he couldn't pop in and say hello?"

"Mum said he needed time to adjust," Ellie replied, shrugging off her coat and placing it, along with her bag, on the counter. "He's been sleeping in her greenhouse."

"Your mother didn't offer him the guest room?" Maggie tutted, scandalised on her son's behalf, despite everything.

"It was his choice," Ellie said, sipping her tea. "Find anything in the book?"

Maggie shook her head and flipped it open, revealing a forest of colourful sticky notes. "Nothing's leapt out yet. The main character might be based on his sister since she's afraid of swimming. It's set in Devon, and someone's been writing her letters."

"'The final letter of importance came on the tenth day of the tenth month,'" Ellie recited, the line flashing back from her glance in the office.

"So you *were* sneaking a peek," Maggie said with a knowing look.

"Just the first page," Ellie replied defensively. "What's the rest like?"

"A paint-by-numbers romance. Girl meets boy, they break up, years later he starts writing her letters about their youth. They reconnect while he grieves his mother's death." Maggie closed the book with a soft *thump*. "It's sweet. Maybe Benjamin *was* a romantic, but if he meant to be cryptic, he wasn't obvious about it."

"He's an accountant," Ellie said, eyeing the plain cover. "A details man. Maybe the clues are in the logic, not the story." She straightened, her hand moving to her coat pocket. "But that can wait. I found something else."

She pulled out the stack of envelopes and laid them gently on the counter. "These were in Dad's bag. Letters going back to the 1970s. Threatening ones."

Maggie's face drained of colour. Her hand hovered above the pile, as if the yellowed envelopes might bite.

"Threatening him? What on earth…"

"Read them," Ellie said, spreading the dozens of

letters across the counter, nudging aside pots of pens and souvenir Wiltshire bookmarks to make room.

Oliver reached for one from the middle, postmarked 1993. Maggie took the oldest, its paper brittle with age, stamped 1975. Ellie kept the most recent, her fingers lingering over the typed address. No return address. Just like all the others.

"'You're doing well keeping your mouth shut, Peter. See that it stays that way,'" Oliver read aloud, his voice tight. "'Your little boy's school violin performance was lovely yesterday. The blue jumper suited him.'" He looked up, ashen. "That was my Christmas concert. Someone was *watching* me?"

Maggie's hands shook as she unfolded her letter. "'A reminder that silence is golden,'" she read. "'What a tragedy it would be if something happened to your mother's bookshop. Those old buildings can be so vulnerable to fire.'" Her hand flew to her mouth. "These are *awful*."

"They get worse," Ellie said grimly, eyes scanning the page. "'I see your daughter's settled in Cardiff now. Nice flat, though the street's not the safest after dark.'" She swallowed. "At first they came every few months. Then years apart. Always the same warning: keep quiet about what he saw that night. Never saying what that night was… or what actually happened."

"It's about the pond," Maggie said, rifling through another envelope, distress clouding her features. "It has to be."

"Then he knows something," Oliver added,

spreading several letters across the counter like evidence. "Something worth keeping buried for someone to send these for fifty years."

"Or someone *thinks* he knows something," Ellie countered, leaning forward. "Either way, it explains why he never showed them to the police." She turned to her gran, clutching a letter but staring far off into the middle distance. "Did you know about these letters? They're all addressed to our cottage, gran. Peter Cookson at 3 Cooper's Nook."

Maggie shook her head slowly. "If something came for Peter, I just handed it over. He had pen pals. Birding friends. That's all he said. I never asked more… never had a reason to." Her voice cracked. "He *never* told me."

"He was protecting us," Ellie said softly. "These letters will have scared him. We know what he's like. Scared enough to run when he heard about the book."

Maggie blinked, then looked up. "Are you suggesting Benjamin sent these?"

Ellie hesitated. "I'm not sure. Maybe he wanted to scare Dad into confessing. Or slipping up."

"But these letters warn him not to speak," Oliver pointed out, tapping one. "They're telling him to stay silent, not confess."

"Then it wasn't Benjamin," Ellie said firmly. "Unless he killed his sister—which seems unlikely, considering how *he* died—someone else has been threatening Dad. For fifty years."

"So why run?" Oliver asked, raking a hand through his hair.

Maggie sank onto a nearby stool, her face lined with exhaustion. "You didn't see the worst of it," she said quietly, as if the past might overhear. "It was awful. He was hounded. People needed someone to blame for Sally's death, and Peter was easy to point at." Her gaze wandered to the window, taking in the village beyond. "Eventually, it quieted. But if Benjamin's book threatened to stir it all up again…"

"He ran because it's all he knows," Ellie said softly. "He can't face this any more than we want to. But we have to. For him. For Sally. And for Benjamin."

Maggie sighed, looking over at the book-signing table they'd set up. "Benjamin should've been here today, signing his book." She shook her head. "It doesn't feel real."

"He was meant to be here yesterday," Ellie said gently. "Maybe his paranoia over the stolen books wasn't so paranoid after all. If someone wanted to keep the truth buried—"

"Not just anyone," Maggie cut in, suddenly alert. "He blamed the postman, didn't he? I wonder if we've still got the same one… Oh, what was his name—"

The bell above the door interrupted her as a teenage girl in a Meadowfield Comprehensive uniform stepped hesitantly inside.

"Um, excuse me," she asked. "Do you have *An Inspector Calls*?"

"GCSE time again," Maggie said, slipping

seamlessly into bookseller mode as she stood. "Come with me, dear. We've got a whole shelf of required reading."

As Maggie led the girl away, Ellie watched them go, a pang of nostalgia catching her off guard. It felt like another lifetime that she was that girl. Cramming for exams and thinking coursework was the worst life could throw at you. The memories almost made her smile.

"I can't believe I never knew," she said to Oliver. "About Dad. About any of this."

"I did," Oliver admitted, folding his arms as he leaned on the counter. "You had *your* mother's surname."

"Her married name," Ellie corrected. "Back when she thought 'Eleanor Swan' sounded like an actress, and Ellie Cookson sounded like..."

"A bookshop manager?" Oliver replied with a hint of humour. "Well, I'm a boring old Cookson. And I went to school with the kids of the parents who remembered all about what people said a Cookson once did. Their kids made sure I never forgot it." He gulped, then almost as an after thought, added, "We did go to different schools though."

Ellie let out a dry laugh. "At mine, they were too busy reminding me Mum was the 'washed-up actress' from *that* soap."

They exchanged a look.

Children of old scandal, tied by second-hand shame.

Ellie turned to the window, watching villagers drift

towards the pond. After a long breath, she faced her brother.

"Where would he go, Oli? We need to think like Dad."

Oliver shrugged. "Scotland, maybe? Somewhere open. Somewhere wild. He could handle it."

"That doesn't narrow it down."

She glanced at the letters and manuscript on the counter. Maybe the answers were already there. They just had to learn how to read them.

"If we solve this, we clear Dad's name," she said. "He can stop running."

"But how do we find him?"

Before Ellie could figure that part out, their gran returned with the schoolgirl, who clutched her copy of *An Inspector Calls* as she paid. Once the bell jangled behind her, leaving them alone, Maggie turned, eyes bright with fresh resolve.

"Then we'll clear his name so he can come home with his head held high," she declared. "Because I'm not living through that again." She straightened her cardigan. "We need to be smart. First things first—" She picked up the manuscript. "I'm making a copy. If the truth's in here, someone didn't want it getting out."

She disappeared into the back room. Silence settled between Ellie and Oliver.

"Do you think he did it?" Ellie whispered.

Oliver stiffened. "Are you seriously asking me that?"

"Yes."

He opened his mouth, then closed it again. "I *hope*

he didn't," he said finally. "But… Ellie…" He lowered his voice. "Mum's being cagey, but she says it's not just about witness sightings. There's *evidence*."

"What evidence?" Ellie asked, stomach tightening.

"She wouldn't say," Oliver replied, frustration edging into his voice. "Just that it's serious enough they'll have trouble *not* charging him once they find him."

Ellie's jaw set. "Then we make it hard for them. I need to go back to the beginning—to that night in 1975."

"I've got to get back to the café," Oliver said, checking his watch. "Want to look for him later? After work?"

"Sure," Ellie nodded. "We'll plan it over lunch. I'm meeting Daniel at your place."

"I'll have your tea ready," he promised, squeezing her shoulder before heading out.

"Ellie!" Maggie's voice rang from the back. "The printer's out of ink! How do we make a copy?"

Ellie followed the voice and found her grandmother frowning at the blinking error on the printer screen.

"I can order more, but it won't get here till tomorrow," Ellie said. "We'll have to keep the original safe."

"We still need a backup," Maggie insisted, tapping the desk.

"We'll do what we did with the coffee instructions," Ellie said, pulling out her phone. "I'll photograph each page. That way, we've got a digital copy no one can steal."

As she began photographing the manuscript, a plan started to form.

"Can I take an hour for my lunchbreak?" she asked, not looking up.

"I suppose," Maggie replied warily. "What are you planning?"

"I've got a story to chase."

"The letters?" Maggie asked.

"No. The manor," Ellie said, glancing up. "When I was at the pond, I swear I saw someone watching from those big windows." She returned to photographing, her fingers steady. "Dad finding Sally wasn't the only thing that happened that night. Everyone focused on him—but what about the jewel heist across the road?"

Chapter 6
Mrs Winchester's Lavender Memories

L ater, on her extended lunch break,
Meadowfield Manor loomed into view, its high
red-brick walls striking against the clear spring
sky. A gravel drive curved through immaculately kept
lawns, leading to a house that belonged on a postcard or
in the opening credits of a period drama.

The Winchesters had owned the manor for
generations, ever since one ancestor made a tidy fortune
during the railway boom, supplying timber for sleepers,
back when Meadowfield still had a working station and
ambitions of grandeur.

That money had lasted long enough to buy land,
build the house, and preserve the family's comfortable
obscurity ever since. They'd never been village royalty,
just quiet wealth behind iron gates. A footnote. Present
but apart.

Since moving back, Ellie hadn't been sure who lived
there now. She'd assumed the older woman who'd lived

there when she was a girl had passed away. But perhaps Mrs Winchester still lived within those walls?

She recalled seeing her only once, at the post office years ago. Mrs Winchester had appeared long enough for Ellie to see her gran gasp like she'd spotted a rare bird. Ellie hadn't seen her since. But even then, swathed in fur and jewels, she'd seemed like she'd stepped through a portal from some bygone, gilded era.

Standing at the ornate gates, Ellie hesitated. The manor still felt like a world apart, despite being just one stone wall away from Meadowfield's heart.

She was weighing her next move when someone cleared their throat behind her—loudly, and with intent.

Ellie turned to find Daniel's nan at the bus stop across the street, lips pursed in her usual expression of disapproval. Behind her, police continued their slow, grim sweep of the pond.

"They found your father yet?" Daniel's nan called, making no effort to lower her voice. "It's as good as proved, from what I'm hearing."

"Innocent until proven guilty," Ellie replied evenly, crossing the road to meet her. The words felt hollow, even as she said them.

Daniel's nan perched on the bench, her handbag clutched protectively in her lap. She looked uncomfortable, as if standing too close to Ellie might somehow tarnish her by association.

"Off anywhere nice?" Ellie asked, keeping her tone polite despite the woman's clear disdain.

"What's it to you?" she snapped, but then a grudging answer followed. "If you must know, I'm off to the market in Marlborough. It's fruit and veg day. I'm making Daniel a vegetable soup tonight. That boy still doesn't eat enough greens."

Ellie suppressed a smile at the thought of an adult-aged school teacher being fussed over by his nan like a finicky toddler. But there was something oddly touching about the fierce protectiveness, so she let the snap slide.

She glanced at the manor's gate out of the corner of her eye. "Do you remember anything about the jewel heist? The one that happened here in 1975?"

"Of *course* I do!" Daniel's nan huffed, clearly offended. "What do you take me for? My memory's sharp as a needle." Her eyes drifted to the pond. "Same night your father found Sally." Her lips pinched. The implication hung in the air.

"Do you think the two events were connected?" Ellie asked, ignoring the jab.

"How should I know?" she said briskly, glancing at her watch and peering down the road for the bus. "All I know is my Herbert worked for the paper and he said the Winchesters paid to have the story dropped from future issues. They didn't want the whole village knowing they'd let their guard down."

She leaned forward, voice lowering, eyes glinting. "Meredith and Jonathan Winchester—dead now, mind you—always did things their own way. Cut off their son without a penny but lavished everything on their daughter." She gave a disapproving sniff. "Nasty business, playing favourites with your children."

Then, abruptly, she said, "Speaking of families, what's all that clicking next door?" She mimicked a camera shutter with surprising accuracy. "Day and night it is! I bang on the wall, but they don't pay a blind bit of notice."

"That's probably Auntie Penny photographing my mum," Ellie said. "She's practising for a modelling shoot."

"*Modelling?*" Daniel's nan snorted. "Still trying for that comeback, is she?"

"I don't think she'll ever stop," Ellie replied, almost fondly.

"Well, good luck to her," came the sarcastic reply, followed swiftly by, "And tell them to keep it down. I can barely hear *Deal or No Deal* with all that racket." She rose as a bus rounded the corner. "If you want to know more about that robbery, go talk to Mrs Winchester yourself. The daughter who was in that night—she still lives there."

She shuffled onto the bus, leaving Ellie to return to the gates of Meadowfield Manor, digesting these new nuggets of the story. The daughter who'd been present during the robbery still lived in the house. Perhaps she'd seen something that night. She was sure she'd seen someone watching at the window earlier.

Ellie spotted a small brass intercom set into one of the stone pillars. Before she could talk herself out of it, she pressed the button.

"Yeeesss?" came a man's voice, the drawn-out syllable steeped in boredom and faint judgment.

Ellie hesitated, suddenly unsure what to say. "I'm here to see Mrs Winchester," she managed, trying to sound as though she had a perfectly valid reason.

A pause followed—long enough to fray her nerves. Then, surprisingly, the gates clicked and began to swing open.

"Mrs Winchester and the rest of the guests are having afternoon tea in the garden," the man said, his tone suggesting she was late rather than unexpected.

Guests?

Ellie froze. Was she expected? She considered correcting the obvious misunderstanding—but the gates were open.

And opportunity didn't knock. It rolled back with wrought-iron grace.

Not questioning her good fortune, Ellie slipped through the gates before they could change their mind.

Unlike the village's medieval cottages with their crooked walls and thatched roofs, the Manor was Victorian: red brick with ornate white window frames, grand gables, and tall chimneys that pierced the sky like they were reaching for the clouds.

Despite the owner's age, the house was immaculately kept. A gardener clipped stray leaves from the hedges, someone stood atop a ladder tending to the pointing, and a man in a crisp white shirt waited at the door with the posture of someone who'd been keeping watch for decades.

Ellie hesitated at the base of the stone steps, uncertain—until a burst of laughter drifted around the side of the house. The sound was so unexpected—so alive and warm compared to her grim morning—that she found herself pulled in.

The laughter led her past rose beds swaying gently in the breeze, to a weathered wooden gate half-hidden by ivy. Beyond it, tucked away like a secret from a storybook, was a walled garden. Under the pink blossom of a flowering cherry tree, three women sat around a wrought-iron table, sunlight glinting off their china cups.

Mrs Winchester was the first to notice her. Her head turned with uncanny precision, teacup poised mid-air. She sat with the elegance of someone who'd once hosted garden parties in heels—and never saw a reason to stop. She had to be in her nineties, but her eyes still held a spark, and her stiff posture put Ellie's to shame on a good day. Soft silver waves framed her face, her lipstick was perfectly applied, and a string of pearls gleamed against her collar. She wore a cream blazer, sharp and quietly expensive.

"It seems we're not alone, ladies," she remarked in a soft, commanding voice.

The other two turned in unison. Ellie froze. A familiar face. Miss Mills. The schoolteacher Daniel had reintroduced at the book launch.

Beside her sat a woman in a vicar's collar, almost snow-white hair cut in a neat jaw-length bob. She had to be in her late eighties, at least, but Mrs Winchester felt older. Maybe it was the manor's opulence, trapping her in a bygone era.

"Ellie!" Sarah Mills exclaimed, clearly surprised. "What a lovely coincidence. Ladies, this is Ellie Swan— Maggie's granddaughter, from the bookshop. I taught her back in the day." She gestured to the others. "Ellie, this is my aunt, Vivienne Winchester, and Reverend Catherine Harper from St Mary's."

"Do join us, dear," Mrs Winchester said, gesturing to the empty fourth chair. "Tilly from The Drowsy Duck hasn't shown up for our weekly debriefing. We've saved you some scones."

Feeling oddly off-balance, Ellie took the seat, murmuring thanks as Sarah poured her a cup of tea. Conversation drifted around her as gently as the breeze stirring the cherry blossoms—oddly mundane, given the events of the past day.

"The Clarksons' wheat crop is in terrible trouble this year," the vicar was saying, spreading clotted cream on a scone with quiet precision. "All that early rain in April."

"I always said Frank planted too early," Mrs Winchester replied. "His father would never have made such a mistake."

Ellie sat quietly, stunned by the banality of it all. A man had been found dead in the pond less than twenty-four hours ago, and here they were discussing crops as if nothing had happened. It felt surreal—like she'd stepped into another dimension where tragedy didn't disturb the bubble of afternoon pleasantries.

Then, like a cloud passing across the sun, Mrs Winchester set down her teacup with a decisive clink. "The police were round this morning," she announced, to no one in particular. "Looking for some man in his sixties. Thought he might be hiding in my garden, of all places."

"That would be my father," Ellie said, the words escaping before she could stop them. Even to her own ears, her voice sounded oddly detached. She wasn't sure if it was shock from the murder—or from discussing it over Earl Grey in a secret garden—but everything felt distant.

Sarah's teacup froze mid-air. "There was a drowning in the pond this morning, Aunt. They think Peter might be connected."

"He was seen nearby," Ellie clarified, sitting straighter. "But I doubt he was more involved than that."

"Who was drowned?" Mrs Winchester asked.

"Benjamin Brown," Sarah replied softly.

Mrs Winchester's eyebrows lifted. "Benjamin Brown? But, Sarah, you were engaged to him once, weren't you? Terribly dull man, as I recall… Why didn't you say?"

"I *was* going to get there, Aunt," Sarah said, a flicker of edge in her voice. "I just didn't want to *start* with it. And frankly, it hasn't sunk in. I'm still in shock."

"That's actually why I'm here," Ellie said, seizing the moment. "About the drowning—or rather, the one in 1975. And something else that happened that same night."

"The burglary," Mrs Winchester finished for her, a knowing smile curving her lips.

"Yes," Ellie confirmed, surprised. "I saw both events on the same newspaper front page. I was hoping to find a connection."

"Oh, not this old story again," the vicar said with a forced laugh.

"Yes, *that* old story again," Mrs Winchester snapped. "I told the police back then it must have been connected, and…" She paused, tilting her head. "This drowning—do you think it's connected too?"

"No," the vicar said quickly. "There's no way it could be."

"Actually," Ellie said, sitting forward, "I wouldn't be so sure. Benjamin Brown wrote a book that might expose what happened to his sister—Sally—who drowned that same night in 1975. If you can tell me anything about the burglary, Mrs Winchester, I might be able to piece it together. And clear my father's name."

"Peter…" Mrs Winchester murmured thoughtfully.

"Cookson," Ellie supplied.

"Hmm," she grumbled, her fingers circling the rim of her teacup. "He was the young chap accused back then? Found the girl, didn't he?"

"He did," Sarah confirmed quietly, offering Ellie a small, supportive smile. "He pulled her out."

"He was never convicted," Ellie added. "There was no evidence. But anything you remember—"

"Lavender," Mrs Winchester said suddenly, setting her cup down with a sharp *clink*. "Mother and Father were out that night—went to see *The Mousetrap*. Big fans of Christie, they were." Her lips curled at the memory. "I stayed behind. I was in my forties, newly home after my second divorce, and not in the mood for more theatre. But I *should* have gone. Whoever broke in must've assumed the house was empty."

"But it wasn't?" Ellie asked, the iron chair creaking as she edged forward. "You were here. Did you catch them?"

Vivienne shook her head, her sigh tinged with regret. "I was in my room. Wallowing, I imagine." She let out a dry little laugh. "I heard something in the hall. This old house has always creaked dreadfully, so I thought nothing of it. Then, a little later, I heard footsteps. Heavy ones. I assumed my parents had come home early—but then the steps passed my room, and there were more than two sets. I counted four."

"How could you know that for sure?" the vicar interrupted. "I can't imagine it's easy to tell how many people are walking past a room."

"I counted four," Vivienne repeated, her tone cool and final.

She gestured to the tall windows overlooking the vast lawn. "I moved to the window up there. Father always parked around the back—didn't like to 'advertise,' as he'd say. But his car wasn't there. Then I heard a crash in the other room."

Ellie leaned in, heart thudding. "What did you do? You must've been terrified."

"I was," Vivienne said quietly, and her breath caught just slightly. "I didn't have a phone in my room, despite my repeated requests. I don't think they wanted me back here, not really. But all that changed when they needed someone to care for them."

Her gaze drifted toward the house, the past tugging at the edges of her composure. But she blinked slowly, then looked back to her tea.

"I didn't think about confronting them. I knew by then they were burglars, and I wasn't about to get myself killed. So I thought about where they wouldn't look. I crawled under the bed—wedged between hat boxes."

She closed her eyes as if reliving it.

"Three of them came in. Went straight for the dressing table by the window. Knew exactly which drawers to check. Maybe they were lucky. Maybe they weren't. I listened to them rummage, too scared to breathe. Then one of them started pulling out the hat boxes."

Ellie held her breath.

"They would've found me—if someone hadn't rushed up the stairs just then. Another set of footsteps. And a strong scent of lavender, like a gust of wind. The new addition whispered something, and the others froze. Then they left—quick, quiet. I heard yet another set of footsteps come from my parents' room… and that was that."

The vicar raised an eyebrow, her teacup hovering. "I thought you said there were four sets of footsteps? By my count, that's three in the room, one running up the stairs, and another from your parents' room."

"It was four," Vivienne said, tone like stone. "Then it became five."

The vicar let out a brittle laugh. "Honestly. You're not suggesting Benjamin's sweet sister was part of a burglary?"

"No," Mrs Winchester said firmly.

"She might've witnessed something," Ellie offered. "Something she wasn't meant to see."

Mrs Winchester's smile widened. "Very clever, young one." She nodded approvingly. "I thought the same. Those burglars were clever—they slipped away, never caught." She took a delicate sip of tea. "In the end, I was right about my parents. They returned during the interval—*The Mousetrap*, they'd seen it so many times, no surprises left—and scared off whoever the five were. They ran quickly. Like… children, almost. And the scent of lavender lingered."

"What do you think it was?" Ellie asked.

"Soap," Mrs Winchester said without hesitation. "The same kind we kept in the downstairs bathroom—bought from a little shop on South Street, according to the housemaid at the time. A few days later, I decided to venture out to replace it myself. The teenage girl behind the counter, working there with her mother, looked at me as if I were the Grim Reaper come to carry her off." Her smile turned thin. "From the look in her eyes alone, I *knew* she was involved. I told the police—but they did nothing."

"Well," the vicar interrupted again, "you did have that soap in your own bathroom. One of them might've washed their hands before coming upstairs—"

"Wasn't *your* daughter, Tracey, friends with that soap shop girl?" Mrs Winchester cut in, fixing the vicar with a pointed look.

The vicar faltered. "They were… friendly, yes."

"Joanne Cole," Sarah supplied. "Still runs the place —Lovely Bubbly. She inherited it from her mother."

The vicar checked her watch with theatrical surprise. "Is that the time? I'm afraid I must dash—parish council meeting." She gathered her things, her movements stiff with barely concealed agitation. "The tea and scones were delightful, as always."

Sarah also rose. "I need to get back to school—lunch break's nearly over." She kissed her aunt's cheek. "Same time next week?"

Mrs Winchester nodded. Sarah turned to Ellie. "Coming?"

"Yes," Ellie said, standing. But before she could move, Mrs Winchester reached out and caught her hand in a surprisingly firm grip.

"Do you think you're going to figure out what happened to my jewels?" the older woman asked.

"You've given me a thread to pull," Ellie replied honestly.

"I hope you do," Mrs Winchester said, squeezing her hand. "Not for the jewels—the insurance paid out. I never cared much for them. But that girl… so young. No life."

Ellie swallowed. "I'll try."

"Yes," Mrs Winchester nodded. "I think you will."

Ellie left the garden with much to think about. Sarah was waiting, and the two women walked side by side around the manor, the late morning sun warm on their backs.

"It's noble of you," Sarah said, "wanting to know what happened back then."

Ellie studied her profile. "You'd have been a teenager, right? Did you know Benjamin's sister?"

"I did," Sarah nodded, gaze distant. "We were in teacher training together. She was sweet." A shadow crossed her face. "I saw her that night—at The Old Bell. I had somewhere to be, she stayed. That was the last time. We said, 'See you tomorrow'… and we didn't."

She looked close to tears. Ellie gently changed the subject. "You were engaged to Benjamin?"

"A long time ago," Sarah said. Her laugh was brittle. "I'm devastated about how he died… the irony of it. But like I said—it was a long time ago. He changed after Sally. Became someone else."

"What was he like?"

Sarah checked her watch. "I need to go, but—if you'd like to talk more, lunch tomorrow? Café on South Street?"

"I'd like that," Ellie said.

Sarah slipped through the side gate. Ellie lingered on the gravel path, the manor behind her like a memory she hadn't lived but now somehow carried. The scent of lavender. Five sets of footsteps. A soap shop girl with guilty eyes. The story wasn't collapsing—it was unfolding. A lock turning.

Then—

"*Lunch!*" The word escaped in a gasp. "Daniel!"

She checked her watch and groaned. Half past one. She'd completely lost track of time, and now she was hopelessly late.

Chapter 7
Rumour Has It

When Ellie had worked to the ticking clock of studio schedules, time had been something she could measure down to the second. Scene changes, costume calls, retakes all followed a rhythm she could rely on. But in sleepy Meadowfield, time was elastic. An hour could vanish in the blink of a scone-laden tea, while ten minutes could stretch on like a Dickensian funeral. Today, it had slipped straight through her fingers.

She tore down the long drive of Meadowfield Manor, the stately house shrinking behind her as she hit the pavement at a jog. Her mind still churned with five sets of footsteps, lavender-scented air, and the vicar's abrupt departure at the mention of her daughter. Tracey Harper. The name meant nothing to Ellie.

She shook it off and picked up speed, hoping to salvage something of her missed lunch break.

By the time she burst into the café, flushed and

breathless, Oliver flung his arms wide behind the counter, as though auditioning for a village panto.

"She lives!" he declared to the nearly empty room. "We were about to organise a search party."

Her eyes went straight to Daniel, waiting in their usual corner, laptop half-closed, a nearly empty cup of tea beside a precarious stack of Year Three homework books. His disappointment passed quickly, but not before it landed.

"I am so, so sorry," Ellie said, dropping into the chair with a groan. "I got caught up at the manor. I didn't realise the time."

"It's fine," Daniel replied, already gathering his books. "Really. But I've got to get back. Mock exams in the hall after lunch—I can't miss it." He hesitated. "I'm s-sorry I can't s-stay." The old stutter crept in, soft but unmistakable, before he glanced at his watch. "Drink after work?"

"Perfect," she said quickly. "Just the two of us."

"I can only stay for one," he replied, already rising. "I need to catch up on my marking before half-term."

"I'll be there. On time," she promised, managing a hopeful smile.

He kissed her cheek—brisk, not cold—and hurried out, checking his watch again as the bell jangled behind him.

Oliver slid into the vacated seat with theatrical flourish, planting a cup of strong tea in front of her.

"It broke my heart," he said, placing a hand to his

chest. "Watching his little face glance at the clock every minute. Like a puppy."

"Don't," Ellie groaned, hiding behind her hands. "I genuinely forgot. I got held up trying to help Dad."

"I've been up to my neck in cold tea and tepid theories all morning," Oliver said, his light-hearted expression faltering as he glanced around the café. He leaned in, voice dropping to a whisper. "It's getting bad out there, Ellie. The things people are saying…"

"What things?" Ellie asked, her stomach tightening.

"Dad and Benjamin had a massive row in the pub. That Dad threatened him, and Benjamin was terrified." Oliver's eyes betrayed his worry. "I heard Mrs Hendricks telling everyone she heard from Pam in the post office that Dad was seen by the pond just after midnight. Soaking wet."

"It wasn't a row," Ellie reminded him. "You were there. Dad confronted Benjamin, it went down like a wet balloon, and he left."

"And came back," Oliver added pointedly. "That's what people are saying. He left, then came back and was there all night… biding his time."

Ellie hesitated. Her hands curled around her tea cup, suddenly too warm.

"Oliver… there's something I haven't told you."

His eyes shot up.

"Last night. Dad came to see me. Just before two."

Oliver's eyes narrowed. "What? Are you serious? Why didn't you say anything?"

"I'm saying something now," she replied, more

sharply than intended. She paused, then added more gently, "I didn't know what to make of it. He wasn't making much sense—rambling, apologising, saying he should never have come back. That he was in the wrong place at the wrong time... again." She drew a shaky breath. "Looking back, I think he was trying to warn me. He knew how it would look. Maybe he knew what was coming."

"Well, whatever happened, he was right," Oliver said grimly. "It's like the village has already made up its mind. People are bored and *hungry* for a proper village scandal."

"That's not what this is."

"We know that," Oliver said. "But they don't want the truth, Ellie. They want the *story*."

His words hung between them for a moment before he straightened, as though trying to tuck the worry somewhere it couldn't be seen.

"So?" he said, tone lighter now. "What was worth standing up Teacher of the Year for?"

"Afternoon tea at Meadowfield Manor."

"You're joking." His eyes widened.

"I'm not. I fell down the rabbit hole—and I got a name."

"Well, don't keep me in suspense."

"Know anything about Joanne at the soap shop?"

Oliver shrugged. "Not really. She pops in sometimes. Though now I think about it… she never seems to pay. Someone else always picks up the bill." He narrowed his eyes. "Is she involved?"

"I don't know yet," Ellie said, rising. "I'm going to see what Gran knows."

"So you're not even going to tell me about tea with the Winchester royal family?"

"Another time," she called over her shoulder. "And if you hear from Dad—"

"I'll ring before he's through the door," Oliver promised, waving her off.

Ellie stepped out into the sunshine, her mind racing. A soap shop. A lavender scent. A fifty-year-old burglary. And somehow, her father—threaded through it all.

Back at the bookshop, Ellie pushed through the door and froze. The cheerful jingle of the bell was swallowed by a clamour of voices. The space was packed— shoulder to shoulder, flushed faces hot with excitement or outrage. Pandemonium, and more crowded than launch day.

Her grandmother stood behind the counter, hands raised in a sorry attempt to calm the crowd.

"—as I've *already* explained," Maggie said, voice strained but steady, "the book launch isn't going ahead, for *obvious* reasons."

"But Benjamin announced it at the pub!" shouted a red-faced man near the front, jabbing a finger. "He said the *truth* was in his book! If you've got it, we want it!"

"She's covering up for her son," called a woman

from the romance section, voice thick with accusation. "He was seen at the pond. Everyone knows it!"

"That's right!" another chimed in. "He's done a runner because he's guilty!"

Ellie's midsection flipped. The tide had turned. Her worst nightmare—an angry mob in the shop, and her grandmother facing them alone.

She took a steadying breath, called on years of wrangling temperamental directors and cast members, and stepped forward. Her posture lengthened, voice calm, clear, and cutting through the noise.

"Excuse me."

The room fell still.

"The book launch has been cancelled out of respect for Benjamin Brown," Ellie said, meeting their eyes one by one. "We do not have the books. They were meant to be delivered to Benjamin yesterday, but they weren't. That's why the event didn't happen. That's all we know." She gestured to the shelves and added, "If you'd like to browse our other titles, you're more than welcome to."

The crowd grumbled. A few muttered under their breath, shuffling to the door, disappointed by the lack of drama. But some lingered, their eyes narrowed with suspicion.

A well-dressed woman near the till stepped forward. Clutching her fancy handbag to her chest like armour, she lifted her chin.

"But it's true, isn't it?" she said, her voice ringing through the now-quiet shop. "Your son killed Benjamin.

Just like he killed his sister. That's what's in the book, isn't it?"

"No!" Maggie gasped—her composure cracking for the first time.

"So you *do* know what's in the book?" a man by the window pounced. "You've got it!"

"No," Maggie repeated, her voice catching. "I meant—*no*, that's not what happened. My son hasn't been charged with anything, so if you'll please—"

"That's because he's on the run," someone muttered from the back.

"Enough," Ellie called. Her voice was firm, but there was a plea in it too—reaching for whatever decency still lived in the room. "Like I said: you're welcome to browse, but we're not here to answer questions about the case."

The atmosphere shifted. A few of the mob looked sheepish. Others clung to their anger but began to drift towards the door.

At last—mercifully—the crowd thinned, until only a handful of silent browsers remained, carefully avoiding eye contact with either of them.

Maggie sank onto the stool behind the counter, her face pale.

"Thank you," she whispered as Ellie approached. "They started trickling in, one after another, and when I couldn't give them a book…" She shook her head. "I was beginning to think I'd have to ring Angela."

"I'm sorry I was gone so long," Ellie said, guilt

rushing in. She should have been here—not chasing ghosts across the village.

Maggie waved a trembling hand. "Nonsense. People will believe anything if it sounds wild enough." She took a slow, steadying breath. "What did you find?"

Ellie recapped the manor visit—five burglars, the lavender scent, Mrs Winchester's suspicions about the soap shop girl.

"The Coles," Maggie nodded, leaning in, lowering her voice. "That shop's been in their family for generations. Joanne took it over from her mother not too long ago. She's been struggling lately—behind on rent, according to Martha at the estate agent's."

"Financial troubles?" Ellie mused. "Could be a sign she didn't profit from the robbery?"

"Ellie," Maggie said, her voice dropping, "are you sure you want to pull that thread? Some things might be better left buried."

The words hung in the air—soft, but weighty.

"I have to," Ellie said at last. "Not just for Dad. For the truth. Don't you want to know what really happened? What happened to Sally that night? And again to Benjamin?"

Maggie's shoulders sagged. "The truth isn't always kind, love. Not to those who seek it. And not to those it reveals."

"I can handle it," Ellie said firmly—though a small voice inside her wasn't so sure.

What if the truth wasn't what she hoped for?

What if her father wasn't the gentle man she'd always believed him to be?

No.

She forced the thought away. She had to believe in his innocence. The alternative was unthinkable.

"I should pay Joanne a visit," Ellie said, her resolve sharpening after witnessing the mob's eagerness to condemn her father.

"You should," Maggie agreed, giving Ellie a gentle nudge. "I can manage here."

Ellie stepped out onto South Street and crossed the narrow road to Lovely Bubbly, the soap shop's mint-green front a cheerful contrast to its more muted neighbours. Dried lavender framed the doorway, and the windows brimmed with pastel soaps curled into roses and seashells.

But as she reached the door, her heart sank. A small wooden sign hung in the window: 'Closed for Lunch'

She cupped her hands to the glass and peered inside. The shop was dark. No movement. She tried the handle—locked.

After everything that had happened today, this small setback felt wildly disproportionate. Her frustration flared.

She stepped back, checking her watch. Just past two. Should she wait?

"Looking for Joanne?"

Ellie turned. Zara from the gift shop stood across the street, arms folded, a knowing look in her eyes.

"Yes, actually," Ellie replied, shielding her eyes from the sun. "Do you know where she might be?"

Zara shook her head. "She has been closing up at odd hours lately. Long lunches, early finishes. I think she is scared of that shop—has not a clue what she is doing. Always has a sale on, too. Makes the rest of us look bad." She leaned in slightly, lowering her voice, though no one else was near. "Between you and me, I would be surprised if she makes it through summer."

Ellie thanked her and headed back to the bookshop. She'd try again later.

For now, she had a new bookshop to run, a missing father to worry about—and a growing list of questions that refused to leave her alone.

Chapter 8
Lovely Bubbly

The rest of the day passed in a bit of a blur. Ellie kept herself busy, throwing her energy into the shop, hoping the hum of routine might drown out her racing thoughts. She moved between customers like she'd been doing it for years—not just her second day on the job. Maggie kept up beside her, the two of them slipping through the narrow aisles like they'd always worked together.

After the morning's chaos—the crowd, the accusations, the sideways glances—it was a relief to slip back into the steady hum of bookish conversation. The shop had become a haven again, a quiet place where the loudest voices lived on paper, not in the café down the street.

"Something romantic—but not too sweet," said the young woman hovering uncertainly by the classics shelf, her beret askew and expression hopeful. "I tried Austen once, but couldn't get on with her."

"Then you need the Brontës," Ellie replied, already pulling a copy of *Jane Eyre* from the shelf. "Gothic drama, windswept moors, brooding men full of secrets... Far less matchmaking, far more madness in the attic."

The woman laughed. "That sounds more like it."

"And if you like this, try *The Tenant of Wildfell Hall* next." Ellie handed over the book with a knowing smile. "Anne Brontë doesn't get the attention she deserves compared to her sisters. Think of her as the quiet one who turns out to have the sharpest knife."

A flicker of surprise crossed the woman's face, followed by delight. "That's quite the pitch."

"I do my best," Ellie said. "Oh—and if you want something with a little more bite, *Villette* will take you somewhere strange and melancholy. It's not an easy read, but it stays with you."

The woman left soon after, book in hand and face glowing. The bell jingled as the door closed behind her —the last customer of the day.

Ellie flipped the sign to 'CLOSED' and leaned against the cool glass.

Some small part of her had expected her father to appear—sheepish, bearing peace offerings: custard creams or jelly babies, like he used to when he'd take her down to The Burrows. She'd read while he birdwatched, the two of them settled in the grass with biscuits, sweets, and a flask of tea Maggie had packed just so.

But the street outside remained still.

No sign of him.

"I couldn't help overhearing, but those were perfect recommendations," Maggie called from her seat near the fading fire, Benjamin's manuscript open on her lap. Her pencil hovered, poised to catch anything useful. "I knew you'd be a natural."

"I went through the same phase at her age." Ellie crossed the shop and dropped into the armchair opposite. "Any luck?"

Maggie shook her head, tapping the pencil in quiet frustration.

"Nothing that screams confession or hidden message. Just a romance—girl inherits a cottage, reconnects with an old flame through romantic letters... some lovely reflections on grief and second chances, but nothing that leaps out as a clue."

She shut the book with a sigh.

"There has to be something," Ellie said, flicking through a few pages. "He wouldn't have made such a fuss at the pub over a simple love story. He wanted people to read between the lines. Maybe it's not what's *in* the book, but what it represents."

"Well, if he buried something about Sally, or the pond, or that night... it's deep."

She shuffled into the back room and returned with a well-worn broom.

"Feels good to be open again, but I haven't missed the sweeping."

"Which is why I'll do it," Ellie said, intercepting the

broom. "I'll be twice as quick. You do the cashing up—I still haven't got the hang of that."

"You will," Maggie said, handing it over without protest. "We make quite the team, don't we?"

"I knew we would."

They shared a smile that, for a moment, pushed back the shadows of the day.

Ellie moved through the shop, sweeping the aisles and brushing dust from the day's footprints into a tidy pile. She tipped the dustpan into the bin out back, then returned to find Maggie by the door, cardigan buttoned, keys in hand.

"All ready to lock up?" Maggie asked, jangling the keys.

Ellie nodded, but her gaze had drifted across the street to Lovely Bubbly. Its lights were now glowing. The 'Closed For Lunch' sign had vanished.

"I'll catch Joanne before she closes," she said, zipping her jacket. "Mrs Winchester didn't drop her name for nothing."

"Just… tread carefully," Maggie said, her voice softening. "Joanne lost her mum just after Christmas. It hit her hard. That shop was her mother's life's work, and Joanne's been there since she left school." She slipped the keys into her pocket and gave them a secure pat. "I'll get home and start dinner. I'm thinking lamb chops. We both need a proper meal after today."

Going their separate ways for now, Ellie stepped into Lovely Bubbly and was hit by a wall of scent—lavender, rose, lemon, and something faintly earthy beneath it all. The shop was a riot of colour: soaps shaped like cakes and woodland creatures lined the shelves, while glitter-dusted bath bombs nestled in wicker baskets like sugared sweets.

Behind a small demonstration table stood a woman Ellie guessed must be Joanne Cole. Silver streaked her auburn hair, twisted into a neat bun. She had to be at or past retirement age, with a worn look in her eyes that Ellie only felt after the longest days. She held a fizzing bath bomb aloft, addressing a small group of customers as if unveiling a sacred relic.

"Now, watch closely, children," she said, summoning brightness as she held the purple sphere above a bowl of water. "See how the lavender and chamomile release their essential oils? Perfect after a long day of revision."

Three teenagers slouched on folding chairs, their boredom as thick in the air as the lavender. Nearby, a distracted mother scrolled through her phone.

"Can we go to Costa now, Mum?" asked the tallest girl, already half-turned towards the door.

"Just five more minutes, Chloe. Your nan bought these workshop vouchers for Christmas and they expire in June."

Joanne's smile held, but something in her eyes flickered—a taut glint, like someone watching their passion slip through their fingers. Ellie glanced around. Price tags had been crossed out and replaced with bold red 'CLEARANCE' stickers.

Then Joanne saw her.

The demonstration faltered. The bath bomb slipped

from her hand and dropped into the bowl with a splash, water sloshing over the table's edge.

"Sorry," she mumbled to her unimpressed audience. "Let me just—" She grabbed a roll of paper towels, her hands trembling as she waved to Ellie. "I'll be with you in a moment!"

"Don't mind me," Ellie said, lifting a shopping basket from the stack by the door. "Just browsing." She wandered over to the bath bomb display, pretending to study the pastel spheres. "Could use a good soak after everything that's been going on."

"We've got a lovely new lavender and chamomile," Joanne called, her professional smile firmly back in place. "Perfect for stress relief."

"Lovely," Ellie said, turning a glittery purple bomb in her hand. "Though I suppose nothing compares to the stress of 1975, does it?"

Startled, Joanne knocked half a dozen more off the table and they tumbled into her demonstration bowl, water churning into an explosion of colour and foam.

"Oh! Oh *dear*—" Joanne flailed, reaching for a roll of paper towels just out of reach as the rainbow mess spread across the table.

The tallest teenager jumped back.

"I'm out," she muttered, already texting furiously. "Mum, seriously? This is worse than when Grandad signed us up for magic lessons."

The mother sighed and began steering her daughters towards the door.

"Please do come back anytime!" Joanne called after

them, voice high and tight. "Twenty percent off your next purchase!"

The door thudded shut, leaving only the fizzing of bath bombs and Joanne's uneven breathing.

"I'm sorry," Ellie said, setting down her basket and stepping forward to help mop up the mess. "I didn't mean to startle you."

"It's quite alright," Joanne replied, though her hands trembled as she wrung out a sodden towel. "I think I lost them long before you walked in. I don't know why I thought demonstration vouchers were ever going to work."

Ellie glanced around at the 'CLEARANCE' signs taped to every surface. The shop felt like a ship taking on water—and she'd just added to the storm.

Once they'd cleaned up, Joanne moved to the door. She stood there for a moment, hand hovering near the latch, then flipped the 'OPEN' sign to 'CLOSED' and turned the deadbolt with a soft but final click. Her fingers lingered on the lock.

She didn't turn around.

"Why would you bring up 1975?" she asked.

Ellie's grip tightened around the shopping basket as she scooped it up. The cheerful pastel bath bombs inside looked absurd now—like props from someone else's day.

"It's been on my mind," Ellie said. "Two siblings. Both drowned. Fifty years apart, in the same pond. And then I found out about the burglary at Meadowfield Manor—the same night Sally died—and that's what led me here." She paused as Joanne's breathing turned ragged. "To you."

Joanne inhaled sharply, barely audible. Then she turned and began packing away the demo table, movements brisk, too fast—the kind that belonged to someone who needed their hands to be busy. Anything to avoid stillness.

"I get it," Ellie offered. "I've been exactly like that all day—stacking books that weren't out of stock, sweeping corners that didn't need sweeping. My dad's missing. He's connected to both cases—Sally and Benjamin—and I'm just trying to find the truth. That's all I want."

"I don't know what you think you know," Joanne said, tearing a paper towel with unnecessary force, "but I had nothing to do with any burglary."

Ellie held back her reaction. Of everything she'd said, Joanne had latched onto the burglary. That was where she felt most exposed. Ellie had her on the back foot. Joanne began scrubbing the table in tight, angry circles.

"That's not what I've heard." Ellie kept her tone light, almost conversational, but her gaze held steady. "A very reliable source places you at the manor that night."

Joanne's hand stilled. Silence settled over the shop, thick and awkward. From across the street, Ellie caught the sound of Zara's light and careless laughter drifting through the quiet.

"Phil told you, didn't he?" Joanne said softly—so quiet it was almost to herself.

Ellie filed the name away. Phil. Another new thread. One she hadn't expected.

"Does it matter who told me?" Ellie asked, still calm, watching the way Joanne's throat moved as she swallowed. "You were involved, weren't you?"

Joanne didn't reply. Instead, she strode to the till and began cashing up with unnecessary urgency. She yanked open the drawer, rifled through receipts—there weren't many. Coins clinked as she counted them out, then again, and again, each attempt more distracted than the last.

"I was young and stupid," she said suddenly, eyes fixed on the notes in her hand. "I needed the money."

"I heard you've worked here since you were a teenager?" Ellie asked. "Not for free, I imagine."

"I have, but…" Joanne gulped, then looked up at Ellie, her expression flickering with disbelief—like she couldn't quite believe she was saying it aloud. "… I wanted to be a nurse. But my mother said if I left the family business, I was out on my own, so… I… I was just the lookout, okay?"

Ellie said nothing for a moment. She watched Joanne fumble with the till drawer, watched her shoulders curl in slightly, as if expecting judgement. It was the kind of confession that didn't change the facts —but it shifted the shape of the woman in front of her. Not hardened. Just stuck. Trapped in a decision made a lifetime ago, still paying for it in clearance stickers and chamomile-scented regret.

"But Mrs Winchester smelled lavender in her

bedroom," Ellie said, stepping closer to the counter. "Someone burst in, reeking of it, while she hid under the bed—terrified for her life."

Joanne's head snapped up, panic blooming in her eyes.

"That wasn't—" She stopped herself, gaze flicking around the room, searching for an escape. "She wasn't *supposed* to be at the manor, okay? I was just outside… I…"

She returned to the takings and tried to count the money again, fingers fumbling over notes and coins that wouldn't sit right. She stopped, exhaled, and closed her eyes. One hand stayed on the counter, holding it like an anchor.

"I know you went inside," Ellie said quietly. "I know you're lying."

"You don't know *anything*," Joanne snapped, slamming a jar of bath salts onto the counter with a crack that made Ellie flinch.

"I know you and Phil were involved."

Joanne froze. "I never said Phil was involved. And *I* never said *I* was involved."

"You just did," Ellie replied, voice calm, steady. "One minute ago—*you* admitted *you* were the lookout."

Joanne's composure collapsed like soap left too long in water. Her story crumbled in her hands, truth slipping out in panicked, contradictory bursts. The secret she'd kept buried for decades had bubbled over—impossible to contain.

"Look," Ellie said, softening her tone as Joanne

unravelled, "just tell me what happened. You clearly didn't profit much from the burglary." She gestured to the red stickers dotting the shelves like a rash. "I'm not here to cause trouble. I just want to know what happened—for my father's sake."

Joanne's chin dropped, gaze fixed somewhere on the floor. When she spoke, her voice was flat, hollowed out.

"Months behind on rent," she murmured. "Mother made it look easy, but in just a few months…" She trailed off, lifting a hand in a half-hearted gesture towards the empty shop. "Everyone sells bath bombs and soap now. We're not special anymore. I put my heart into this place, but it's a race to the bottom. Even on sale, people talk about them being too expensive."

She turned and drifted towards the window, stopping just short of the display.

"Meadowfield's tourism is too patchy. We get people passing through, but they're not here to buy soap. They come for the café, to poke around the bookshop—" She glanced at Ellie over her shoulder and added, "—we don't get many fans of that old TV show anymore. And if it weren't for the Americans turning up for the war connection—" Her voice caught, and the rest of the sentence slipped away. Tears tracked silently down her cheeks.

Ellie, unsure what else to do, stepped closer, resting a hand on Joanne's shoulder. Up close, the scent of lavender clung to her—on her clothes, her skin, the very air around her.

"Please," Ellie urged, tightening her fingers. "Just

tell me what happened that night. Was Sally there? Did you see her?"

At Sally's name, something shifted in Joanne's face. Grief hardened into something sharper. Anger.

"S-Sally?" She jerked away from Ellie's touch like it burned. "Whatever I did or didn't do that night, it had nothing—*nothing*—to do with Sally." Her voice rose, splintered with emotion. "That was a coincidence. A horrible, awful coincidence."

"But—"

"I think you should go." The warmth vanished, replaced by something blazing.

"Please, I'm just trying to understand—"

"*Go!*" The word cracked through the air like thunder. Ellie stumbled back.

Heart pounding, she backed towards the door. Her hand hovered on the handle. Had she pushed too hard? Maybe. Joanne had looked ready to crack open—and then she'd slammed shut. But one thing was certain—she'd flinched harder at Sally's name than at the burglary. She wasn't just guarding an old mistake. This was something deeper. Something that truly frightened her.

Ellie swallowed, her mouth dry. Her fingers tingled from the adrenaline, and she didn't realise she'd been gripping the basket until she set it down with a soft clatter.

Phil. The name circled like a leaf in a puddle. Who was he, and why had Joanne tried to cover for him after letting his involvement slip?

She stepped outside, blinking against the pale gold of the early evening light. The air was cool on her flushed cheeks. For a moment, she stood there, breathing it in—trying to ground herself in the scent of spring, of blossom, of something ordinary.

Joanne was in her late sixties now, which would have made her a late-teenager, in the mid-seventies. Ellie assumed the same of Phil, and perhaps everyone else involved. Breaking into a manor late one night during a storm seemed like something only someone under twenty-five—unless they were a career criminal—would cook up.

She exhaled, leaving Lovely Bubbly behind.

The street was quiet. Too quiet. A postcard version of peace.

Then—movement.

At the top of South Street, just past Meadowfield Books, a figure stood half-hidden around the corner. Dark coat. High collar pulled up, despite the mild spring breeze.

Ellie froze, heart thudding.

"Dad?" she called.

Chapter 9
Lost in the Post

The figure in black jumped—then slipped out of sight.

Ellie ran towards the bookshop on the corner, her red Converse slapping against the cobbles.

"Wait!" she shouted, nearly tripping over a startled black cat. She rounded the corner at speed, grazing the postbox as she passed.

She turned in a slow circle, scanning doorways and shadows. Whoever had been watching was gone.

The street was empty.

"Dad?" she called again, her voice smaller than she meant it to be.

No reply—just the echo of her own voice bouncing off ancient stone walls. A cold prickle settled at the back of her neck, the feeling of being watched still clinging. She drew a breath to steady herself—and caught something unexpected on the air. Not her father's familiar woodsy scent. Something fresher. Clean. Expensive.

She crossed her arms, suddenly aware of how exposed she felt. First Joanne's collapse. Now this.

The streets of Meadowfield weren't just quiet tonight. They were listening.

Before she could decide what to do next, the door to Bramble & Brie swung open. The bell sang, and Sylvia stepped out.

"Ellie, was that you I heard calling out?" she asked, turning the key with an exaggerated twist.

"It was," Ellie said, folding her arms against an evening chill that hadn't quite arrived. "I think someone was following me."

Sylvia didn't hesitate. Her sturdy heels clacked as she hurried over without a flicker of doubt.

"Did you see who it was?" Sylvia asked, eyes scanning the street like a hawk.

"No. Just a figure. But I caught a trace of aftershave."

"Youthful," Sylvia said, sniffing the air. "Almost *definitely* Chanel."

Ellie's eyebrows rose higher. "How do you know?"

"My fourth husband was obsessed with smelling like a twenty-year-old," Sylvia said, waving the memory away. "Hoped it would distract from his second facelift." She leaned in and whispered, "It didn't."

Despite the tension, Ellie laughed. Sylvia kept surprising her—never more than when she was talking about whatever life she'd led before moving to Meadowfield.

But Sylvia wasn't laughing. She squinted into the shadows between buildings, tense as a cat ready to spring.

"Whoever it was, they've scarpered now," Sylvia declared, pulling Ellie in close. "And if they've got any sense, they won't come sniffing around again."

Ellie's chest warmed at Sylvia's ready loyalty—no questions, just instinctive protection. It gave her the courage to ask the question that had been burning since Lovely Bubbly.

"Sylvia, do you know someone called Phil?"

Sylvia's face scrunched in thought, one coral-painted finger tapping her lips.

"Phil… There's Phil who owns that quirky record shop in Marlborough. And Phil who manages those posh retirement flats up the hill." She tilted her head. "Oh! My postman's called Phil."

Ellie's breath caught.

"Postman Phil?"

"Yes—he does my route. Why?"

"Remember what you heard when Benjamin and my gran were arguing in the back room?" Ellie asked as she rounded the corner of South Street, going nowhere in particular—but going there together, and with purpose. "Benjamin said he thought someone had stolen his books and blamed it on the post."

"That's right!" Sylvia clicked her fingers. "But by all accounts, Phil is lovely. Always on time and hides parcels so I don't get the dreaded red slip of doom. I bought him a bottle of fizz at Christmas. Why do you ask?"

"Because Joanne from the soap shop mentioned his name. And I was sent there by Mrs Winchester, who brought her up in connection with a burglary that happened the same night Sally died. Joanne just admitted she was the lookout—and when I mentioned Sally Brown, she panicked and threw me out." Ellie paused to catch her breath. "But before that, she slipped up. She assumed Phil had already told me."

Sylvia's eyes widened with delight. "Goodness. You have had a busy day!"

"So… do you know where Phil lives?"

"No," Sylvia said, and Ellie's heart sank. "But I know where he *might* be."

She pulled out her phone and tapped quickly, fingers surprisingly nimble across the screen.

"He takes evening delivery slots—overnight parcels. He dropped my new cheese knife at my house exactly…" She squinted at the screen. "Six minutes ago, according to the app."

Ellie blinked, impressed.

"If we hurry," Sylvia said, already marching off, "we might catch him. He usually does a few houses in my little cul-de-sac."

Before Ellie could form a better plan, Sylvia grabbed her arm and swept her away from South Street, past darkened shop windows and shuttered doors. They turned left at the old war memorial—fresh daffodils nodding in the breeze—then right down a narrow lane Ellie had rarely walked.

"Where exactly are we going?" she asked, breathless, trying to match Sylvia's determined pace.

"Avonbeck Way," Sylvia replied, as if that explained everything. "It's a lovely little hideaway."

The cobbles gave way to smooth tarmac as the road climbed. The cottages grew grander—set back behind manicured hedges and ornate gates, their windows like watching eyes. Stone walls rose higher, shielding sprawling gardens where not a blade of grass dared lean the wrong way. This was Meadowfield's hidden wealth: off the tourist map and rarely mentioned by locals, who mostly had no reason to visit. These were the people who came down into the village only when absolutely necessary—rare birds in their own roosts.

At the crest of the hill, Sylvia slowed and raised a finger to her lips.

"There," she whispered, pointing to a red delivery van parked outside a neat detached house, its white-painted porch columns glowing gold in the last of the sun. "He's with Tracey. Number six."

She ducked behind a tall hedge, peering through the leaves with the precision of someone long-trained in curtain twitching. "And look at that—she's usually quiet as a church mouse."

Ellie froze.

"Tracey?" The name rang like a bell. "Tracey Harper? The vicar's daughter?"

"Yes, that's her. Do you know her?"

"No," Ellie admitted. "But Mrs Winchester mentioned her to the vicar. Well—it was more of an accusation. She said Tracey was friendly with Joanne from the soap shop." She dropped her voice. "It felt like a warning."

Sylvia gasped, eyes sparkling.

"And Joanne mentioned Phil," Ellie continued. "And now Phil's chatting with Tracey. The dots are connecting themselves."

"The conspiracy deepens!" Sylvia said, gripping Ellie's arm. "What do we do? Confront them?"

"No, no," Ellie said quickly, placing a calming hand on Sylvia's shoulder. "I pushed too hard at the soap shop and got thrown out. I doubt I'd be welcomed back." She took a steadying breath. "I just want to talk —see how they react. What they let slip."

"Deep undercover," Sylvia nodded, tapping the side of her nose. "I like it. At least let me introduce you."

Before Ellie could protest, Sylvia had linked arms with her and was boldly marching them up to the pristine garden fence. On the doorstep stood a man in Royal Mail red, deep in conversation with a silver-haired woman.

Phil looked to be around seventy—wiry and compact, and not much taller than five feet. His uniform jacket hung a little loose at the shoulders, and his red cap was pushed back to reveal thinning hair and a forehead furrowed like a map. His stance was relaxed, but his eyes missed nothing.

Tracey, by contrast, was all nervous energy. She

wore a pale jumper and pressed trousers, neat as a pin, but her fingers twisted at a chain around her neck, and she shifted from foot to foot like she couldn't decide whether to stay or bolt.

Their conversation cut off at once as Sylvia and Ellie approached.

"Hello there, Tracey!" Sylvia called, radiating the confidence of someone who'd never once knocked before entering. "Small world, isn't it? My friend, Ellie, here was just at afternoon tea with your mother!"

Tracey's eyes widened, darting between them. Alarm flashed across her face before she forced a polite smile.

"And if it isn't Phil," Sylvia added, beaming at the postman. "Still out doing evening rounds?"

"Already dropped off at yours," Phil replied, voice low and gruff—rough as rust but not unfriendly.

"And glowing reviews incoming," Sylvia assured him. "Did I mention this was Ellie?"

They both nodded. Wary. Unsure.

Not quite the introduction Ellie had expected from someone as socially adept as Sylvia. Less 'deep undercover', more 'thrown in at the deep end.'

Phil's gaze lingered. It sharpened as he looked at Ellie, a flicker of recognition tightening his mouth.

"You're Peter Cookson's daughter," he said. Not a question.

"I am," Ellie replied, though her skin prickled. Being recognised by someone she'd never spoken to— someone who'd always hovered on the village's periphery—was unsettling. And now she placed him: the postman Benjamin had been arguing with outside the bookshop the morning the launch was delayed.

"Your father drowned Benjamin," Tracey blurted, her voice high and taut.

Phil exhaled, the kind of sigh that said she'd gone too far.

Tracey's foot tapped the step in a frantic rhythm, her bottom lip caught between her teeth. Ellie saw it clearly: Tracey hated silence. She'd fill it, if given even a second.

So Ellie said nothing.

Neither did Sylvia.

Three seconds passed.

"I took the picture," Tracey burst out, the words tumbling like waves.

"You took what picture?" Ellie asked, keeping her voice even.

Tracey's hands fluttered like trapped birds. "I saw him at the pond and took the photo. I gave it to the police."

"Christ, Tracey," Phil muttered, shooting her a look as sharp as flint. "You don't have to say anything else."

Ellie steadied herself. "You saw my father drowning Benjamin in the pond—and took a picture?"

Tracey nodded, eyes downcast.

"Well," Ellie said, clearing her throat, "I wasn't sure how to approach this, but thank you for being so honest. Because now I know this wasn't a coincidence." She held Tracey's gaze. "You were involved in the burglary at Meadowfield Manor the night Sally drowned. Mrs Winchester knows it. And now, so do I."

"Who told you?" Tracey gasped, the colour draining from her face.

"Christ, Tracey!" Phil snapped, his composure cracking. "Keep your mouth shut!"

"But *someone* told her," Tracey whispered, turning to him, eyes wide and pleading. "How else would she know?"

Ellie pressed her advantage.

"You, Joanne, Phil—and two others—broke into the manor while the Winchesters were supposed to be at the theatre in London. Whose idea was it?"

Silence folded in, soft and suffocating.

"I'm guessing you didn't walk away with a fortune —unless you spent it all?" Ellie continued, her eyes shifting between them. "Phil, you're still working extra shifts. And Tracey—" She nodded towards the curtain twitching behind the window. "You're still living at home. Something went wrong, didn't it?"

"I don't have to listen to this," Phil growled, brushing past them. "I've got parcels to deliver."

The van door slammed, rattling on its hinges. Gravel sprayed as he tore off down the road.

Tracey stood trembling on the doorstep—a woman unravelling by the second.

"Tracey, dear," came a voice from inside—gentle, insistent. The vicar, Ellie guessed. Reverend Catherine Harper. "Come in, your dinner's getting cold."

"Tracey," Ellie said gently, stepping closer. "If you know anything about that night—about Sally—"

"Talk to the mechanic," Tracey whispered. "He was her ex. The plan…" She swallowed. "It was his idea."

Before Ellie could speak again, Tracey slipped inside. The door clicked shut. Curtains swept closed, cutting off the scene like the final act of a play.

Ellie stared at the door, heart pounding.

She hadn't expected it—not like this. A name, a link, a piece that fit too neatly to be coincidence. Sally's ex-boyfriend. A mechanic. And the plan had been *his*. It wasn't just guilt by association or afternoon tea gossip anymore. It was a clear and undeniable link between the night of the burglary and Sally's death.

"Ellie, dear," Sylvia said lightly as they turned back down the drive, "I don't want to alarm you—and don't turn around—but we were followed here."

Ellie froze.

"What?"

"Hooded man. By the bushes," Sylvia replied calmly, as if discussing a change in the weather. "Terrible at blending in." She leaned closer, her floral perfume tickling Ellie's nostrils. "My second husband once hired a PI to follow me. I spotted him in two days —despite ten days' pay. I hired him myself after that. Paid double. Found out where my husband really went when he said he was playing golf." She moved her neck side to side, cracking it with casual precision. "Confront or lose? I'm happy either way."

"Neither," Ellie said, mind racing. "Let's see what

they want. They've slipped up twice already—maybe third time's the charm."

She checked her watch. The light was beginning to fade.

"I need to find this mechanic before it gets too late."

"I'm coming," Sylvia said firmly, looping her arm through Ellie's. "No arguments. If the mechanic is who I think it is, you do *not* want to meet him alone."

"Why?" Ellie asked, half-dreading the answer.

Sylvia leaned in with a conspiratorial smile. "Because if Tracey was talking about Terry, he has the most unscrupulous reputation for being the biggest thief in Meadowfield."

Chapter 10
Mechanics of the Heart

Meadowfield had fully quietened into evening by the time Ellie and Sylvia made their way back to the centre. It wasn't late, but the village had already folded in on itself—like a cat curling up for the night.

They passed the pond outside The Drowsy Duck—now free of police tape. A handful of bouquets rested by the water's edge, weighed down with small stones and hand-penned notes. Ellie slowed, drawn to them.

A spray of white chrysanthemums from the accountancy firm Benjamin had worked for. A smaller bunch wrapped in foil from the church. Another, tied with ribbon, bore the logo of a local men's mental health charity.

Ellie crouched beside a bouquet of pristine white roses. The card was plain and unsigned but the message read:

I wish things had ended differently. I really do. – Your Sarah

Sarah Mills.

Ellie straightened slowly, her mind turning. Her Year Six teacher. And Benjamin Brown's first fiancée.

"Poor man," Sylvia murmured beside her. "He didn't seem the type to stir up all this. Quiet ones, though. Always more going on under the surface."

Somewhere down a narrow side street, a rhythmic clanking rang out—sharp, metallic, and out of place in the hush of evening.

They rounded the corner and found the source: a squat garage tucked behind the shopping street. Its bay doors stood open, stark lights spilling onto the weed-infested courtyard where a man in oil-slicked overalls leaned over the exposed engine of an ancient Volvo.

"That's Terry Ford," Sylvia murmured, slowing to a stop. "From what people say, he's been a mechanic since leaving school—but everyone *knows* he's a thief."

She cast another glance at him, still bent over the engine, unaware of their scrutiny.

"I can't prove it, but I'm nearly certain he broke into my conservatory last spring and pinched my digital radio. Oily smudges on the door handle." She rubbed her thumb and forefinger together, as if she could still feel the residue. "I did leave the door unlocked—my mistake," she added after a pause. "But wouldn't you know it, Mrs Clark—Daniel's nan—was offered a suspiciously similar radio in the pub the very next night. She seriously considered buying it, according to eyewitnesses."

"What did you do?" Ellie asked, watching Terry work, oblivious to their approach.

"I told the police," she said. "They didn't think there was a case since I couldn't prove it. The man is past seventy and still creeping around the village like a sticky-fingered cat burglar half his age. Being a mechanic in a small village must not pay well, and I said as much when I confronted him—"

"You confronted him?"

"I most certainly did!" Sylvia drew herself up, puffing out her chest. "I was sorely tempted to perform a citizen's arrest, but he didn't seem terribly keen on the idea."

Ellie gently freed her arm. "Then maybe don't come with me this time. I'd like a clean start."

Sylvia gave a brisk salute. "Say no more. I'll be right here by this plant pot, keeping a very close eye on you. And if anything kicks off, I'm in there like a flash."

"Thanks," Ellie replied, privately unsure what help Sylvia could offer if things did kick off.

She took a breath and walked towards the garage. The scent of oil and metal thickened with each step. Terry looked up at the sound of her approach across the courtyard, slowly straightening from the engine. His sharp, assessing gaze swept over her as he wiped his hands on a rag.

His sparse white air hinted at his seventies, but he

had the build of someone who'd spent decades lifting engines and muscling through seized bolts. His face was weathered—leather worn by a life spent outdoors.

"You got a car parked up?" he asked, his voice rasping with years of cigarettes. His yellowed fingers clutched the rag like it was an extension of his hand.

"No," Ellie replied, unsure of her plan.

After Postman Phil had stormed off, she'd vowed to be more subtle. Tracey had cracked under pressure— but this man was all brick and stubbornness, baked solid.

"I'm not here about a car," she continued, choosing her words with care. "I'm here about… something else."

Terry's expression shifted. A flicker passed across his eyes. He glanced around, then gave a short, knowing nod.

"Gotcha," he said, still wiping his hands. After a quick check that they were alone, he jerked his head towards the back of the garage. "Caught your drift. Kids, is it?"

"I'm… sorry?" Ellie faltered, trailing after him.

"You got kids?" he asked over his shoulder, already halfway to the door.

"Oh. No," she said, bewildered. "Is that… important?"

"Not really. Just get a lot of women your age in here asking for stuff, usually for their kids. Can't afford much. Times are hard. So—what're you after?"

He opened the door, and Ellie stopped still.

Inside was a makeshift electronics showroom—rows of televisions, speakers, fridges, and coffee machines. Air fryers still had price tags; kettles sat untouched in their boxes. The whole place had the polished sleaze of a pop-up car boot sale in a layby, lit dimly by naked bulbs swinging from chains dangling from the exposed ceiling.

"Mind if I have a look around?"

"Yeah, go on. Shopping, are you?" Terry eyed her like a half-solved puzzle. "Just don't take all day—I've got to get that Volvo running before seven." He patted a gleaming fridge on his way out. "This Smeg's just in. Bit dusty, but near new."

As Terry disappeared back into the garage, she moved towards the fridge. Cheerful letter magnets dotted the door, spelling out a crooked reminder: 'biNs On tUEsdAy!' A shopping list was pinned beneath a faded rollercoaster snapshot from a decade ago.

Her fingers trembled slightly as she opened it. Cold air rolled out. Inside—milk, still slightly chilled.

"You like it?"

Ellie jumped and slammed the door shut.

She turned. Terry was back in the doorway, a wrench resting in one hand.

"It fell off the back of a lorry," he said, catching her glance at the tool. "No one got hurt."

"There's a shopping list," Ellie said, voice steadier now. "Cheese. Bread. Ham…"

Terry's expression darkened. "I thought you knew what this was." His voice dropped—husky, with a warning burning the edges. "You want cheap, you don't get new, sweetheart. You after a fridge or not?"

"No," Ellie said firmly, stepping back. "I'm not here for your Aladdin's cave of stolen goods."

She met his eyes. He stared right back.

"I prefer the term *acquired goods*," he said, tipping his head. "Are you police? Because if you're police, you have to tell me if I ask."

"I'm not police," Ellie replied, swallowing the stone lodged in her throat. "I'm here to ask about 1975."

She lifted her chin and met his gaze, steady now.

"What about it?" he said, voice stiff as steel.

"The heist. Sally's death. She was your ex-girlfriend, wasn't she?"

"*Boyfriend* when she died," he snapped. Colour flushed his face. "Ain't no *ex* about it." He crossed his arms—the wrench still clutched tight. "You a journalist?"

"No. I'm Peter Cookson's daughter." Her voice held steady, though her heart thudded like a struck drum. "I know you planned the manor heist. And that your girlfriend died that same night—"

"If you want answers, darlin'," Terry cut in, voice rising, "look no further than *your* old man. Everyone knows Peter drowned her. And now he's done it again."

Ellie's stomach twisted at the bluntness of it. "Why would my father want to kill Sally?"

"Because he was *sweet* on her. Obvious, wasn't it?" Terry spat the words. "They'd go off 'birdwatching'—

but I knew what he was after. He was a boy. I was a man. No contest."

"And yet Sally still chose to be friends with him," Ellie said, calm but unyielding. "They had things in common, didn't they?"

"Yeah, so what?" Terry snapped, leaning closer. "He was a weirdo. Always flinching, wouldn't look you in the eye. Creeped me out."

"He's shy," Ellie replied, heat rising in her chest. "Always has been. Maybe that's why people thought he was guilty—because he didn't know how to defend himself." She paused to catch her breath. "But there's no evidence he killed Sally."

"Yeah? And where's the evidence *I* did anything, huh?" Terry barked, jabbing the wrench like a sword. "There isn't any. So why don't you run along, little girl, and leave this to the grown-ups."

Ellie edged towards the door, recognising the pointlessness of continuing to question him—but unwilling to leave empty-handed.

"I know you planned the heist," Ellie said, reaching the threshold.

"Do you?" Terry's voice echoed across the cluttered space. "Then you might want to talk to someone in the grande dame's inner circle—find out where the idea *really* came from." He held her gaze, unblinking. "Little girl, you don't know a damn thing."

Ellie didn't move. "What about Benjamin Brown?" she pushed. "Did he know something? Did he say anything to you before he died?"

Terry snorted. "That pompous pillock? Thought he was the smartest man in the room. Always quoting something or other—like he thought the rest of us couldn't read." He shook his head. "I didn't have time for him."

"But you agreed with him," Ellie pressed. "You think my dad killed Sally."

"I didn't *agree*. I said it makes sense." Terry's eyes flashed. "She died. He was there. He was *always* there. Always sniffing round where he wasn't wanted."

"Did you know anything about Benjamin's book? About what he might have found—what made him leave clues behind?"

Terry hesitated, jaw tightening. "You know Sally wanted to be a writer," he said, quieter now. "She talked about it all the time. Said she'd write a book one day. A kids' book or maybe a romance. Said she'd focus on it after her teacher training."

"But she never got there," Ellie said. "She never got the chance."

Terry said nothing.

Ellie narrowed her eyes. "You didn't answer my question. Do you know what Benjamin was writing about?"

He scowled. "Who says I've gotta answer anything?"

"You don't," Ellie replied, surprising herself with the calm in her voice. "You know, by all accounts, Sally seems to have been a sweet woman. Bright. Kind."

Terry swallowed. "She was."

Ellie tilted her head. "I'm just not sure what she ever saw in you."

The wrench came down hard on the metal counter with a crash that echoed through the garage. Ellie flinched.

Terry pointed the wrench at her like a warning. "Get out."

She didn't wait for a second invitation.

"You're not half as scary as you think you are," she said over her shoulder, then slipped through the door and out into the evening.

The sharp air hit her like a wall. Her hands trembled.

Terry hadn't denied being involved—only denied being in charge. That mattered.

She replayed his words as she reached the street, turning them over like puzzle pieces. The *'grande dame's* inner circle.' That must be Mrs Winchester. Who had been pulling strings? And had she pushed Terry too far?

A blur of movement cut across her thoughts.

Sylvia came charging down the street, handbag swinging, breath ragged.

"I saw him again!" she puffed, skidding to a halt. "The man in the black hood. I gave chase the moment I spotted him, and I nearly caught him!"

Ellie reached out to steady her while she caught her breath. "Did you see his face?"

"No—but he dropped this." Sylvia reached into her handbag and pulled out a sleek metal baton. With a flick of her wrist, it extended with a satisfying click.

Ellie blinked as Sylvia gave it a few brisk swings, then collapsed it and tucked it back into her bag as if it had always been there.

"Better in *my* hands than *his*," Sylvia said, fastening the clasp with a crisp snap. "So? What did you find out?"

Ellie glanced back at the mechanic's courtyard, relieved to be out of it.

"Terry all but admitted it," she said as they set off up South Street, the streetlamps blinking to life one by one. "And you were right—he's got a whole warehouse of stolen appliances back there. Thought I was there to buy a fridge."

"Of *course* he did," Sylvia said, with smug satisfaction. "Didn't see my radio, did you?"

"Afraid not."

"Ah well. Never mind." She sighed. "What happened next?"

"I mentioned my dad, and things escalated. But he slipped—said he wasn't the one who planned it. He didn't deny being involved."

"Sounds like you've done what the police never managed," Sylvia said, eyes bright with admiration. "You've found the heist crew."

"All but one."

Ellie's gaze drifted towards the silhouette of Meadowfield Manor, rising dark against the sky. Terry's parting hint about the 'inner circle' echoed in her mind.

They slowed near the gates. The iron bars loomed in the fading light.

Ellie's hand hovered near the buzzer, but the manor sat quiet, the path bathed in hazy shadows. It was too late to disturb Mrs Winchester.

"Tomorrow," she whispered.

A promise.

And a plan.

* * *

As she walked through the village with Sylvia, Ellie's thoughts spun—mostly around that cryptic mention of someone in Mrs Winchester's inner circle. She was so tangled in the spiral, she nearly missed the familiar figure outside The Old Bell.

DS Angela Cookson paced beneath the pub's string lights, phone pressed tight to her ear, voice cutting clean through the quiet.

"I wonder if there's been an update?" Sylvia murmured, unlooping her arm from Ellie's before giving her a firm nudge through the pub gate. "You're practically family. She'll tell you."

"'Practically' is doing a lot of heavy lifting in that sentence," Ellie replied—but it was too late. Angela had already spotted her, and the familiar frustration was already obvious.

"Fill me in tomorrow," Sylvia called, already waving and backing away. "I'm teaching a cheesemaking workshop at the night school in Marlborough, and if I don't leave now, I'll miss the bus."

She gave Ellie a wink, then turned on her heel and scuttled off down the lane.

Ellie took a breath and moved closer.

"Do what it takes," Angela snapped into the phone, half-turned away. "There's tracking info, a delivery record—boxes of books don't just vanish—"

She ended the call with a sharp tap and turned to face her.

"Evening."

"Ellie." A nod. "Any luck finding your father?"

"No," Ellie admitted, hands going into her pockets. "But I have something I think you want."

Angela's brow lifted, her interest barely concealed beneath the detective's calm. The old tension between them still hummed—an echo of silences and sharp glances—but time had worn it down at the edges.

"Well?" Angela snapped. "Are you waiting for me to offer you something in return? Because that's not how this works. If you know something of importance, I expect you—"

"If you don't mind receiving 345 photos to your phone," Ellie cut in, pulling out her mobile, "I can send you a copy of Benjamin's book. Or at least, the manuscript he gave my gran for approval a few weeks ago."

She met Angela's gaze, steady now.

"There's nothing in it that ties to my dad," Ellie continued, glancing at her shoes. "But if you think you can crack some hidden message in there—good luck."

For a moment, surprise flickered across Angela's

face before she smoothed it back into professional neutrality.

"That's why you want it, isn't it?" Ellie pressed. "You've probably had half the pub offering to recite Benjamin's speech word for word."

Angela didn't answer immediately. Then she nodded at Ellie's phone. "How do we do this?"

"Turn on your AirDrop—I'll send them over."

Angela stared blankly at her device.

Ellie reached out. "Here, let me."

With obvious reluctance, Angela handed it over. Ellie tapped through the settings—but as she scrolled, a notification lit up the screen:

PC FINN WALSH

Tracey Harper wants to report witness intimidation. Says Peter's daughter…

Angela snatched the phone back before Ellie could read more.

Ellie said nothing and finished sending the images. Angela turned away, stiff as a snapped twig, and headed for the pub entrance.

Ellie caught the door before it closed and followed her inside.

The Old Bell was the sleepier of Meadowfield's two pubs—low-ceilinged and snug, with a crooked charm earned from centuries of leaning into the wind. A battered piano slouched in the corner beneath a faded sign reading 'LIVE MUSIC MOSTLY ON

PURPOSE', and the fireplace still held a faint whiff of winter's smoke.

Ellie liked it best on quiet nights.

Tonight, a few tables were full—locals nursing pints and sharing bags of crisps. She trailed Angela to the bar, watching her scroll through the photos, squinting at the tiny text.

"According to Tracey," Angela said, eyes still on her phone, "Peter's daughter visited her today and harassed her. Now, unless my son's father has another child he hasn't told me about—care to explain?"

Ellie slid onto the stool beside her. "I asked her a few questions," she said evenly. "She told me she took a photo of my dad drowning Benjamin."

Angela sighed and set the phone down. "Yes."

"So… she saw the whole thing?"

Angela glanced around the pub. Her gaze settled on Sammie, the young landlady, who was pulling a pint at the far end of the bar.

"Tracey claims she was out walking," Angela said, turning slightly into Ellie, as if reluctant to let the whole pub overhear. "She reports that she saw something at the pond, took a photo… and only realised what it was when she heard about the drowning the next day. That's when she came in."

"What?" Ellie couldn't hold in her confused laughter. "She saw someone being drowned and her first thought was to take a photo? Not to shout, or call for help?" She waited for the penny to drop, but Angela was avoiding her gaze. "You know Tracey is connected to the heist? At the manor the night Sally died fifty years ago?"

"Unconnected," Angela replied, finally catching Sammie's eye and gesturing for a drink.

"Phil the postman, Terry the mechanic, Joanne at the soap shop—they were all involved. Tracey too." Ellie could hear the pleading creep into her voice. "Need I go on? That's four other people you could be looking into."

"*Instead* of your father, you mean?"

"As well as," Ellie said. "There's someone else, too. I'm still working on the fifth."

Angela finally turned to face her. "I don't need you to work out anything, Ellie. Just focus on finding him."

But Ellie wasn't backing down. "Did you already know those names?"

Angela turned away. "Many people were questioned back then about the burglary. But there was no evidence linking it to Sally's death."

"Tracey said Terry planned it. And Terry was Sally's boyfriend. That is your connection."

Sammie approached, towel slung over one shoulder. "Evening, ladies. What can I get you?"

"Large glass of the house red," Angela said, then glanced at Ellie.

"Nothing, thanks," Ellie murmured. She was too focused to drink.

As Sammie moved off, Angela leaned in, her voice low. "Listen, Ellie. We're looking for your father because that's where the evidence points. You can bring me every name in Meadowfield, but unless you've got something to *prove* your theory—what exactly do you want me to do?" Her expression softened, just for a moment. "The evidence says your dad killed Benjamin. Do you think I *want* that? The father of my son—a murderer?"

Ellie's throat tightened.

"Did you know about the 1975 rumours?"

Angela gave the smallest of nods.

"So you didn't believe them back then?"

A pause. Then the faintest shake of her head.

"Then don't believe them now," Ellie urged. "Not until we know."

Angela hesitated, then pulled out her phone. She tapped the screen and held it out.

The photo showed a figure in a green coat and a flat cap, bent over the pond. Another body lay half-submerged in the dark water. Grainy. Poorly lit. But to anyone who knew Peter Cookson—it was unmistakable.

"How can I ignore that?" Angela's voice was barely above a whisper. "It's as good as a confession." She met Ellie's gaze. "If you find him—you know what to do."

Sammie returned with the wine. Angela slid a few pounds onto the bar, took her glass, and moved to a quiet corner. Conversation over.

Ellie remained at the bar, stunned. The figure looked like her father—the coat, the stoop of his shoulders—but no face. And if Tracey had truly witnessed a murder… why wait until morning to report it? Why say nothing at the time? And what was she doing out walking so late?

She sighed, eyes drifting up to the pub's framed photographs—snapshots of Meadowfield in sepia and faded colour. As a child, she'd studied those pictures while her father nursed a half-pint. Local history, right on her doorstep.

One frame caught her eye.

'The Great Storm of 1975.'

Ellie slid off her stool and moved closer. In the background—a small camera crew. And there, unmistakable: her mother, youthful and picture-perfect. She remembered her mentioning a storm and a lock-in at the pub during a night shoot.

She lifted the frame carefully. Among the crowd, the face from the old front page—Sally, smiling. And beside her… a younger Sarah Mills. Her hair longer, but her posture recognisable. In the background, clustered around pints, she found younger versions of Tracey, Phil, and Terry.

"Sammie," Ellie called. "What's the story behind this photo?"

The landlady joined her, wiping down the bar. "That was a wild night, according to my mum. Lock-in here 'til the storm passed. Singing, storytelling. Went on 'til the early hours, for those who didn't sneak out. I think your mum was one."

"She was," Ellie said, replacing the frame. "Thanks."

As Sammie moved away, Ellie stared at the photo.

There was the moment Sarah had mentioned. The last time she saw Sally. They'd parted at the pub with a promise to see each other the following day, and never did.

And suddenly, it clicked.

Sarah wasn't just a friend of Sally's—she was part of the inner circle Terry had hinted at. She knew some of the others. And she was close to Mrs Winchester.

Ellie snapped a picture of the framed photo. She had lunch with Sarah tomorrow. A perfect opportunity to press her for answers.

As she slipped her phone into her pocket, Ellie noticed Angela watching her from across the room. The detective's face was unreadable in the dim light—but her gaze was sharp. Unblinking.

Something in that stare sent a chill down Ellie's spine.

It wasn't a warning. It was resignation. A look that said: *give up, this is already over.*

But Ellie couldn't.

Not while the past was still whispering.

Ellie stepped out of The Old Bell, her head still full of unfinished sentences. Angela hadn't just sounded tired —she'd sounded done. Like someone who'd already packed up her hope and filed it away.

The door swung shut behind her, muting the low murmur of the pub. Meadowfield was mostly quiet now, save for the clink of cutlery through a half-open kitchen window and the faint scuff of footsteps on South Street.

Across the road, Auntie Penny was out walking Duchess. The lurcher's pale coat shimmered like wet paint under the streetlamps. Ellie raised a hand in greeting, meaning to cross.

But then she saw movement by the cottage next door.

Daniel, barefoot and in pyjamas, was crouching to place two empty milk bottles on the doorstep. He straightened, and his eyes met hers across the street. The brief flash of hurt on his face was impossible to miss, though he quickly masked it with a neutral expression. This time, he looked a little less forgiving than his usual easygoing self.

Her heart dipped.

The drink. The plan. She'd forgotten all of it, chasing soap shop confessions and flickering clues instead. Twice in one day.

Ellie crossed the green, offering a sheepish smile. "Please don't tell me you waited too long," she said, the words tumbling out. "I completely forgot."

"It's fine," Daniel replied, with a shrug that suggested it wasn't.

"It isn't," Ellie said gently. "And it's alright that it isn't."

Daniel exhaled, the tension in his shoulders easing as her honesty cut through the awkwardness. A genuine smile broke through at last.

"I waited twenty minutes at the Duck before I checked the Bell, just in case," he said, leaning in the doorway. "Been home ever since, marking Year Three's 'Who I Will Be in Ten Years' essays. A lot of them are planning careers in TikTok stardom and competitive slime-making."

Ellie laughed, the sound light with relief. "I won't keep you," she said. "But I am sorry. Really."

"Really, it's fine," he said—and this time, it sounded like he meant it. "Let's just meet up when you're actually free." He grinned. "I'm not going anywhere."

She stepped closer, drawn by the warmth behind his teasing. The kiss they shared on the doorstep was brief but sure—soft, forgiving, and more honest than words.

From somewhere inside, a voice rang out:

"Daniel! You're letting all the heat out!"

"It's a warm night!" he shouted back.

Before he turned to go inside, Ellie caught his arm.

"What's Sarah Mills really like?"

He frowned. "Why?"

"Because she keeps popping up," Ellie said. "And I'm trying to figure out where she connects."

Daniel hesitated, shifting his weight. "She's a good teacher..."

Ellie studied his face. "But?"

He sighed. "She plays favourites—with the staff, I mean. The head's hands-off, so Sarah's quietly running the place as deputy. If you're in her good books, you get less lunch duties, fewer after-school clubs. That sort of thing." He ran a hand through his hair. "But honestly, every school has politics. It's still a good place to work. She's capable—organised, clear with the kids, all that."

Ellie didn't speak. He gave her a faintly apologetic look.

"I'm sorry—I don't know what you want me to say."

"What's she like outside of school?"

Daniel blinked. "Outside?"

"You know. What she does when she's not marking spelling tests."

He scratched the back of his neck. "She's in the church choir, I think. Pretty active at St Mary's." He cast a finger up the street to the church looming over the green. "I'm fairly sure she's co-master of the choir with someone. She's mentioned her a few times... Tracey, maybe? Tina?"

Ellie stilled. "Tracey Harper? The reverend's daughter?"

"I think so?" Daniel squinted, brow furrowed. "I'm not sure. I don't really get involved with the church stuff, to be honest."

He glanced over his shoulder at the glow from his hallway. "Look, Ellie—I really do have a lot to do. Staff meeting in the morning, and I've still got ten of these homework books to get through."

Ellie gave a small nod, her thoughts already spinning. "Of course. Thanks for telling me."

Daniel leaned against the doorframe again, that familiar, easy smile returning. "Let's try again soon. Properly."

She returned the smile. "We will."

He stepped back inside, pausing just long enough to meet her gaze once more. "Goodnight, Ellie."

"Goodnight," she said softly, watching as the door closed.

The village was quiet now, the air hushed and still as she set off up the lane. By the time she reached the cottage, the last of the twilight had faded. She pushed the door open to find her grandmother waiting, arms crossed, eyes sharp.

"Good news, is it?" Maggie asked, nodding toward the faint smile Ellie hadn't realised she was still wearing, "I thought you were coming straight home after the soap shop?"

"I got a little… sidetracked," Ellie said, the weight of the day slipping back onto her shoulders like a too-familiar coat. "It's been a weird one, actually."

"And it's not going to get any better," Maggie said, leading her into the kitchen, where a tray of charcoal-blackened shapes sat forlornly on the counter. "I've burnt the lamb chops."

"Beans on toast it is," Ellie said, gently steering her gran to a chair. "You sit. I'll do it. And I've got a lot to fill you in on."

She reached for the tin opener, her mind already leaping ahead to tomorrow. The manor. Mrs Winchester. Sarah Mills.

Somewhere in that tangle of people and half-truths lay the answer about her father.

She was getting closer. She had to be.

Chapter 11
Return to Meadowfield Manor

The bell above the door hadn't rung in over an hour.

Ellie pretended not to notice as she sat behind the counter, pen in hand, staring down at her notes. She'd spent the morning so far writing summaries for *The Last Love Letter*. Most of the first half of the manuscript, all neatly written, underlined—and not a single one pointing to anything remotely suspicious.

She read aloud, more to herself than to her gran, who was busy wiping down the coffee machine.

"Margaret inherits a house in Devon from a great-aunt she barely knew. She moves in, meets the local vet, and tries not to fall for his dimples. Letters start arriving from her ex-boyfriend, begging her to come back. He turns up unexpectedly and ruins a perfectly nice garden party. Against all sensible judgement, they go for a walk on the moors and decide to give things another go."

Ellie dropped her pen. "So far, our mysterious author has produced the world's most innocent romance."

Maggie didn't look up. "He wasn't exactly Mr Hearts and Flowers."

"But why write this? If he was trying to *hide* a message—he's doing an excellent job."

Maggie gave the steam wand a final hiss and wiped it down. "Not every day's full of secrets and scandal. Some are just quiet. Like this one." She gestured around the empty shop. "I'm used to quiet mornings. You, on the other hand, are itching to get up to the manor. Go on. You said you wanted to after breakfast. I can manage things here."

"You sure?"

"I'll send up smoke signals if an angry mob blows in, but I'm not sure one is forecast."

Ellie stood, stretched, and wandered over to the fiction shelves. Her eyes drifted, almost on autopilot, to the Christie section. Nestled between the usual suspects was a slim, gold-tooled Folio Society edition of *The Moving Finger*.

"Hello," she murmured, pulling it free. She traced the embossed title with her thumb, then glanced over at Maggie.

"Take it," her gran said, not even looking up. "You said Mrs Winchester's parents were fans. Might loosen a few memories."

"Exactly my thinking." Ellie slipped the book into her backpack. "I'll be back before the lunchtime stampede."

The book tucked safely in her bag, Ellie set off for Meadowfield Manor.

She'd spent half the night tossing and turning, her mind spinning with questions, hoping that Mrs Winchester had more to say without her afternoon tea buddies around.

Or perhaps she'd slam the door in Ellie's face for even suggesting her niece might be involved.

The manor looked different in the morning light—less imposing, more stately, the red brick warmed by sunshine. Ellie pressed the buzzer at the gate, half-expecting resistance after her abrupt departure the day before.

To her surprise, the gate clicked open.

As she walked up the driveway, Ellie spotted a police car parked discreetly to one side. Her stomach tightened. Had something happened?

The butler opened the front door before she could knock, his face a careful mask of professional detachment.

"Mrs Winchester is in the drawing room," he announced, stepping aside. "She's expecting you."

"She is?" Ellie blinked, caught off guard.

The butler merely inclined his head and gestured for her to follow.

The drawing room was gracious and still, awash with late-morning sun and the quiet gleam of antique furniture. Mrs Winchester sat in a wingback chair by the window, looking more drawn than she had at the garden party where Ellie had first stumbled into her orbit.

"Mrs Winchester," Ellie began, "I wanted to apologise if I overstepped—"

"Nonsense, child." The older woman waved the words away. "Come in, come in. And please, call me Vivienne. We're hardly strangers anymore."

Ellie approached, retrieving the book from her bag. "I brought you something."

Vivienne accepted the gift, her eyes widening slightly as she took in the elegant binding.

For a moment, Ellie wondered if she'd misjudged things. Was a book too obvious? Too intimate? But then Vivienne's fingers curled around the spine with something like reverence, and Ellie breathed out.

"An Agatha Christie? You remembered." Vivienne ran her fingers over the embossed cover. "Folio Society —first edition reprint. A lovely copy."

"I thought you might enjoy it," Ellie said, watching as Vivienne turned the book over in her hands.

"This is… very thoughtful," Vivienne said, her voice gentler than Ellie had yet heard. "It's been a long time since anyone gave me anything."

Ellie glanced around the opulent room—the oil paintings, the crystal decanters, the careful hush of money well aged. She'd imagined a woman like Vivienne received gifts regularly.

"Please, sit," Vivienne said, gesturing to a nearby chair. "We've had quite a morning of it."

"Oh?" Ellie asked, settling in.

"Would you believe," Vivienne leaned forward, lowering her voice, "that given everything we spoke of the other day… I'm dealing with this *again*?"

"This?" Ellie asked, settling into the chair.

In answer, Vivienne gestured towards the far corner of the room, where two uniformed police officers were dusting for fingerprints around an antique writing desk. Ellie hadn't noticed them when she'd first entered, but now she saw the opened drawers, the scattered papers, the unmistakable signs of a careful search.

"The house was broken into last night," Vivienne said, lifting her teacup with steady hands. "And this time, I didn't wake up. But when dear Jeremy brought in my toast this morning and informed me of the break-in, I knew straight away what they'd taken."

Ellie followed her gaze to an empty space on a nearby bookshelf.

"What was it?"

"Benjamin's book." Vivienne exhaled slowly. "He visited about a month ago to give me an advance copy."

She glanced at the officers, then leaned closer to Ellie.

"He told me—in confidence—that he was convinced there was a link between the robbery here and what happened to his sister. I think he always suspected as much, deep down. But he was so fixed on your father, he never really examined the other possibilities."

"What changed his mind?" Ellie asked, leaning forward.

"He wouldn't say. He was vague—deliberately so, I think—but he said he'd written something that would explain it all. Then he gave me the manuscript and made me swear not to tell a soul I had it."

Ellie shook her head. "Someone clearly knew. Someone who wanted it badly enough to break in."

"I urged him to go to the police with whatever he'd found," Vivienne said. "But he'd given up hope. I think he was counting on the book to do the talking for him. But alas—" she tapped her temple lightly "—I'm not as sharp as I once was. I didn't see it."

"My gran neither," Ellie admitted. "Or me. I read more this morning. I'd tell you which chapter I'm on, but… there are no chapter numbers. No titles."

Vivienne straightened slightly, her eyes brightening. "Oh, I think there were in mine. Yes—I'm sure of it. Some of the chapter titles were oddly worded. Curious, even."

Her brow furrowed.

"There was something strange in the middle. A scene set during a storm—like *that* night. I remember hiding under the bed, watching purple lightning flash across the room while the wind howled down the chimney something wicked." She paused, gaze distant. "There's a scene just like it. And the characters… they were talking about a robbery." She glanced at Ellie with those steely eyes. "But they weren't the same characters from the rest of the book. It didn't seem to belong."

"I haven't got to that part yet," Ellie said, shuffling

to the edge of her seat. "Do you remember which chapter it was?"

"I wasn't altogether sure why he'd included it," Vivienne murmured, ignoring the question. "But now… perhaps it meant more than I realised." She sighed. "I'm afraid I didn't make a copy."

"I have one," Ellie said. "Gran's. But it's missing the chapter titles. Do you happen to remember any of them?"

Vivienne closed her eyes, brow creasing with concentration. After a long moment, she gave a small, apologetic shake of her head.

"I'm sorry. Nothing comes to mind."

Ellie bit her lip, wondering how many more people out there had been given an advance copy. She glanced at the police officers, now packing up their equipment. How many people had Benjamin trusted with his secrets?

"Actually," she said, shifting gears, "I came today because I found something interesting—and it lines up perfectly with what you just told me about the storm."

She pulled out her phone and showed Vivienne the photograph she'd taken at the pub.

"This was hanging in The Old Bell—from the night of the storm. The same night as the robbery and Sally's drowning."

Vivienne leaned forward, squinting at the screen.

"Sarah told me she was there that night with Sally," Ellie went on. "But she didn't mention the others. That's Joanne from the soap shop in the corner."

"Did you talk to her?" Vivienne cut in, eyes sharp.

"I did. She admitted she was involved. Said she was just the lookout—and it doesn't sound like she walked away with any money. But you were right to suspect her."

"I suppose I should feel vindicated after all these years," Vivienne murmured, though her voice held little satisfaction. "Did she tell you what happened?"

"Not exactly," Ellie said. "But she slipped up—pointed me towards Phil the postman."

Ellie zoomed in on the photo. "Benjamin thought his postman had stolen his books, and when I tracked Phil down, he was chatting with Tracey—"

"Reverend Harper's daughter," Vivienne interjected, her eyes lighting up. "You *did* pick up on my hint! Did you notice how quickly she changed the subject when I mentioned her?"

"I did," Ellie admitted.

"That's why I suspect her," Vivienne said, satisfied. "Catherine had the same reaction in 1975 when I mentioned I'd been to see Joanne—and pointed out that Tracey was her friend. She all but called me a liar. And I don't think I ever saw those girls together again." She gave a brisk nod. "I wouldn't be surprised if Catherine knows more about that night than she'll ever admit, but you've done a marvellous job so far."

"There's more," Ellie said, slipping the phone back into her pocket. "I spoke to Terry. He's a mechanic, and he was Sally's boyfriend when she died. An admitted thief. Tracey said the robbery was *his* plan." She hesitated. "But he told me to look closer to _your_ inner circle."

Vivienne's brow lifted, expectant. Ellie hesitated.

One sentence, and she might lose Vivienne's trust entirely. But the truth had to matter more than manners.

"Your niece," Ellie said quietly. "Sarah. She was in the pub that night with Sally. Along with the others I believe were involved in the robbery."

Vivienne's expression snapped shut like a trap.

"No," she said, her voice suddenly cold. "Sarah wasn't involved. She's been my closest confidante for years." She stood abruptly, smoothing her skirt. "I commend your investigation so far, but I won't have you tarnishing my niece's name."

"Vivienne, if I could—"

"I've just remembered." She glanced at her watch with theatrical precision. "Bridge club. Half an hour. I must get ready." Her smile was as ornate as the setting. "And thank you for the lovely book, Ellie."

Vivienne swept from the room, leaving Ellie sitting with the distinct feeling she'd just been shown the door.

Jeremy, the butler, appeared in the doorway. "This way, miss."

Ellie followed him into the hallway. The house was hushed now, each footstep echoing softly through its cavernous grandeur.

"Jeremy," she said, catching up to walk beside him. "May I ask—were you working here the day of the robbery? In 1975?"

He glanced at her sidelong, expression unreadable. "Yes, miss. I was."

"But not overnight?"

"No, miss. I've never worked the night shift. I was in my own home by then."

Ellie hesitated, then said lightly, "But you're in the inner circle, aren't you?"

Jeremy stopped at the front door, hand resting on the polished brass handle. "What exactly are you suggesting, miss?"

"Only that if the butler had done it… he probably wouldn't still be here."

That earned the faintest twitch of his moustache. "Indeed, miss."

She tilted her head. "What about Mrs Winchester's niece—Sarah? What do you make of her?"

There was a long pause.

"If you're asking for my personal opinion of my employer's niece, with respect, I don't think that would be appropriate to share."

He opened the door, letting in the scent of freshly cut grass, the distant murmur of the mower drifting across the lawn as the gardener moved in neat lines back and forth.

But just as Ellie stepped over the threshold, he added, "I do, however, have one observation to share. June 1975 marked the beginning of Miss Sarah's regular visits to the manor. Before that, they were more… infrequent." He nodded politely. "Good day, miss."

The door clicked shut behind her.

Ellie paused on the front step, one hand resting on the strap of her bag. She swung it around, pulled out her notepad and pen, and scribbled his parting observation—quiet, precise, and deliberate. Just like Jeremy himself.

Back on the gravel drive, keeping pace with the gardener and his mower, Ellie checked her watch.

Three hours until her lunch with Sarah Mills.

Three hours to review her notes, refine her questions, and decide just how hard she was willing to push Mrs Winchester's niece.

Chapter 12
Ashes by the River

E llie pushed open the door to Meadowfield Books. Behind her, South Street was humming —shoppers crossing the street with bags, prams wheeling by, a pair of teenagers laughing too loudly outside the bakery. Inside the shop, the air felt still.

A couple browsed quietly near the travel section. A young boy sat cross-legged in front of the picture books. Near the till, a man in a flat cap turned the pages of a military history volume as if searching for an old friend.

Maggie stood behind the counter, offering a smile that didn't quite reach her eyes. The coffee machine hissed obligingly as she wrestled it into producing two cappuccinos.

Ellie stepped inside, but her mind was still back at the manor. Vivienne Winchester's sudden frost, the clipped goodbye, the door quietly closing behind her— it all circled in her thoughts like a flock refusing to land.

At the back of the shop, someone bounced on their toes with barely concealed impatience.

Sylvia.

She was lurking in the thrillers, clutching a paperback by the spine and peering towards the counter like she might combust if forced to wait another minute. The moment she spotted Ellie, her whole face lit up.

"*There* you are!" she exclaimed, abandoning the thrillers to rush over. She seized Ellie's arm and dragged her into the quieter gloom of the classics section. "I've been waiting."

"Is everything okay?" Ellie asked, noting the barely contained fizz of excitement in Sylvia's expression.

"I put the feelers out about those missing books," Sylvia whispered, all but vibrating with delight. "And someone in the dog-walking group chat says they found a box of *burnt books* down by the river. They didn't get a closer look."

Ellie blinked, trying to keep up. "I didn't know you had a dog?"

"I don't," Sylvia said breezily. "But I posted about it online, and your Auntie Penny cross-posted it to the dog-walking groups. I bumped into her on the way home when she was out with Duchess after I got back from my cheese-making class, which was once again sold out, I might add." She paused to offer a small bow. "Your auntie said if anyone can find something odd, it's the dog walkers." She nodded sagely. "They notice everything."

A spark of hope flickered in Ellie's chest. "Do you think it could be Benjamin's missing delivery?"

"Only one way to find out," Sylvia said, tossing a devious wink towards the door. "I know the way."

Ellie glanced at her gran, who was pouring a flawless rosetta into a cappuccino while chatting to the man with his military book.

The shop, as always, was in capable hands.

"How far is it?" Ellie asked, though she was already reaching for her coat.

"Ten-minute round trip," Sylvia promised, halfway to the door. "Fifteen minutes, tops."

Thirty-five minutes later, Ellie clung to a gnarled tree root, inching her way down the slippery embankment that led to the river.

"Careful of those loose stones," Sylvia called from below, wielding her telescopic baton like a walking stick. She looked perfectly at home scrambling down the muddy slope, despite her cashmere cardigan and knee-length skirt.

Ellie tightened her grip on the thick branch she'd found to steady herself. One wrong step and she'd be in the water. By the time she reached the bottom, her trousers were streaked with mud and leaves clung to her jumper.

"Well, this brings back memories," Sylvia said

cheerfully, brushing dirt from her knees. "Reminds me of my days as a Duke of Edinburgh Award leader. All those earnest teenagers slogging through bogs with compasses and misguided optimism." She glanced over. "Did you take part when you were younger?"

"No, I was more 'hide in the library'," Ellie admitted, flicking a particularly stubborn clump of mud from her trainer.

"Nothing wrong with that," Sylvia said, already striding along the riverbank like it wasn't sloped at a forty-five-degree angle. "Though I do love the great outdoors. There's very little a walk by the water won't cure… temporarily, at least." She stopped suddenly, consulting her phone "Ah! There it is, just ahead." She paused, comparing their surroundings to the photo on the screen. "The trees line up. And look! The box hasn't moved. Thank the dog walkers!"

"Thank them indeed," Ellie murmured, catching sight of it.

A scorched cardboard box lay tucked against the trunk of a fallen tree. Even from several feet away, she could see the blackened corners of books inside, their spines blistered, pages curled like dried petals.

They approached cautiously, as if the ashes might scatter at a breath.

Ellie knelt beside it, heart sinking. "It's the missing box of Benjamin's books," she said, carefully lifting the top flap. "Most of them are destroyed."

She began tipping the remnants out onto a

relatively dry patch of ground. Burned edges flaked away with each touch, the titles almost illegible.

Then her hand froze.

There, just inside the lid, printed in bold black marker: 1 of 2.

Ellie looked up. "This is box one."

Sylvia stepped closer, squinting at the writing. "Which means there's a second box out there somewhere."

While Sylvia scanned the banks, Ellie sifted through the ruins, unsure of what she was looking for. Preferably something she could walk away with. Her fingers closed around a volume where the top half had survived the flames. She peeled it open carefully, revealing a partially intact contents page, then flipped through the remaining pages.

"This one has titles for the chapters," she said, excitement rising despite the destruction around her. "*Tender Kiss. Love Unveil. Heartswell. Amour Amici…* these titles are—"

"Avant garde," Sylvia remarked.

"Ten chapters in total."

"Is that important?" Sylvia asked, crouching beside her.

"The manuscript I've been reading doesn't even have chapter numbers, let alone titles." Ellie turned back to the first page and read the first line aloud: "'The final letter of importance came on the tenth day of the tenth month.'" She tapped the page. "That repetition of ten—"

"Ten clues, perhaps?" Sylvia offered.

"Or ten suspects?" Ellie managed a dry laugh, though it felt hollow. "If so, I *might* have five."

The pages crumbled at the edges as she turned them, and frustration began to prickle under her skin. If they couldn't find the second box, this might have been the only batch Benjamin ever printed. She searched the box again, hoping to find another copy in better condition, but the one in her hands seemed the least damaged by far.

"It's something," she said, snapping a photo of the contents page and sending it to DS Cookson along with their location. Whatever her suspicions about Tracey's photo, Angela needed to see this.

They gathered the burnt books back into the box, leaving it where they'd found it for the police to collect.

As they started back up the embankment, Ellie noticed a weathered wooden signpost half-lost beneath the brambles: THE BURROWS NATURE RESERVE – PUBLIC FOOTPATH THIS WAY.

The sight of it caught her like a string pulled tight. A rush of childhood memories surged up: her father's warm hand around hers, the quiet hush of the woods, pausing every few minutes so he could point out birdsong, the weight of borrowed binoculars thumping against her chest as she kept up, the book under her arm threatening to slip.

"The Burrows," she murmured. "Dad used to take me there birdwatching all the time."

"Have you looked for him there?" Sylvia asked, following her gaze.

Ellie shook her head. "It hadn't crossed my mind. But if he's hiding anywhere…" She trailed off.

They crested the slope and emerged onto the path that curved beside the river. Sylvia paused, making a show of wiping down her baton with a tissue from her handbag.

"You go on ahead," she said, collapsing the metal rod and looping its wrist strap rather than putting it away. "I need to catch my breath."

Something in her tone made Ellie turn.

Sylvia gave the faintest nod towards the trees behind them. "Our friend in black is back."

Ellie's heart stuttered, resisting the urge to turn and stare. "Shouldn't we stay together?"

"You go ahead," Sylvia repeated, that sharp gleam returning to her eyes. "I'll give him a taste of his own medicine."

Before Ellie could protest, Sylvia had already turned back, swift, purposeful, and utterly undaunted.

For a moment, the only sounds were the rustle of leaves and the distant burble of the river. Then Ellie turned, following the dirt track as it curled away from the bank and into the countryside.

The Burrows.

She hadn't been back in years. The trees had grown thicker, the hedgerows wilder. The quiet was the same. Familiar. A little eerie.

She walked slowly at first, unsure of what she hoped

to find. A footprint? A campsite? Her father, sitting on a log roasting marshmallows as if this were all perfectly normal?

She didn't know what she'd say if she saw him. Not really.

But she kept walking anyway, each step carrying her deeper into the trees—towards whatever, or whoever, might be waiting in the quiet.

Chapter 13
Mountain Out of a Molehill

The Burrows Nature Reserve brought with it a familiar, guilty pang, like bumping into someone you hadn't thought about in years but suddenly missed the moment they were right in front of you.

The swaying grass had grown wild since Ellie last walked these paths. It brushed at her fingertips, taller and thicker than she remembered. Or maybe her memory was playing tricks on her. Time had a way of turning places into stories, softening the corners, adding fuzzy warmth where there hadn't been much. It was easy to wear rose-tinted glasses when looking back at your own childhood, and most of Ellie's memories of The Burrows wore that glow.

At nine, this place had been a kingdom during an endless summer.

Her mother had been away filming a doomed horror film in Bulgaria, full of prosthetic fangs, wandering accents, and barely a budget. She'd sworn it was her big break, but the film never made it past the editing suite.

Ellie had stayed with Granny Maggie and spent every day with her father. Morning after morning, once breakfast in the garden was cleared away, they'd trek to The Burrows through sunshine and showers. She'd tear across the mounded hills, her father always a step behind, as if she were leading him to his usual spots.

"Giant mole tunnels," he'd once told her as they rounded one of the mounds, earnest apart from the twinkle in his eyes. "That's how this place got its name. The moles were the size of cars. Very territorial."

She'd laughed, knowing it was nonsense, and loving it all the more for that.

Mostly, she remembered the quiet. Not silence, but the hush of birdsong and rustling leaves. No reading lines with her mother, no endless errands with Auntie Penny. Just peace. She'd curl up with a book beneath the shade of a tree while her father wandered off with his binoculars and leather notebook, scribbling down sightings like a one-man ornithological MI5.

A twig snapped.

Ellie spun, heart leaping.

Her father? Or the mystery follower, finally closing in?

The undergrowth rustled again—and out hopped a robin, tilting its head like it had been expecting her.

Ellie let out a breath. Just a robin. It blinked once,

then disappeared into the brambles, busy with its own hunt for lunch.

She glanced at her phone.

No message from Sylvia.

But there was a message from Daniel, reminding her about lunch with Sarah at the café. She'd forgotten, off chasing ghosts in The Burrows.

Half an hour to get to the café. If she didn't find her father in fifteen minutes, she'd head back to the village.

Turning deeper into the woods, she paused at the fork in the path. To the right, a well-trodden trail led to the pond where birdwatchers gathered behind wooden screens. To the left, the path narrowed, winding into the quieter woodland that peppered the valley's edge. Her father had always preferred to be away from chattering tourists and overeager photographers with their enormous lenses.

She veered left, ducking beneath low branches. The ground grew uneven, roots snaking across the path like petrified snakes. After a short climb, the trees began to thin, and the path opened onto a clearing framed by giant oaks as old as the buildings in the village below.

Meadowfield lay spread out like a map, St Mary's church spire rising above the patchwork of honeyed stone and greenery. She could just make out the tip of the shop's thatched roof, peeking from the top of South Street. The pond was nothing more than a still blot from up here.

This had been their lunch spot. Her father would

lay out the threadbare tartan blanket, and Ellie would unpack the flask of tea that was too hot to drink straight away. Always the same cheese sandwiches in wax paper, slightly squashed, always perfect. At nine, Ellie had believed they could live like that forever, the two of them, under open skies, as long as the sandwiches kept coming.

Something caught her eye at the edge of the clearing.

A flash of faded green canvas, half-hidden among the branches.

She held her breath.

She knew that tent.

A relic passed down from her grandfather, patched so often it looked more like a quilt than a proper shelter.

She stepped closer. The campsite was tidy: a compact stove beside the tent flap, a pair of muddy boots neatly placed on a groundsheet, a shirt fluttering on a clothesline strung between two trees. And on a small fold-out chair, a plastic plate bearing the crusts of abandoned cheese sandwiches.

"Dad?" she called.

A twig snapped behind her.

She turned—and nearly collided with him.

Peter stood in front of her, binoculars raised in one hand, frozen mid-focus. Somewhere in the trees, a warbler's cry cut short as a blur of feathers disappeared into the canopy.

He lowered the binoculars, disappointment flickering across his face. Not anger, not irritation, just the quiet deflation of a moment missed. That hadn't ever been a rule, exactly, but Ellie had always known when to keep quiet and still.

But the disappointment faded as he took her in. His face, weathered and gaunt, twisted with something between hope and disbelief.

"Sparrow?" he whispered, as though afraid she might vanish. He glanced over his shoulder, like a man expecting pursuit. "How did you find me?"

"This was our spot."

"That summer," he said with a nod. Something in his face softened. "Do you remember the day we strayed too far east and ended up in Old Billy's farm?"

"I remember his rifle," Ellie said, laughter escaping before she could stop it. "That was the first time I'd seen a gun in real life."

"He said he was after the fox that got his hens." His gaze drifted east. "But I'm sure he was a pig farmer."

Their laughter faded, and the years stretched between them—cavernous, awkward. It wasn't that he'd never visited her in Cardiff, or that she hadn't returned to Meadowfield at least once a year. But it had never been quite enough. She could feel the difference now, the distance grown between them. Yet here they were, their paths crossing back in The Burrows.

Peter shuffled to a fallen log beside the camping stove, brushed away a patch of moss, and sat down with a quiet grunt.

"Tea?" he asked, picking up the enamel mug at his feet, as though he'd left it there mid-bird chase. "There should be enough left in the pot for a cup, if you don't mind it black. Ran out of milk."

Ellie couldn't believe he was asking if she wanted tea. She did, but it wasn't the reaction she'd expected. "That would be nice," she said anyway.

"I thought about going to the shop," he added, almost absently, "but I didn't want to risk being seen."

Ellie's throat tightened. He'd been missing for days, and all he could worry about was the milk. But the tremor in his hands and how his eyes darted restlessly through the trees told a story of sleepless nights and mounting dread.

"If I'd known, I'd have brought some," she said instead, swallowing the urge to let her worry spill out. "You could have called me."

"I know, Sparrow. I just… didn't want to drag you into it."

She poured herself a cup of tea, the enamel warm against her palms. So many questions pressed at her, but she didn't want to spook him. Instead, she moved aside the sandwich crusts and sat in the foldout chair. As she swung her backpack forward, the zip shifted open, revealing the stack of letters inside, still bound with an elastic band.

"You've made yourself at home," she said, glancing around the campsite. "Impressive, considering you left your bag in my mother's greenhouse."

Peter didn't answer. Instead, he brightened, like a radio picking up a clearer signal, and said, "Do you remember the hawfinch?"

"I do," Ellie said, smiling. "You got so excited you fell into the brook."

"My second bath of the day, after you pushed me into that puddle on the way here."

"I did *not* push you!" she protested, just like she had then. "You tripped on your shoelaces."

"Well, it was either you or a woodland fairy."

She glanced down at his worn trainers, the laces still dangling over the edges. They could sit there for hours, swapping stories like a game of ping pong. As comforting as it was to reminisce, that wasn't why she'd taken the gamble of checking The Burrows.

"Angela's looking for you," she said.

Peter's smile faded. He looked down at his tea, steam curling between his fingers.

"I suspected she might be," he said quietly, running a hand over his stubbly jaw as he took in his makeshift home. "The bag I left at your mum's was my everyday bag. I stashed my camping gear here in case I needed to—"

"Run again?" Ellie interrupted. "But not before throwing stones at my window. Dad… what happened that night? Did you—"

She couldn't finish the question, but the weight of it hung in the air.

"No," he offered. "I didn't kill him."

"But you know Benjamin is dead?"

He nodded.

"Did you… see something?"

"I *found* him, Ellie," he whispered, his eyes darting

around the tree edge as something rustled. "Like how I found Sally all those years ago. He was in the pond and I…"

He couldn't get the words out.

"What happened?"

"I'd just left The Drowsy Duck," he started, squinting into his tea as he struggled through his memories. "I thought I was seeing things from all the whisky, but then Benjamin snapped into focus. Floating. Face down in the pond, just like Sally. Only it wasn't raining this time, and I wasn't *meant* to be there."

"Meant?" Ellie echoed. "Were you meant to be there in 1975?"

Peter swallowed hard, scratching his neck. He took a long gulp of tea, then closed his eyes like he was hunting for the words. None came. He slurped more tea, buying time.

"Please."

"I'm building up to it, Sparrow," he said, setting his mug on the ground. "I've told this story so many times in interview rooms, but I never thought I'd have to tell you."

He glanced up, his gaze brushing hers, then falling away again.

"It's just me, Dad," she said, ducking to offer him a smile.

He nodded. "She called me that night."

"Sally?"

"Yes. She needed to talk to someone she could trust, but she wouldn't tell me why over the phone.

Remember that old phone box on the corner by the bus stop? She was in there." He cast his distant gaze in the direction of the village. "Gone now."

Ellie did remember it, and she hadn't noticed it had vanished since her return. "What did she say?"

"The rain was hammering down," he said, straining his head like he was trying to pick up on a faraway noise. "It sounded like she was calling from a shower. I could barely make her out, but she was scared. I could hear it in her voice. Shaking out of control, and I'd never heard her so scared before."

Ellie could hear the tremor in her dad's voice now. "Did she hint at anything?" she pushed.

"No, but she told me to meet her under the tree by the pond," he stated. "I told her to keep dry, that I'd be there in five minutes. I ran faster than I think I ever have. I was soaked, but I think I made it in under five minutes. And when I got there..." His voice cracked. He looked away. "She was in the water. There was nothing I could do. I... I tried... but..."

"But you got there too late," Ellie said softly. "Do you remember what time it was?"

"Not long after ten," he replied. "Your gran had just gone to bed, and ten o'clock was sacred back when she was teaching."

Ellie glanced at her bag, thinking of the letters. "Did you see anything suspicious once you got there?"

He shook his head. "I couldn't look away from her until the police came. Like I couldn't believe what I was seeing." He stared at the ground, then clenched his eyes shut. "I'd seen Sally that afternoon. She was heading to the school across the green, and I was off to South Street to find a new hat. I'd left mine on the bus. You'd never have guessed a storm was coming. It was a day as nice as today." He looked up at the sky, where bright blue patches were breaking through the trees. "She was giddy about a robin that had flown through her bedroom window and hopped onto her dresser while she was brushing her hair." He paused, eyes glassy. "The last thing she said to me in person was that she planned to ride out the storm at the pub with her boyfriend and someone she didn't like from work. And that was it. How could she be dead when I'd just spoken to her five minutes earlier?"

"Did you tell the police all of this?"

"Every detail. And they believed me at first. I told them about the call from the phone box, running through the rain, finding her, but…" His voice drifted away.

"You're doing good," she said, catching his eye and offering a smile. "What happened next?"

"They took me into the pub and someone wrapped me in a blanket. Even gave me half a pint. I wasn't old enough, but I think they were just being kind. I was in shock. Nothing made sense, and the beer tasted like old pennies. And then Benjamin turned up." His shoulders clenched up. "Everything changed after that."

Ellie left her black tea and joined him on the log. He hunched forward, exhaling like the telling had taken what little strength he had left.

"He said you had a crush on her?" she asked gently.

Peter nodded, seeming grateful not to have to say it himself. "He made it sound like I was obsessed… like I was following her around." He shook his head. "I'd never even spoken to him before that night. Sally told me he was a drunk in a band, so I stayed clear."

"Benjamin Brown?" Ellie asked, surprised. "In a band?"

"A rock band," Peter confirmed. "Back then he went by Ben. Fifty years is a long time, and he wasn't the man you saw recently. After Sally died, something broke. People thought he'd spiral—drink, disappear—but he gave up the music, cut his hair, and got a job where he never left his suit. But that old anger never went away. I couldn't pass him in the street without him shouting at me, always loud enough for everyone to hear." He rubbed his face, worn-out from remembering. "I went to the police," he continued. "It was harassment. But they didn't take me seriously. I could tell they thought I'd killed her too. The same officers who'd wrapped me in a blanket and told me everything would be alright if I just told the truth. So, I did. Over and *over*."

"But the truth about Sally didn't come," Ellie said quietly. "And Benjamin filled in the gaps with something that sounded plausible." She tilted on the log to face him. "But Sally Brown called you that night. Not Benjamin. Not Terry. You."

"Terry thought I did it too," he said, almost flinching at the name. "Even when Sally was alive, he hated me. Told me to stay away more than once. And for a while, I did. But Sally and I kept bumping into each other. Birdwatching, mostly." He gestured towards the trees. "We met when she took the last spot on a birding platform near the pond. You know how it is—you settle in, start chatting. She realised I knew my stuff. Her grandfather got her into it, and there wasn't a bird she couldn't name. She gave me the confidence to leave the main paths, to explore. Until that night, she only ever rang to share sightings or walking routes."

"So, a friendship?" Ellie concluded.

"That's all it was," he said certainly. "But to Terry and Benjamin, I was the only thing in Sally's life that didn't make sense to them. No matter what I said to defend myself, they were always louder." He paused, tucking his chin in to face her before whispering, "I saw Terry."

Ellie straightened. "You saw him?"

"That night on my way to the pond," he said. "He nearly ran me over, speeding out of the village in a car full of people."

"How could you be sure it was him?" Ellie asked.

Peter gave a dry laugh. "Because of the rain? That's exactly what the police asked. But it was Terry. I'd know that car anywhere. He had this bright orange Allegro. A real eyesore. I once heard someone say the thing had a fake licence plate and that it was stolen. Wouldn't surprise me—he's always had a reputation."

Ellie hesitated, deciding not to mention she'd already met Terry and experienced the heat of that reputation. "So, you did see something strange that night," she said, mulling over the letters in the bag. "Someone has thought that for fifty years, haven't they? That you witnessed something important?"

His face dropped. "How did you—"

"The greenhouse," she reminded him, nudging his arm with hers. "The letters threatening you and everyone you care about."

"You read them?" he asked in a small voice. "I was always so careful to keep them hidden."

"I had to."

"I don't know why I kept them all this time," he said. "They scared me at first. For a while, actually, but then I came to expect them. A constant reminder of that night."

"They must have given you a strange sense of continuity," she said, glad he was opening up without running. "And you never showed anyone? Not even the police?"

"How could I?" he said, almost pleading. "As the years rolled by, I started to think they were just empty threats, but I wasn't going to call their bluff, was I? They were threatening me to cover their backs because whatever that person thinks I saw—"

"But it could have been Terry," Ellie pointed out. "You saw him."

"I told the police about him, and he was questioned almost as much as I was. Benjamin didn't like him either. He looked down on Terry. But whoever sent those letters, I have no idea."

"What about their relationship?" Ellie pushed, eager to pry more into Sally's involvement with the thieving mechanic. "They seem like an odd match to me."

He hesitated. "We mostly talked about birds, but sometimes we'd talk about other things. Family. Life. The weather. The usual stuff. Her parents ran off to be roadies for some glam rock band, and Benjamin thought he was the next Iggy Pop. She was the odd one out. Quiet. Shy. And she loved to read. You would have liked her." A warm smile lifted his tired eyes. "She told me one of her favourite books was *Peril at End House*."

"A Christie classic based in Devon."

His smile lifted. "That's the one. All she wanted was to move to Devon, live by the sea, and spend her days fending off seagulls, just like in Christie's book."

"And Benjamin's book," Ellie said quietly, narrowing her eyes as the dots connected. "The main character moves to Devon, but can't escape her past—or her ex-boyfriend."

"I did get the impression she wanted to go to the coast to start again *alone*." He paused, delving deeper into the fog of memory. "Benjamin said something about Sally and Devon. Last night. That Sally helped him write the book. When the truth came out, he'd move to Devon for both of them. He'd found something." He exhaled, as if the detail was returning for the first time since drinking with Benjamin. "The locket."

"What locket?" Ellie asked.

"It was one of the only pieces of evidence at the time," he said, his hand rising to his collarbone. "She always wore this silver locket with a little robin etched on the front. She never took it off, and you'd notice it because she had this habit of always pulling it out from under her jumper, like she didn't like wearing jewellery but made an exception."

"It must have been special to her."

"A gift from her grandfather. It had a photo of the two of them inside. I think he'd not long died in '75." Any trace of a smile faded. "When I pulled her from the water, it wasn't there. I noticed. Everyone who knew her noticed. The police searched your gran's house three times." He tightened at the thought. "The third search was the only time I ever saw your granddad properly lose his temper."

He exhaled, letting the years go.

"Everyone was so tired by then," he continued. "Tired of the questions, the rumours. I started to wonder if the police were trying to stitch me up. If they'd come out of my room with the locket in their hands and say it had been there all along." He shook his head slowly. "But it never turned up. Not until recently."

Ellie leaned in. "How recently?"

"Benjamin had it."

"In the pub?" Her mouth dropped open. "How?"

"He pulled it out of his pocket like it was nothing." He repeated the motion, holding out his empty palm. "He couldn't open it, and he wouldn't let me look properly. I think he was afraid someone might see. Kept glancing over his shoulder." He did the same as a soft breeze rustled the leaves around them. "He said the locket proved I was innocent."

Ellie searched her father's face. "How?"

"He was being cryptic. He had this fizzing, nervous energy—like he'd been dying to tell someone, but he couldn't get to the point. He kept saying when people cracked the code, the timebomb would go off—but not on either of us." Peter gave a faint, bewildered smile. "I'd spent half my life afraid of him. But that night, he was just another Meadowling I was having a pint with. And I could see how much he still grieved for Sally. I don't think he ever forgave himself for not being around more when she was alive. They were just so different."

"What was the code?" she asked, edging closer. "What did he tell you?"

His face fell. "I can't remember the details. The whisky... it's all foggy. He said something about going back to front. That he didn't want to write anything that could get him sued."

Ellie's stomach dipped. "So, he wasn't certain?"

"I suppose," Peter said, squinting as if the memory might sharpen. "But he didn't sound uncertain. Said it was a numbers game. That once people worked it out and started saying the same name, the police wouldn't have a choice but to reopen the case."

She glanced at her bag again, this time thinking about the charred top half of the finished book she'd found earlier. "He really thought his book would be enough?"

"He said he showed the locket to the police first, but they weren't interested. But it wasn't about the locket—it was *where* he found it. Somewhere only one person could've put it, which is what finally ruled me out for—"

Peter froze mid-sentence.

A shout tore through the clearing.

Ellie's head snapped up as a blur of beige cashmere burst from the trees, all flailing limbs and righteous fury. Sylvia hurled herself at a hooded figure emerging from behind an oak, her handbag flapping like a war banner, the found baton raised high.

"Gotcha, you skulking little—!"

Her words dissolved into a grunt as she tackled the figure to the ground. They went down hard in a patch of bluebells, limbs thrashing, petals flying.

Chapter 14
Arrested Development

Peter lurched to his feet, but Ellie was already moving, sprinting towards the chaos. Sylvia, like it was no work at all, had the figure pinned —one knee pressed into his back, the baton locked around his throat.

"Stop wriggling, you slippery little ferret!" she commanded. "I am performing a citizen's arrest!"

Ellie seized the figure's hood and yanked it back.

The tousled brunette hair was unmistakable.

It wasn't an attacker at all, but somebody she knew.

"PC Finn Walsh?" she said, arching a brow.

"Get her off me!" Finn squeaked, his voice several octaves higher than usual. "This is highly illegal!"

"Sylvia, let go," Ellie called, trying not to laugh. "It's Finn."

Sylvia paused, baton still tight in her grip. "You're sure? He was following us."

"I'm sure."

With clear reluctance, Sylvia released him. She kept the baton poised as PC Walsh staggered to his feet, twigs and leaf litter clinging to his civilian clothes. He dusted them down, half-keeled over as he flashed his badge at Sylvia.

"I'd wager this is still harassment," she sniffed, adjusting her cardigan with all the dignity she could summon. "Lurking in the woods like some criminal from a penny dreadful. I almost had you when you were creeping around at the garage!"

"I wasn't creeping," PC Walsh said, brushing dirt from his knees. He fixed Peter with a stern look that his youthful face couldn't commit to. "DS Cookson had a hunch Ellie might lead us to him." He turned to Ellie. "Which you have."

He then eyed Sylvia warily as she hovered nearby, still wielding her new baton like she might change her mind about using it at any moment. The young officer held out his hand.

"Miss Fortescue, that's a police-issued weapon."

Sylvia didn't move. "Finders keepers."

"It's illegal for you to even be holding that right now," he replied, reaching for the second pair of handcuffs. "And I can arrest you for using it." In a lower voice, he pleaded, "C'mon, Sylvia. Sergeant will have my head if she finds out I lost it, and I'm always buying cheese at your shop."

"Hmm." Sylvia gave the baton a final, thoughtful look, then collapsed it against a tree and tossed it to him. "I still don't think it's right, following young Ellie all over the countryside like you have been. How do you think that made her feel?"

"I can assure you, she was in no danger," he said, fumbling to clip the baton back onto his belt.

"But she didn't know that," Sylvia said pointedly. "And, actually, on second thought, I'd like to make a formal—"

"It's fine, Sylvia," Ellie cut in, holding up her hands. "Stalking forgiven." She nodded at the radio on his belt. "Are you going to alert DS Cookson to your golden egg find, or was this goose chase all for nothing?"

Finn blinked another silent apology, then unclipped the radio.

"This is PC Walsh," he said after clearing his throat. "Suspect Peter Cookson has been located at The Burrows Nature Reserve. Preparing for arrest and requesting backup and transport." He turned slightly away, lowering his voice. "And let DS Cookson know. She'll want to be informed."

He reattached the radio, his expression hardening as he pulled out the handcuffs once more.

"Mr Cookson," he said, turning back to Peter, "please don't make this harder than it needs to be."

Ellie saw it immediately—that flicker of panic in her father's eyes, the look of something wild and cornered. Fight. Flight. Freeze. He'd never been a fighter, and had proved he knew the second option very well.

"You're going to cooperate, aren't you, Dad?" she said, firm but gentle. "Because if you keep running, it's only going to make things worse. You know how this looks." She leaned closer, her voice dropping to a whisper. "They've got a picture, Dad, and I still have so much I need to ask you." She searched his eyes, tears obscuring her vision. "Please. Promise me you didn't drown him."

He clenched her hands in his. "I swear, I didn't do it."

"But why did you find him?"

"I was in the pub," he recalled, his voice shaking as the words came out faster, eyes darting like he might run at any second. "Benjamin said he was off to the loo, and he never came back. I looked for him, but he wasn't in the bathroom. When I got back to the bar, there was a handwritten note under my glass."

Sirens howled in the distance, growing louder with each passing second.

"It said, 'Meet me by the pond.' No name. I thought it might be Benjamin. But when I got there…"

His breath hitched.

"He was already in the water?" Ellie finished for him.

"Yes." Peter's voice thickened. "I dragged him out. His coat was heavy with water—it pulled me off balance, nearly took me under too. I was staggering, slipping, but I got him onto the bank somehow." He paused, swallowing hard. "He was already gone. And I... I panicked. I called the police from the phone box near the post office—then I ran." He rubbed a hand over his face, fingers trembling. "I walked for ages. No idea where I was going. Just wandering in circles, soaked and stunned. And then I came to see you. I needed you to know I was sorry. Before I…" He trailed off, eyes scanning the trees as if trying to remember where he'd meant to go next. "I didn't have a plan. Maybe deep down I knew it was the end of the road. That I wouldn't outrun this a second time."

"Dad, I—"

"I didn't want people thinking I'd found someone *again*," he said, almost in disbelief. "I didn't want to put that idea in their heads. I was drunk, and scared. But I promise you, Ellie—I didn't drown him. If I'm guilty, it's of being a coward. I couldn't. You know I couldn't."

A police car pulled up at the edge of the reserve. DS Angela Cookson stepped out and began making her way across the uneven ground, her pace brisk, expression unreadable.

"You know I'm innocent, Sparrow," Peter murmured as Finn gently eased them apart. "You know I didn't do this." Then, almost as an afterthought—so quiet she nearly missed it—he whispered, "The envelope. Under my sleeping bag. It's all in there. Give it to your gran."

Ellie nodded as the handcuffs closed with a soft click.

"We'll fix this," she said, voice steady. "I'll fix this."

Angela reached her former husband as he was being led to the police car. She said something Ellie couldn't hear. Peter nodded, his face drawn with resignation.

"Wishing him luck?" Ellie asked as Angela turned to face her.

Angela's face was stony. "You think I'm enjoying this? I told him not to say anything until he'd spoken to a solicitor. I told him that as a friend, not as his ex-wife."

"Maybe you're not impartial enough."

Angela didn't flinch. "You think this would be easier with a detective who didn't know him? Who didn't understand what he's like?"

"Maybe they'd be looking into other suspects to make sure they had the right one," Ellie fired back. "I gave you names, and you brushed them off."

Angela looked away, jaw tightening.

Ellie didn't stop. "And thanks for having me followed, by the way."

"I knew you'd lead us to him," Angela said quietly. She dragged a hand through her hair, looking worn down. "And you did." She hesitated, as if weighing up whether to keep going. "It's over, Ellie. I'm sorry, but—"

"But you have the photo, don't you?" Ellie cut in. "The one Tracey took? Case closed, right?"

Angela met her gaze, then turned without answering and walked back towards her waiting car.

Ellie stood a moment longer, fists clenched at her sides as the police car pulled away. Her father didn't look back.

Before the lingering officers moved them on, Ellie slipped away into the clearing. The tent's zip creaked as she knelt beside it and let herself inside.

The inside was small and sparse. A rolled towel, wash bag, carefully folded clothes stacked in piles. The battered notebook where he still logged birds. He'd set a clean shirt out for the next day.

It wasn't much of a life, even for a man who preferred the simpler things.

Beneath the sleeping bag, she found the envelope. She held it for a moment, weighing the choice in her hands. Whatever was inside was thick. She could open it, find out what he'd left behind. But he'd been specific about giving it to her gran.

With a reluctant sigh, Ellie tucked it into her bag just as Sylvia appeared in the tent's entrance.

"I'm sorry it had to end like this," Sylvia said, helping Ellie to her feet. "It's the last thing anyone wants to see happen to their parent."

"I know he didn't do it," she said quietly. "He promised. And until it's proven otherwise, I have to believe he's been set up."

"And rightly so!" Sylvia patted her on the back. "But it seems someone in this village really wants it to look like your father is guilty."

Ellie glanced back at the trees, the tent, the place where it had all fallen apart. She'd found her father and was leaving without him while a police car drove him to Marlborough Police Station. But at least she had some answers—and some new threads to pull on.

She didn't know how it would all unravel. But she'd start pulling. She owed him that much.

"Your hunch about this place was spot-on!" Sylvia

said out of the blue as The Burrows faded into the grass behind them. "You keep listening to that sharp gut of yours, and you'll uncover this elaborate ruse in no time." She looped her arm through Ellie's and asked brightly, "So, Sherlock, where to next? Another interview? A stake-out?"

"The bookshop," Ellie said, glancing at her watch. "Ten minutes to check that box of burnt books has turned into an hour. My gran should hear about my father from me."

The walk back from The Burrows was accompanied by Sylvia's steady stream of chatter, but Ellie only half-listened, her mind replaying her father's desperate pleas and the cold click of handcuffs.

"…might as well have been a ghost, the way he popped up in those trees," Sylvia was saying as they passed Meadowfield Manor, crossing the road and heading towards the pond. "I've never moved so fast in my life. Bet that young constable will think twice before sneaking up on someone again. One of my many brothers-in-law was in the Territorial Army, you know. Taught me a thing or two about self-defence."

"What would I do without you?" Ellie said absently, her gaze drifting to the pond. The water was placid now, reflecting the clear blue sky as if nothing terrible had ever happened there. Twice.

"Let's consider the stalker case closed, because this

is where I leave you," Sylvia announced, checking her watch. "I've left poor Marcus minding the shop far too long, and we've got the wine from France being delivered today. You're sure you'll be alright?"

"I'll be fine." Ellie mustered a smile. "Thank you. For everything."

"Don't mention it." Sylvia squeezed her arm. "That's what village family is for. And Ellie?" Her voice softened. "Trust your gut."

With a final nod, Sylvia headed down South Street.

Ellie stood alone at the crossroads, the envelope pressing against her side through her bag. Her gran needed to see it, but the thought of walking into the bookshop with this news made her stomach clench. She needed a moment—just one moment to breathe before everything changed again.

Almost without thinking, she wandered towards Meadowfield Primary. The afternoon bell hadn't rung yet, and the playground buzzed with activity—children racing, shrieking, skipping in blurred ropes of colour and noise.

Daniel stood at the edge of the playground, his glasses slightly askew, hair blown by the breeze. Just the sight of him steadied something inside her.

She knew she shouldn't distract him, but she lingered by the fence anyway, her fingers curling around the cold metal links. As if sensing her, Daniel turned. His smile came slowly, then slipped into a frown, like he could tell something was off even from a distance.

He said something to another teacher, then made his way over.

"Ellie?" His voice was low, careful. "What's happened?"

"I found him," she said simply.

His eyes widened. "Your dad? Where?"

"The Burrows." She swallowed. "The police have him now. They're taking him to Marlborough."

Daniel's hand twitched at his side, like he wasn't sure if he should reach for her in full view of the whole school. "Are you okay?"

She let out a breath that was too close to a laugh. "Not really."

A group of Year 5 girls had stopped to watch, whispering behind cupped hands. One of them stage-whispered, "*Mr Clark's got a girlfriend!*"

Daniel angled himself slightly, blocking their view. "What can I do?" he asked. "Tell me how to help."

"Have some answers?" she said, attempting a smile. "Kidding, obviously. This is my father, my family. My mess." She shook her head. "What's going on with you? I feel like I haven't asked that in days."

"Nothing to report," he said with a small shrug. "Looking after Nan. Searching the school top to bottom for the missing chimney sweep costume. Mrs Jenkins thinks it's sabotage because Mr Rodgers wanted to do *Oliver!* instead of *Mary Poppins*."

"The Case of the Missing Costume," Ellie said, matching his smile. "Meadowfield's crime wave continues."

After a moment, he said, "I might have some answers, actually. Or some information, at least. My nan remembered something. She didn't realise it was around the time Benjamin was killed at first—she just got up in the night. Her water tablets aren't working and—on her way back to bed she heard raised voices on the green. Thought it was pub-goers staggering home at first, so she went to the window to tell them to quieten down, but she swears one of them was Tracey."

"Tracey Harper?" Ellie confirmed, glancing at St Mary's next door. "How could she tell?"

"She recognised the walk," he whispered, glancing around. "And these are my nan's words—she 'walks like a duck' and could spot her a mile away."

Ellie blinked. "Does she?"

"I'm not sure. They're in the choir together and… you know what my nan is like," he said, and he didn't need to elaborate. "She said it looked like Tracey was" —he cleared his throat, cheeks flushing—"*waddling* back towards the church. Nan checked the clock on her way back to bed—it was twenty-five to one."

"So, Tracey and someone else were arguing on the green just after she supposedly took that picture." Ellie's voice steadied. "That's helpful. Very, very helpful. Thank you, Daniel. I need to get back to the bookshop, and you're at work, so… drink later?"

"How about we don't make a plan," he said, squinting one eye. "I said I'd help with rehearsals tonight. But if you're around about seven, come and find me."

"Deal," she said, then corrected herself. "I'll try."

He flashed a smile and, checking no one was watching, dipped across the railing to give her a quick kiss before turning on his heel and heading back to work.

Ellie turned towards South Street, heart and head still too full.

She wasn't juggling this well. The bookshop, the murder, her father, Daniel. It wasn't a balancing act she ever wanted to master.

She needed to shorten the list.

The murder. The truth.

Maybe there were answers in the envelope she'd found under her father's sleeping bag. She quickened her pace, the bookshop coming into view.

"We should've checked there," Maggie announced as Ellie stepped into the quiet bookshop, pen poised over a crossword. "The Burrows. Always was his thinking place."

"You've heard already?"

"Five minutes ago," she said, glancing over her reading glasses at the antique clock—one of her charity shop finds. "Zara burst in asking if I'd heard about Peter's arrest. I hadn't, of course, but she was good enough to relay the full account—colourful commentary and all." She laid down her pen on the counter. "I suppose Sylvia was her source. Zara mentioned she was at the scene with you." Her brow lifted, a glimmer of dry amusement surfacing. "And here I was thinking you were popping out to visit Meadowfield Manor."

"I was," Ellie said, stepping up to the counter. "I did. And I came back, but Sylvia was here and we… found him. Almost by chance, really."

She couldn't read her gran's face. Maggie was deep in thought, guarding herself.

"How was he?" she asked at last, as though she'd cycled through a dozen opening questions.

"Surviving. He had a camp set up." She added, "He's already run out of milk for his tea."

"Barbaric." Maggie removed her glasses and folded them with care, the metal frame clicking softly shut. "Did he get in touch with you?"

"No, I saw a sign."

Maggie raised an eyebrow. "From above?"

Ellie smiled, grateful for her gran's steady humour. "No angelic trumpets, sadly. We were following up on the missing books—which we found, by the way—and I saw a sign for The Burrows. I had to follow it. He was looking for a warbler."

"Of course," Maggie said, a chuckle slipping out through.

"He opened up more, and then… then Sylvia tackled a constable and almost got arrested for carrying a weapon, and everything since has been a bit of a blur."

"You found Benjamin's books *and* your father in one

swoop?" Maggie asked, leaning back in her chair as she folded her arms. "Top of the class. I'm impressed. Where were the books?"

Ellie swung her bag around and carefully pulled out the scorched remains of the novel.

"Down by the river, and they were mostly burned up." Ellie laid the remains gently on the counter as though even a breath might reduce them to dust. "This was the best one I could find. I thought it might help to compare with the copy Benjamin gave you."

Maggie brushed ash from the brittle edges and peeled the pages apart with care. "Chapter titles," she noted, her voice low, as if afraid of disturbing what was left. "Interesting."

"Dad said something about reading it 'back to front,' but he couldn't remember the details. He spent the night with Benjamin at The Drowsy Duck."

"Something to explore," Maggie said thoughtfully. She set the charred manuscript aside and looked up again, her eyes meeting Ellie's with quiet intent. "How are you, love?"

Ellie leaned on the counter, elbows resting on either side of her notebook, chin in her hands.

"I don't know," she admitted. "I didn't mean to lead the police right to him. I've had PC Walsh following me around since yesterday." She hesitated, then said, "I'm... relieved."

"It's for the best, love. They can't charge him without evidence. Oh, they'll give him the run-around, try to catch him out, see if he stumbles. But if he tells the truth, and sticks to it—"

"They've got a photograph, Gran," Ellie cut in. "A convincing one. Tracey took it, but that's not the only strange thing going on with her. Daniel's nan thinks she saw Tracey arguing with someone on the green just minutes after that photo was supposedly taken."

Maggie's brows lifted, unimpressed. "What does a photograph prove these days? I saw a video last week where someone made their cat play the violin."

Ellie huffed a laugh, caught off guard. "Was it any good?"

"Utterly dreadful. But that's not the point." Maggie's voice firmed as she reached for the kettle. "We don't give up on your father now. It sounds like Tracey Harper is up to something, and someone's gone to an awful lot of trouble to make him look guilty." She turned toward the coffee station, reaching for the cups. "Now, I'll make us a proper cup of tea, and you can tell me what my son had to say for himself."

While Maggie rattled about with mugs and the reassuring clink of teaspoons, Ellie opened her notebook and began scribbling everything she could remember from her father's confession: his version of that dreadful night, Terry's bright orange Allegro, Benjamin's cryptic warnings, the endless letters that had followed him since.

"He said someone slipped a note under his pint glass," Ellie said, her gold pen tapping against the page.

"Told him to meet them by the pond. That's why *he* found Benjamin."

Maggie narrowed her eyes. "Could it be the same person who's been sending those letters all these years?"

"It would line up," Ellie murmured.

"Regardless, it sounds like a stitch-up," Maggie said, placing a hot mug beside Ellie's elbow. She peered down at the notes, upside down. "What's this about an old Allegro? Haven't seen one of those in a while."

"Dad saw Terry speeding out of the village in one. Bright orange. He nearly ran Dad over. Said there were other people in the car. I think Terry was the getaway driver in '75."

"I always said that man was shifty," Maggie muttered, blowing on her tea. "We had a bunch of televisions go missing from the school back in the '80s, and his name came up then too. Nobody could prove anything, but everyone knew."

"And he's still getting away with it," Ellie said, reaching for her tea. "But if you need a cheap fridge…" As she leaned, her bag tipped off the counter, its contents spilling out. The envelope slid loose and came to rest against Maggie's foot.

Ellie stared at it for a moment, remembering her father's parting words. She crouched to pick it up and brushed a thumb across the crease.

"From Dad," she said. "It's all in there, apparently."

Maggie accepted the envelope, brow gathering as she broke the seal. She peered inside but offered no hint of what she saw.

"Is it a clue?" Ellie asked. "A confession?"

"Not quite," Maggie said at last, with a relieved smile. "It's an apology." She tugged a modest wedge of colourful banknotes from the envelope. A few hundred, at least. "The savings your father took from my biscuit tin before he left. Every penny, I'd imagine." She clutched it to her chest for a moment, then said, "We'd best get him out of that police station so I can let him know he's forgiven to his face. I always told him it was for emergencies. I suppose in his mind, he finally had one."

They sat in silence for a moment—the kind that didn't need filling.

Then Ellie stirred. "Dad did give me a clue, though. He mentioned a silver locket that Sally used to wear?"

"The one with the engraved robin?" Maggie nodded knowingly. "The one they turned my cottage upside down for. They never found it."

"Benjamin did," Ellie revealed. "He showed it to Dad in the pub last night."

"He must have trusted your father."

"As good as an apology."

"About time," Maggie sniffed, old resentment flickering in her tone. "That's what the book launch was meant to be about. Fixing burned bridges. When Benjamin first came to me asking to launch the book here, he was man enough to admit he'd got it wrong. I told him Peter wasn't around, but he promised the book wouldn't drag him into it. I like that they reached common ground—in the end."

"Thanks to the locket."

"Perhaps the police have it?" Maggie suggested. "There could be a clue inside?"

"Maybe," Ellie said, though she doubted Angela would've kept that detail to herself. Still, she could ask. "I don't think the locket itself is the clue, though."

"Its reappearance is," Maggie countered.

"Dad said it was *where* Benjamin found it that made him certain only one person could've put it there."

"Oh. That is interesting." Maggie hummed, tapping her abandoned pen against the edge of the magazine. "I wonder if there's a way to find out where that was."

"Mrs Winchester might know," Ellie mused. "He gave her an advance copy of the manuscript, but she didn't find anything we haven't."

"But if Benjamin entrusted Mrs Winchester with an early copy, it's further proof Sally's murder and the robbery at Meadowfield Manor that night *are* connected." Maggie exhaled a heavy breath before sipping her tea. "Oh, Ellie, you've bound those two stories together rather neatly."

"I haven't bound anything," Ellie said. "The stories of that night have just been hiding in plain sight. The quick-to-snap postman, the mousy vicar's daughter, the sketchy mechanic, the nervous soap shop owner—and the stoic niece."

"You think Sarah's involved?"

She thought back to Jeremy's parting words as she'd left the manor that morning—already feeling like days ago.

"According to the butler," she recalled, "Sarah's visits to the manor increased after the jewels were stolen."

"Guilty conscience?" Maggie suggested, reaching into the envelope and plucking out a twenty-pound note. "If we're going to crack this case, we'll need lunch. My treat. I hate to send you out again, but I'm getting along with this crossword." She picked up her pen, then paused. "I think we should gather everyone who cares about your father as soon as possible. Tonight. The more eyes we have working on this, the better."

"Good idea," Ellie agreed, taking the money—only for her gaze to flick to the clock behind the counter.

Her face dropped. She shot to her feet.

"What is it?" Maggie asked.

"Lunch," she croaked. "Oh no—Sarah!"

Chapter 15
Hats Off

The café bell jingled violently as Ellie burst through the door.

"Late again?" Oliver called from behind the counter, not looking up. He was elbow-deep in steam wands and metal nozzles, dismantling his state-of-the-art coffee machine with the weary air of a man engaged in daily battle. "Once is an instance, twice is a hobby."

"Then I won't tell you about the third time," Ellie replied, breathless. "I've been a little busy."

"Well, you just missed Sarah."

Ellie spun towards the door. "How long ago?"

"Three minutes? Maybe four." He wiped his hands on a tea towel already patterned with espresso streaks. "She said she had errands before heading back to school."

"Did she leave a message?"

"That you should buy a watch." He finally looked

up, smudged and scowling affectionately. "Okay, she didn't say that. But do you want to share with the class why you're late again?"

Ellie swallowed. "Have you heard about Dad?"

His grin dropped. "What now?"

"I found him," she said. "He's fine. He's probably at the station right now being processed, but—" she checked the clock. "Really only three minutes?"

"More like five now," he said, returning to the beast of a coffee machine with a sigh. "You found him? Where? Is he alright?"

"I… I need to go," she called over her shoulder. "Ask your mum!"

"*Seriously*, Ellie?"

But she was already gone, the café door swinging shut behind her.

Sarah was out doing errands, which could mean anything, and anywhere. Ellie's best chance was to head towards the school taking the route Sarah would walk. She scanned every shop window as she passed, but there was no sign of her. In the bookshop, she glimpsed her gran at the counter, back to inspecting the scorched manuscript.

Ellie hurried past the pond, heart thudding, and rounded the corner by The Drowsy Duck—and there she was.

Sarah stood, half-blocked by Penny and Duchess, who was doing a spirited dance around a brown paper bag hooked over Sarah's arm. Penny wrestled gently with the lead, trying to restore order.

"Duchess, please," Auntie Penny pleaded. "Sarah, I am sorry—she's usually so much calmer—"

Ellie's arrival distracted the dog. Duchess let out a delighted bark and bounded towards her. Ellie crouched to greet her, ruffling the white Maltese's ears.

"Oh—Ellie," Sarah said, her tone polite but brisk. "Good to see you. I'm sorry, I couldn't wait any longer, but I really do need to get on."

Penny turned, eyes wide. "Ellie… is it true? About your father being arrested?"

But Ellie didn't answer. She was already slipping past them, catching up with Sarah before she could disappear again.

The school was just a stone's throw away—but long enough for a conversation. Or at least the start of one.

"I need to get back before the bell," Sarah instructed, quickening her pace. "I'm covering for Mrs White in Year Two. She's having her wisdom teeth out."

"Can I walk with you?" Ellie asked, already falling into step beside her.

Sarah sighed. "Fine. But when we reach the gates, that's it."

"Fair enough," Ellie said.

The school loomed ahead, the playground alive with the squeals and scuffles of children who didn't want their break to end. A football bounced over the fence and rolled away down the alley behind the cottages.

Sarah paused at the groans of disappointment from

the other side of the railings. "I suppose we can at least get their ball."

Without waiting, she pivoted towards the alley. Ellie followed, her heart pounding slightly faster—the stray football had bought her a few more moments.

"What is it you want to know?" Sarah asked as they rounded the corner into the narrow cut-through. The noise of the playground faded behind them.

Ellie glanced sideways. "I need to ask you about the night at the pub."

Sarah didn't look at her. "What about it?"

"You said you were there with Sally during the storm."

"I was."

"And Terry?"

"Yes."

"And Tracey. Joanne. Phil. All six of you."

Sarah's step faltered—barely—but Ellie caught the twitch. "What exactly are you suggesting?" she asked, her voice sharpening. "Half the village was in there that night."

"I'm getting at the fact that I know at least four of those people were involved in the robbery at your aunt's manor." Ellie crouched to retrieve the ball, now settled between Daniel's nan's bins. "So if they all met up there beforehand, I can't help but wonder how they knew no one would be home that night."

Sarah snatched the ball from her just as the school bell rang out, shrill and sudden. She set off again, climbing the alley at double speed.

"Did you know the Winchesters wouldn't be at home?" Ellie called after her. "Did one of them tell you about the theatre trip?"

"If I mentioned my aunt wasn't home," Sarah said, lowering her voice but not her pace, "it would've been in passing."

If, Ellie noted.

Sarah's gaze flicked to hers—cool, controlled.

But Ellie didn't flinch.

"Where did you go after you left Sally in the pub?"

"I'm sorry?" Sarah blinked.

"You told me that you parted ways with a promise to see each other the next day, and that day never came. Where did you go afterwards?"

"I…" Sarah's fingers tightened around the ball as they reached the school gates. "I got tired of trying to outlast the storm. I went home."

"Alone?"

"Yes. Alone." Her smile reappeared, brittle at the edges. "Now, Ellie, if you don't mind, I thought we were supposed to be having lunch to talk about what I knew of Benjamin Brown during the brief period our lives overlapped. I wasn't under the impression this would be an interrogation." She pushed open the gates as the last of the children were herded inside. "I really must—"

"What do you think of Tracey?"

"Excuse me?"

"Tracey Harper," Ellie said, nodding towards the church. One last long shot. "Do you think her photograph is real?"

Without missing a breath, Sarah said, "Are you asking if I think Tracey is a liar? Because, I do not. We're in the choir together. She's someone I trust."

"Any idea who she might've been arguing with on the green after taking that picture?"

"Why would I know that?" she replied curtly. "Now, if you'll excuse—"

"What time do you finish?"

"I'm co-directing rehearsals for the summer play after school. Bert and Jane still need a lot of work. And then I've got my ladies' choir." She gave a tight, professional smile. "That's why I suggested we met at *lunch*."

With that, she strode through the gates and across the playground, merging into a loose cluster of teachers and pupils at the entrance.

Ellie stayed where she was, watching until Sarah disappeared inside.

She replayed the conversation, word by word. Every answer had been smooth. Except for that pause. That half-second when Ellie had asked where she went after leaving Sally.

Not long—but enough.

What had Sarah Mills been doing after she walked away from Sally Brown on the night of the storm?

And why, nearly fifty years later, did she seem so afraid of that question?

After her strange confrontation with Sarah, Ellie returned to the bookshop and tucked herself away in the snug with her pad. Her conversation with her father had filled in enough gaps for her to start drafting a rough timeline of the night Benjamin died, but the pieces still refused to sit neatly.

Peter had been seen arguing with Benjamin around six o'clock. Ellie had been there herself, trying to get answers even then. Peter had left, then returned at some unspecified time. That much was clear. The two had spent a few hours together—talking, drinking, unburdening.

Then Benjamin had gone to the bathroom and never returned.

Peter, after waiting a while, had gone to look for him, only to find the bathroom empty.

Ellie sighed and rubbed her temples.

"Cake?" Maggie's voice broke the silence as she appeared in the doorway, a small plate in hand. Ellie hadn't heard her creep upstairs.

"Oliver dropped it off. Caramel honey loaf. Still warm. He's been whipping up new concoctions all day."

Ellie took the plate gratefully. "Thanks."

"I think it's how he's coping with everything," Maggie added, almost to herself. "He can't fix it, so he's feeding it." She lingered in the doorway a moment longer and added, "It's nearly closing time."

"Any more customers?"

"Only one," Maggie said with a shrug. "But better than none, right?"

Ellie smiled faintly and took a bite. The sugar helped the bitter feeling an empty bookshop brought.

Maggie peered over her shoulder at the notes. "Do you think there's another door in the Gents?" she suggested. "Or Benjamin left without being seen?"

Ellie nodded, licking the crumbs from her lips. "Right. And when Dad got back to his pint, there was a note under his glass. By then, Benjamin was already in the pond."

"So, let's say your father waited—fifteen minutes? Half an hour, to be polite?" Maggie tapped a finger against the timeline. "That's your window. In that time, someone drowns Benjamin in the pond outside, leaves him floating there, and slips away unnoticed."

"Tracey's photograph puts the drowning at around half past midnight," Ellie added, her voice reluctant. "What time does the pub close?"

"It was a Saturday, so… anytime between one and two. And it's all well and good knowing the timeline, but what are we going to do with it?"

Ellie stood and brushed crumbs from her trousers, the uneaten edge of the caramel loaf forgotten on her plate.

"We read between the lines," she said. "And we look in the margins. There are gaps—and I think I know where to look to fill some in." She closed her notepad and dropped it back into her backpack. "Let's close early. Drink at the pub. Manager's treat."

Maggie raised an eyebrow. "Are you sure? People will stare."

"I don't think hiding away will help."

Maggie didn't argue. She fetched her coat, and together they tidied the shop and turned off the lights. It didn't take long—there hadn't been enough customers to undo yesterday's clean.

The wind had picked up outside, carrying a hint of approaching rain as they made their way down South Street. The village green was nearly empty now, the last of the dog walkers retreating. Ellie kept her head down, aware of every curtain twitch.

When they reached The Drowsy Duck, they were greeted by a sudden lull, like a room inhaling. Heads turned. A few phones were hurriedly lowered, though not before Ellie caught a glimpse of the now-familiar image: Tracey's photo.

"So, this is where everyone's been hiding," Maggie murmured, striding for the bar with purpose. "Nothing brings the village out like scandal."

Harold, the landlord, caught sight of them and gave a nod, his weathered face apologetic as he reached beneath the counter for two glasses.

"The determined Miss Swan and her equally stubborn grandmother," he said, already pouring Maggie a gin and tonic without asking. "What can I get you, Ellie?"

"Just a cider," she replied, leaning an elbow on the bar.

At a nearby table, Zara from the gift shop sat

hunched over her phone with three others, their faces lit blue by the screen's glow. They glanced up in unison, then quickly looked away. Ellie didn't need to see what they were looking at.

"It's everywhere, isn't it?" she said quietly to Harold.

His expression tightened as he slid their drinks across.

"Had it sent to me three times already," he admitted. "Flying round faster than the flu."

"Mind if I see what everyone's gawping at?" Maggie asked, already sidling up to a young man at the end of the bar. He jumped slightly as she appeared at his elbow.

"I—I wasn't—" he stammered, but she'd already plucked the phone from his hand.

She studied the photo, lips pressed into a thin line.

"Grainy nonsense," she declared, loudly enough for the nearest tables to hear. "You couldn't identify a rhinoceros in this lighting, let alone my son." She handed the phone back with a sniff. "Shame on you."

The young man flushed scarlet and tucked the phone away like it had bitten him.

Ellie turned back to Harold. "I need to ask about the night Benjamin died. You saw my dad with him, didn't you?"

Harold leaned against the bar with both hands, eyes flicking to the curious faces not-so-subtly listening in.

"I did," he said at last.

"How did they seem?"

He shrugged. "Friendly enough. Which surprised me, all things considered."

"Did you hear what they were talking about?" Maggie asked, calmer now.

"Not really. I wasn't eavesdropping. But they were sat about where you are now, both putting the drinks away, and it sounded like they had a fair bit of history to get through."

"And did you see Benjamin leave?" Ellie pressed.

"No," he grunted, before stating, "And I told the police the same. First I knew anything was wrong was when the ambulance arrived—about half past midnight, just before I called last orders. We all went out to find a man lying on the embankment of the pond."

"I see," Maggie said, taking in the pub as though she could see that night playing out around them like interactive theatre. "Do you know what time Peter left?"

"I do, as it happens," Harold said, exhaling like a man grateful for a concrete fact. "He kept asking for the time while he was waiting. The last update I gave him was at a few minutes before midnight. That's when he went off to the Gents. He came back to the bar, then went outside, and he…" He trailed off, his finger wagging. "Wait here."

With that, Harold disappeared into the back room.

"Tracey says she took her picture at half past twelve," Ellie whispered. She could feel eyes lingering on them from every corner. "But if Dad left the pub around midnight, what was he doing for thirty minutes?"

"The more important question," Maggie said thoughtfully, "is how the ambulance got here so quickly. If Tracey's time is accurate, how could she have captured a photo of your father drowning Benjamin mere moments before the ambulance arrived?" She paused. "When I broke my hip, they took forty minutes, and that was in broad daylight."

Harold returned, something folded in his hand.

"Here," he said, holding out a worn brown flat cap. "For when he gets out. Your dad left this on the bar."

Ellie took it. The same cap he'd been wearing when he turned up at the bookshop. The brim was creased just the way she remembered—soft and familiar with age. He hadn't been wearing a hat at The Burrows.

"When did he take it off?" she asked, turning it over in her hands.

Harold shrugged. "Dunno. He came in wearing it."

"Did he return at all?" Maggie asked. "After he left at midnight?"

"I don't think so." Harold wiped his brow. "No—he didn't," he said, more certain now. "I was stuck behind the bar with some fella chewing my ear off about starting his own microbrewery in his shed. I noticed the hat not long after Peter left, so if he'd have come back for it, I would have seen him and saved you a job of getting it back to him."

Ellie turned the cap over again, her fingers tracing the worn stitching.

"What if it's not him at all?" she thought aloud.

Maggie searched her face. "Not him?"

"We can't see his face in the photo, just the back of someone in a coat and a cap. But he left it behind." She lifted the hat slightly, as if it might whisper the truth. "Which begs the question, why is there a hat in the picture?"

Harold gave a short, uncertain laugh. "What if he had a second hat? In his pocket?"

Ellie shook her head. "No. He wasn't wearing a hat when he came to see me that night."

She didn't elaborate. She hadn't told the police about his early-hours visit.

"Look, I know it sounds far-fetched," she continued, voice low but steady. "But what if Tracey didn't witness anything real? What if someone staged it to make it look like my dad drowned Benjamin?"

Harold scoffed again, but with less conviction. "Who'd go to all that effort?"

Ellie met his eyes. "The same person who's been sending him threatening letters for fifty years. The same person who got away with killing Sally." She caught her breath, feeling the desperation creeping in. "If you remember anything else from that night…"

Harold hesitated, then gave a small shake of the head. "Look, that's all I know. It sounds like you need to talk to Tracey about that picture. My mum's just gone to choir practice. Tracey's tone-deaf, apparently, but her mum's the vicar, so no one dares say anything."

"If we hurry," Maggie said, already on the move,

"we might catch her before they've finished warming up."

Ellie nodded and clutched the cap tighter. "Thanks, Harold. For this."

As they stepped out into the cooling evening, Ellie looked down at the familiar tweed in her hands. A hat left behind... yet worn in the photograph Tracey had given the police.

It was a continuity mistake. A contradiction in plain sight. A prop that shouldn't be in the scene.

Her father couldn't have been wearing it if he hadn't had it.

For the first time all day, it felt like a victory. Small, yes—but real. Tangible. The first crack in the image they'd all been told to believe.

"We should tread carefully," she said, rounding the corner with her gran as the steeple of St Mary's came into view. "The last time I spoke to Tracey, she told the police I was harassing her."

"The chance would be a fine thing," Maggie replied, undeterred. "We need to get through her mother first."

Chapter 16
An Almighty Find

The sound of voices drifted out onto the green as Ellie and Maggie neared St Mary's. Not a hymn exactly, more of a warm-up that hadn't quite agreed on its key.

They slipped inside, the thick wooden door groaning just enough to draw a glance from the pew-polishing ladies near the back.

Up front, the choir was clustered in loose formation: Harold's mother, Tilly, was there, belting from her chest; Daniel's nan stood mid-row, mouthing along gamely; while Tracey and Sarah flanked opposite ends of the group.

Before Ellie could take another step, Reverend Catherine Harper emerged from the vestry corridor, swishing towards them in her black robes. Aside from noticing her peering through the curtains, Ellie hadn't seen the vicar since her accidental afternoon tea at the manor.

"I'm afraid this is a closed rehearsal," she said coolly, stepping into the archway and blocking their path like she'd been expecting them. "Choir members only."

Her eyes locked on Ellie. A gatekeeper's glare. And a warning.

Ellie met it. "How did you find out?" she asked quietly.

The vicar blinked. "Find out what?"

"That your daughter was part of the group that ransacked Meadowfield Manor," Ellie said, with so much certainty, it didn't sound like a question at all. "That's why you're so protective of her, isn't it?" She waited, but the vicar only stared, caught on the back foot. "Did she confess her sins to you, or did you work it out for yourself?"

"You have quite the imagination!" she replied, rocking on her heels.

"You gave yourself away at Mrs Winchester's garden party," Ellie continued anyway. "Only I didn't quite know what I was dealing with then."

"And you do now?" The Reverend's composure flickered, a twitch at the side of her eye as she tried to hold it all back. "I'm quite sorry, but I'm afraid I have no idea what you're talking about." Her gaze sharpened. "I saw you yesterday, harassing my daughter on her own doorstep. I won't hesitate to call the police again."

"Good," Ellie replied. "I'd welcome it. Then she

can explain the mystery of the reappearing hat in her star witness photograph."

Confusion crossed Catherine's face—just briefly—but Ellie had struck a nerve. The vicar drew in a breath, attempting to steady herself.

"We only want to speak with her," Maggie offered, her tone softer. "Not in front of everyone, if it can be helped. If she's got nothing to hide, what's wrong with a few questions?"

"Because you're *his* family," Catherine hissed.

"Isn't there a bit in the Bible about not judging your neighbours?" Maggie snapped, her voice rising to match the vicar's. "And what about casting stones without sin? My son hasn't been charged with anything." In a more even tone, she said, "You can call this witness harassment—or you can see it, mother to mother, for what it is. I just want to know what happened that night. Your daughter is the only person who claims to have been present at the scene of a murder that my son has been accused of committing."

Up front, the singing had faltered into silence. A few choir members had stopped pretending not to stare; others muttered quietly among themselves.

"Let's take a tea break, everyone," Sarah called out, her clapping hands echoing across the grand stone space. "Five minutes."

"Ask your questions." Catherine's nostrils flared as she glanced at Tracey. "Just be fair. Don't lead her astray to catch her out. She has never been all that… independent."

With that, the vicar strode down the aisle towards her daughter. The group began to scatter. Tracey, after some coaxing from her mother, reluctantly peeled away and followed Ellie and Maggie to a pew near the side altar. She perched at its edge in the dappled light of the setting sun, stained glass colouring her expression something like remorse—or defiance. Ellie couldn't yet tell.

Her fingers found a chain at her neck, twisting it round and round.

"What do you want?" she asked, not meeting their eyes.

"Your photograph," Ellie said, keeping her voice level. "The one circulating around the village. The one that supposedly shows my father drowning Benjamin."

Tracey's fingers stilled on the chain.

"I didn't mean for it to get around," she muttered. "I gave it to the police. That's all."

"And who else?" Maggie asked.

Tracey's eyes flicked up, then away.

"Terry. He asked to see it."

"Terry," Ellie repeated, letting the name settle between them. "The mechanic. You pointed me at him. You said he planned things."

"He knew what to do," she said, her voice shrinking.

"And you took the picture at half past midnight?" Maggie pushed.

Tracey nodded, so Ellie reached into her bag and drew out the flat cap, setting it carefully on the pew between them.

"Do you recognise this?"

Tracey glanced down. "It's a hat."

"It's my father's hat," Ellie corrected. "The one he was wearing in the pub. The one he *left* in the pub."

Tracey's eyes widened. "So?"

"The figure in your photograph is wearing a hat. If this is the one he left behind, how could he be wearing it in your photo?"

Tracey opened her mouth, then closed it again.

"I... I don't know," she stuttered finally. "Maybe he had another one?"

"But it doesn't add up," Ellie said, shifting closer. Her silhouette blocked the coloured light spilling through the stained glass, casting Tracey's face into shadow. "You said you didn't realise what you'd captured. That you didn't report it until the morning. But you stopped to take the photo. At half past twelve. At the pond. Why?"

Tracey's eyes darted towards the rest of the choir, milling just beyond earshot. At the back, Reverend Catherine Harper stood with her hands clasped, her gaze steady. The break wouldn't last long.

"What were you doing out that late?" Ellie pressed. "Walking alone in the dark?"

Tracey's lips pressed into a hard line. Her posture stiffened. Her gaze fixed somewhere near the hymn board.

"But you weren't alone," Ellie revealed, and this time, Tracey flinched. "You were seen arguing with someone on the village green five minutes later, and then you parted ways and came here. Who was that person, Tracey?"

Still, nothing. Tracey folded inward, avoiding their eyes as if willing the moment to pass.

Ellie glanced at her gran. This might be a dead end after all.

But Maggie shifted beside her. "Did someone put you up to taking that picture, dear?"

Tracey didn't move. Then—barely—a hitch in her breath. And the faintest nod.

For a moment, no one spoke.

Then something caught the light: a glint at Tracey's throat as she fiddled with the chain.

A locket.

A silver locket.

Ellie's stomach turned. She couldn't be certain, but it looked like a robin was etched on the front. She nudged her gran and nodded at Tracey's neck.

"That locket…" Maggie whispered.

Tracey's hands flew to her neck, fingers closing protectively around the silver pendant.

"Why do you have that?" Ellie asked.

"A… friend gave it to me," Tracey said at last, her voice barely audible.

"Can I see it?" Ellie reached out.

But Tracey tucked the locket beneath the neckline of her blouse.

"What's inside it?" Ellie tried instead. "Is there a picture?"

"I don't know." She drew her red cardigan tighter around her like armour. "It won't open."

"Just like Sally's," Ellie said softly, her father's voice echoing in her mind—how Sally never took it off, how it vanished the night she died. "Who gave you that locket, Tracey?"

Her voice carried, faintly echoing through the church's stone arches.

"I'm sorry," Ellie added quickly. "I just need to know—"

"Alright, shall we continue?" Sarah's voice rang out from the front.

"Fantastic idea!" the vicar chimed in, far too brightly. She clapped her hands together with forced cheer. "I came here for some singing. Tracey, up front. I want to hear you!"

The choir began to shuffle back into position. Tracey slipped into her spot at the back left, head bowed. Just before she turned away, she glanced back at Ellie with a fleeting look—sharp with something.

Fear? Regret?

"Was that Sally's locket?" Ellie asked, her head spinning. "And if it was—"

"Why does Tracey have it?" Maggie said. "And did you see how she reacted when I asked if someone put her up to taking that picture? It was subtle—but did she nod?"

"I saw a nod."

"I've seen that fear before," Maggie murmured as they

walked slowly down the aisle. "It's the look a student gives when they're keeping secrets for someone else. Usually a bully. She's itching to say something, but she's scared to."

"And she was last time," Ellie agreed. "There must be a way to get her alone. She wants to talk—"

"—but not here," Maggie finished. "Not in front of her mother. And not while they're all watching."

They turned to leave. But as they reached the heavy oak door, Ellie paused—someone had followed them down the aisle.

Sarah.

She stepped forward, her expression carefully composed, but there was something softer in it now. A shift. An opening.

"I wanted to apologise for earlier," Sarah offered. "I may have been a little snappy about the lunch situation."

Ellie nodded, not quite sure how to respond to the sudden change in tone. "Thank you. I didn't mean to waste your time."

"It's fine, I—I actually need to correct a comment I made," Sarah said suddenly, lifting her chin a fraction.

"Correct?" Ellie prompted.

Sarah drew in a breath, her fingers worrying the hem of her cardigan. She glanced back towards the choir, waiting for her return with polite impatience.

"I wasn't entirely honest with you," she said, meeting Ellie's eyes. "The truth is, I was embarrassed. You caught me off-guard when you asked if I'd mentioned knowing that Meadowfield Manor would be empty that night."

Ellie was intrigued to know where this was going.

"When you hypothetically told me that *if* you did," Ellie said, "it wouldn't have been on purpose."

"Exactly. Like I said, I wasn't expecting the question." Sarah offered a tight smile. "There's no *if*. I know I mentioned it. And I've spent fifty years feeling awful about it. Maybe we were talking about theatre or Agatha Christie or something, and it just… came out in conversation. Almost like a joke, and—"

A pointed throat-clear interrupted her. Reverend Harper stood by the rear pews, her expression pinched with disapproval. The church welcomed all, but Ellie and Maggie were clearly stretching that welcome.

"I'll find you tomorrow," Sarah said quickly, already retreating. "I've got an idea. Something that might help, if I can get the right people to agree."

And then she was gone, hurrying back to the front as the choir launched once more into their uncertain harmonies, wobbly but enthusiastic.

Ellie and Maggie didn't linger. They stepped out into the still night, the church door shutting behind them with a soft thud that seemed to close more than just a rehearsal.

"What did she mean by that?" Maggie asked as they started down the path. "The right people?"

"I'm not sure," Ellie replied, mind already turning over Sarah's words. "But if she keeps her word, I'll find out tomorrow."

"I think we've had quite enough revelations for one evening," Maggie declared. "Let's go home."

"Actually," Ellie said, glancing at her watch, "I'm not in the mood to cook. Fancy The Golden Sun?"

"Perfect. Their crispy duck is the only thing that might salvage this day."

"I'll have my usual special fried rice," Ellie called, already setting off. "I'll catch you up, I just need to check something first."

Maggie narrowed her eyes. "Don't be long. You know how Mei gets when the food's left waiting."

As Maggie set off towards the takeaway, Ellie turned and made her way in the opposite direction, down the narrow lane to the garage she'd visited with Sylvia. The main lights were off, but a faint amber glow flickered deeper inside the workshop. She approached cautiously, remembering the wrench Terry had nearly thrown.

A sharp voice sliced through the quiet, halting her in her tracks.

"You keep your mouth shut, got it?" The voice—low, furious—was unmistakably Terry's. "I know you're not a thick bloke. What's so hard to get?"

"Terry, I—"

Ellie strained her ears. She didn't recognise the other voice.

"What did I tell you back then?" Terry continued. "Loose lips sink ships. You sink, we all sink. Don't you get that?"

"Terry, I just want—"

There was a scuffle, followed by the sickening sound of a punch and a guttural groan. Before Ellie could decide what to do, hurried footsteps tore through the shadows. A figure broke from the dark and ran right past her.

Phil. Postman Phil.

He looked rattled, eyes wide, lip bleeding. He brushed past Ellie without so much as a glance, dabbing at his mouth as he half-walked, half-jogged up the street and around the corner.

She considered following him. But she'd come to speak to Terry.

Ellie stepped into the garage's threshold. The air smelled of oil and cold metal.

"What was that about?" she asked.

Terry spun round, startled. "Didn't I make myself clear the other day?" His chest rose and fell with leftover fury. "I have nothing to say to you."

"Why did you ask to see Tracey's picture?" Ellie pressed, keeping her voice steady. "The one supposedly showing my dad at the pond."

Terry grabbed a rag and scrubbed at his hands. "Because I wanted to see proof. Proof of what I've always known." He threw the rag down. "That your dad is a murderer."

Ellie didn't flinch. "Funny, coming from the getaway driver."

His jaw twitched.

"You were all in the pub that night," Ellie said, watching as he noisily cleared tools from a bench to a toolbox. "Sarah let slip the Winchesters had left the manor vacant. Someone saw an opportunity, and before the night's over, your girlfriend is dead." She stepped closer. "So unless *you're* behind this... don't you want to know what really happened to her?"

Terry turned and closed the length of the garage in a few strides. Ellie tensed, half-expecting him to reach for something heavy.

"Why does Tracey have Sally's locket?" she asked anyway. "Do you know where Benjamin found it? Was it in here? Or back there in your secret shop?"

Instead, Terry grabbed the chain by the entrance and yanked it down without another word.

The metal shutter clattered down between them, the sound sharp and decisive.

Outside, Ellie glanced up and down the lane for any signs of Phil, but he'd long gone. She turned away from the garage, Terry's words still echoed in her ears.

"Loose lips sink ships," she repeated aloud.

Whatever Phil knew, it had rattled Terry.

Another splintered shard bleeding through from the past, jagged, incomplete. But where did it fit in the broken mirror she was piecing back together?

By the time she reached The Golden Sun, her gran was waiting outside, a takeaway bag in hand. The warm scent of garlic and ginger drifted into the night like an invitation, and Ellie's stomach grumbled.

"There you are," Maggie said, the worry on her face softening. "Everything alright?"

"Not even close," Ellie replied, taking the warm bag

from her. "The jewel thieves are unravelling out in the open. I just walked in on Terry threatening Phil, and Tracey has a suspiciously familiar locket hanging round her neck."

"You know what that sounds like to me?" Maggie said, hooking their arms together as they set off. "We're going to have to split this takeaway three ways, *if* Angela can pull herself away from interrogating your father. Because if everything we learned today isn't enough, I don't know what will be."

The takeaway tubs littered the cottage's kitchen like debris. Angela hadn't bothered with a plate, eating straight from the carton like someone too used to meals on the go. Ellie and Maggie picked at what was left of their shared portions.

They'd laid it all out—the hat, the timeline, the locket now dangling from Tracey's neck. Angela had listened, the way police officers do when they're not giving anything away, but her fork had stilled the moment Ellie mentioned the locket.

"So, what you're saying," Angela said, setting down her noodles, "is that Tracey's photograph can't be trusted because your father left his hat at the pub? And she's wearing a necklace that might or might not have belonged to Sally?" She dabbed her mouth with a piece of kitchen roll, immediately screwing it up. "The metadata of that image confirms the photo was taken at half past midnight. Tracey wasn't lying about that."

"But Dad was seen leaving the pub nearly half an hour before that," Ellie said again.

Angela's jaw tightened. "That's not enough, Ellie."

"And this isn't?" Maggie held up Peter's tweed cap in her fist.

The room fell quiet. The ticking of the grandfather clock in the hallway suddenly felt too loud. Ellie didn't want this to spiral into a row. Her father's future hung on too fine a thread, and Angela was still their best hope of pulling it taut.

"Do you know what time the ambulance was called?" Ellie asked, keeping her voice low. "Dad said he used a phonebox near the post office."

Angela stabbed her fork around in the noodles. "Not off the top of my head."

"You haven't checked?" Maggie asked sharply.

"We have," Angela fired back. "The information's there, I just don't—"

"Check it," Ellie said. "Because if my dad called before half past midnight, how can that be him in that photo? Nobody calls ahead for an ambulance for someone they're about to drown." She set her fork down and met Angela's wandering gaze. "I should have told you this sooner, but he came here that night. He wasn't wearing a hat, and—"

"I don't care if he was wearing a hat or not." Angela's fork froze mid-air, the noodles dangling down.

"Peter came here *after* Benjamin was already dead, and you didn't think to mention that to me?"

Ellie and Maggie exchanged glances. Maybe Ellie should have kept that to herself.

"He was terrified. Barely making sense," she said, failing to keep the defensiveness from her voice. "He wanted me to know he was in the wrong place at the wrong time."

Angela let out a breath and rubbed her forehead, fingers pressing into her temples. For a moment, her polished composure slipped. She looked tired.

The case was weighing on her shoulders just as heavily as it was on Ellie's and Maggie's.

But it still felt like they were playing for different teams.

"Do you know where Benjamin found the locket?" Maggie asked.

"Until now, we weren't looking at the locket. That was Sally's case. We're working on Benjamin's."

Maggie's spoon clattered against her plate. "You haven't reopened the cold case?"

"It's not my call." Angela's voice rose before she caught herself. "I see the link, but my hands are tied until there's something other than circumstance to tie these two murders together." She sat back, the distance sliding back into place. "I'll look into what you've told me."

She nudged her food aside. Whatever appetite she'd started with was long gone. She flung on her jacket, already moving towards the hallway.

"There's something you should know about how the original case was handled," Angela said as she fidgeted with her jacket in the doorway. "Off the record, the DI in charge of Sally's case—DI Perkins—had a connection to one of the suspects."

"Who?" Ellie asked.

"Terrance."

Ellie blinked. "Terry? The mechanic?"

Angela nodded. "I've spoken to a few older officers still at the station from then. No one wanted to say anything outright, but the implication was that DI Perkins looked the other way when it came to his nephew's criminal activity."

"Are you suggesting the DI at the time let Terry get away with murder?" Maggie choked out.

"'I'm saying there was a connection that wasn't officially acknowledged at the time."

"But you *are* looking elsewhere," Maggie pleaded. "You're trying to help Peter."

Angela checked her watch and said, "I'm trying to do my job." She doubled back to pick up Peter's hat. "I'll look into the photo," she said. "But until I've got something concrete, there are still grounds to charge him."

"Tell him we're trying," Ellie said.

Angela paused, her hand resting on the handle. "He knows," she said quietly. Then she was gone.

The front door clicked shut behind her, leaving the kitchen oddly quiet.

"Do you think we made a difference?" Ellie asked, starting to gather up the leftovers.

"We told her," Maggie said, digging around in the scraps at the bottom of the bag of prawn crackers. "That's all we can do for tonight."

As Ellie wrapped foil around her half-eaten special fried rice, she noticed her backpack slouched against the kitchen chair, half-open. The charred edge of the book peeked out from inside—her second biggest find of the day.

An idea formed.

There was still something she could do tonight.

Alone in her bedroom, Ellie sat cross-legged on the duvet. The scent of soy sauce still lingered on her fingers, and her limbs felt heavy after the trek out to The Burrows, but sleep wasn't coming with everything still circling.

Dinner had ended with more questions than comfort, and Angela's visit had left behind an unsettled energy. Ellie needed to make sense of something—anything.

She opened the scanned pages of *The Last Love Letter* on her phone and placed it beside the half-burnt print edition, both versions carefully arranged across the bed. One digital and neatly typed. The other a crispy artefact, its curling edges a reminder that someone had tried to erase it.

Peeling back the burnt pages one by one, she jotted down the ten chapter titles:

1. Tender Kiss
2. Love Unveil
3. Heartswell
4. Amour Amici

"You still up, love?" her gran's soft voice followed a creak on the landing. "Don't stay up too late."

"I won't, Gran," Ellie called into the dark. "Goodnight."

"Night, love. Good job on your finds today."

Footsteps padded gently down the hall. Ellie hadn't even heard her gran approach—she'd been lost in the titles. She turned back to the charred book and continued:

5. Forever Him
6. Lovers Path
7. Beloved Ada
8. Forever Her

"Did you put the bin out?" her gran's voice whispered through the door again.

"I forgot."

"It's alright, love," she replied, already padding away. "Isn't that full."

Pen still in hand, Ellie nearly went back to her list. But last time they'd skipped bin night, they'd waited a whole month. The rubbish had started to smell long before then. In this May heat, she couldn't risk it.

Leaving her list, she crept downstairs and dragged the bin to the front of the cottage.

She lingered a moment as the village lay still around her. A cool, refreshing breeze slipped down the lane, a long exhale after a strange day. Her thoughts turned to her father in his cell, but also on that night. Running from the village, soaked from trying to save Benjamin, not knowing where to go but ending up at Ellie's window. He must have been a wreck.

She sighed.

"I hope they're not going too hard on you," she whispered into the night, then slipped back inside.

Back in her room, she sat cross-legged on her bed and finished her list:

9. Love's Drama
10. Heartsouls

She read them several times. They were odd, and she couldn't quite put her finger on why.

For one, nobody kissed in the first chapter. And *Amour Amici*, from chapter four, turned out to be Italian for a romance that blossoms from friendship. It might nod to the early flirtations between Margaret and the village vet, but otherwise, the titles felt scattered. Romantic, yes. But vague. Mismatched.

She thought about her father's version of Sally's life. He'd spoken of distant parents, and a brother who wanted to belong to another world. And that quiet dream of finding peace in Devon.

A place to start over.

Benjamin had mentioned following in her footsteps.

Neither of them had made it.

The ex-boyfriend writing letters in the novel—was that meant to be Terry? The past Margaret couldn't quite shake? The same Terry who'd had a powerful uncle the year he was spotted fleeing the village in a getaway car? The night his girlfriend drowned.

Ellie pinched the bridge of her nose and yawned. Benjamin's signal was still scrambled. She couldn't yet separate what mattered from what didn't.

She flipped through the digital pages, scanning until she reached the section matching the 'Beloved Ada' chapter—the one Vivienne Winchester had mentioned.

The chapter set during the storm.

Ellie began to read:

Rain lashed the windows of the Harbormaster's Arms so fiercely Margaret half expected the old glass to give in. Thunder rumbled overhead, making the oak beams groan. A puddle had already spread across the floor from under the door, creeping in like it belonged.

"Another round for the storm-stayed!" called the landlord.

Margaret glanced at her watch—10:15. Looked like she'd be stuck for a while. Across the room, Dr Hamilton, the village vet, caught her eye and raised his glass. He'd been nothing but kind since she'd arrived in Seavale. The exact opposite of Richard, and everything she'd left behind. Maybe, in time.

The door blew open with a gust, and a woman stepped inside, soaked to the skin as she scanned the room.

"Quite the evening," she said to no one in particular, shrugging off her dripping coat.

"Ada," the landlord nodded. "Your usual?"

Ada offered a thin smile and hopped onto the empty stool beside Margaret. Up close, her eyes were a curious grey.

"Not from around here, are you?" she asked.

"Is it that obvious?"

"We don't get many new faces," Ada said. "Especially ones who look like they're running from something."

The words landed hard. Margaret flinched.

Their conversation ambled along from there— village oddities, the weather, the kind of small talk people lean on when they're not sure where things are going. Margaret found herself saying more than she meant to. About home. About Richard. About the unexpected comfort of Dr Hamilton.

"Men," Ada said. "Always making things harder than they need to be."

Her own story surfaced in pieces. The flour mill her family ran, now gone. Fields ruined by floods. Rising costs. Failing machinery.

"The Millers' place sits empty now," Ada said.

"Big old farmhouse out on the edge of town. Owner's away till Tuesday. Funny how they always leave the porch light on, like that'll stop anyone who might fancy a look inside."

Margaret frowned. "Sorry?"

"Antiques. Heirlooms. All just sitting there. No one would notice. We could be in and out in twenty minutes. Split it. Could be enough to start over somewhere. Solve a few problems."

Margaret stared. "Are you serious?"

"Just a thought."

Margaret set her glass down. "I should go. Rain seems to be easing."

The storm had quieted. She gathered her things, avoiding Ada's eyes.

"Think about it," Ada called after her.

No, I won't, Margaret thought as she left.

Ellie flicked through the rest of the book. As Vivienne had said, Ada and the mysterious farmhouse were never mentioned again. The narrative returned to Margaret's coastal romance as if the strange encounter in the pub had never happened.

One chapter. One storm. One quiet suggestion.

It had to be Benjamin's way of alluding to that night. He'd followed the same stale breadcrumbs Ellie was now tracing. He must have seen what she was only just beginning to grasp about that night. A chance gathering. Perhaps Ada represented one of the group. Or the group itself.

Or Sarah. She'd admitted she let it slip. Terry knew the ins and outs. But Joanne, Phil, and Tracey? They seemed as unlikely to be involved in a manor heist as Sally. And yet... they had been.

Had Sally been involved too? Another pair of feet Mrs Winchester hadn't noticed? Somehow, Ellie didn't think so.

Her eyelids grew heavy. She set the book aside and slipped beneath the duvet, but her mind refused to settle.

Her thoughts turned to her father. By now, he was probably curled up in a stark cell, head down on a cold bench. If not there, slumped in some cramped interview room beneath a blinding light. Either way, he had a long night ahead.

Guilt stirred in her chest. She was tucked beneath a familiar quilt, safe and warm, while he faced a sleepless night behind a locked door.

And yet, maybe he was the safest of them all.

Someone was trying to rewrite the present with the lies of the past, and after fifty years of freedom, they were still one step ahead.

But Ellie was closing in.

Her sharp gut—in Sylvia's words—told her that much.

Chapter 17
The Sound of Silence

The next morning, Ellie attacked the shop window, the microfibre cloth squeaking against glass already clean enough to vanish. A pointless task, but it gave her hands something to do while her mind worked in circles about Tracey and the locket.

How many lockets were there with an etching of a robin in one village? And how many of those people were connected to that night.

It was the same locket. It had to be.

But how could *she* have it if Benjamin was supposed to have had it on him when he died?

South Street bustled around her with an unexpected early morning shopping crowd. The fine weather had coaxed everyone out, but for the second day in a row, not into the bookshop. Three customers since opening —two American tourists looking for a bathroom and directions to the war museum, and Sylvia, who had dropped off one of her spontaneous plates of spare cheese samples.

What the shop lacked in footfall, it more than made up for in stares and glares.

Tracey's photo had done its damage.

At the bottom of the street, a flash of royal red caught Ellie's eye. Phil. The postman. He trudged uphill with his familiar slouch, his canvas bag dragging him down.

Ellie needed to speak with him after what she'd seen last night at Terry's garage.

She looked at her now-spotless window, then at Phil's steady progress up South Street. If she kept scrubbing, she'd wear through the glass before he reached her.

Abandoning her cloth and spray, she joined her gran in the shop.

Maggie sat behind the counter, the advanced and scorched copies of Benjamin's manuscript spread before her as she continued to try and crack the code.

"Still at it?" Ellie asked, sliding the vinegar bottle beneath the counter.

"Mmm," Maggie replied, not looking up. "Benjamin certainly liked his metaphors. The man never met a sunset he didn't compare to a wound." She tapped her pen against the page. "It's quiet again today."

"A little," Ellie agreed. "It's a gorgeous day. South Street's bustling. And yet..." She watched a mother gently steer her child past the shop. "Do you think the gossip's sticking to us?"

"Like tar," Maggie sighed, removing her glasses. "Not exactly the grand reopening we imagined, is it?"

"Not exactly. But there's nothing for it now but to clear Dad's name."

"How's that looking?"

"We've got until the afternoon before they have to charge him," Ellie said, glancing at the clock. Ten past nine. "If the police have nothing else to go on but that photo, they'll push him right up to the line in the hopes he confesses."

"And when he doesn't?"

"They'll have to let him go." Ellie grabbed her notebook from beside the till. "I need to speak to them all again," she said, flipping pages. "Everyone who was involved in that heist. That'll be harder now, but it's the only way I'll catch one of them out. Tracey's the most likely to break, but I doubt the vicar will let us get close enough. Terry's slammed the garage door in my face. Joanne, maybe, but—"

The bell jingled.

Phil stepped inside. His thin face creased into a smile that barely touched his eyes, and even that was brief. His lip was no longer bleeding but he had a cut to prove Terry had punched him. He held a small parcel wrapped in brown paper, setting it on the counter without a word. He glanced at Maggie, but he didn't acknowledge Ellie.

"That'll be the handmade tip jar I ordered,"

Maggie explained in a cheery voice. "Local potter, but everything is online now, isn't it?"

Phil gave a tight nod and a hint of a smile, eyes scanning the counter as he dug out his scanner. Something caused him to double back. The charred remains of Benjamin's book beside the manuscript.

"Recognise that?" Ellie asked, stepping closer. "I found it in a box someone tried to turn to ash down by the river. You wouldn't know anything about that, would you?" Phil fumbled his scanner, nearly dropping it. "I heard Benjamin was sure the box got lost in the post."

Still, he said nothing.

"Busy day?" Maggie asked. "It's nice out."

Phil held out the device and she signed a sloppy signature with her forefinger, but still he didn't respond. He slid the scanner back into his bag and turned to leave.

Ellie followed him to the door. "What happened last night?" she asked, keeping her voice low. "At the garage with Terry? I saw you, Phil. He threatened you… told you to keep quiet. What about?"

But he walked on, head down, as though she'd spoken to a lamppost. He didn't look back.

"Looks like the postman's taken a vow of silence," Maggie suggested.

Ellie hovered by the door, half in the shop, half out.

"This is going to be even harder than I thought," she said, turning back into the hush of the shop. "Can I go and check something?"

"Fine by me." Maggie gestured around the empty shop. "Where are you going?"

"Following another hunch."

Shielding her eyes from the bright glare, Ellie hurried down South Street, the vinegar tang still lingering on her t-shirt. She stopped outside Lovely Bubbly. Through the window, she saw Joanne scrubbing the inside glass, the word 'CLEARANCE' nearly vanished.

Ellie stepped inside where the trend continued. The red stickers that had peppered the shop on her last visit were gone.

Had Joanne had a reversal of fortunes?

"Good morning," Ellie said.

Silence.

"What are these called?" Ellie asked, gesturing to the baskets of bathbombs, now being sold at full price. "Did you make them?"

No response.

"What day is it?" Ellie continued, folding her arms. "What country do we live in? What colour is the sky above our heads?"

Joanne wrung out her cloth with a bit too much force, took her time dunking it back into the soapy water, then resumed her silent scrubbing.

Ellie sighed. "Alright, since you're not going to talk, I'll talk. Here's what I think."

Joanne didn't look up, but her shoulders stiffened.

"Terry was the planner and the getaway driver. And you were the lookout, weren't you?" Ellie paused, though she knew no reply would come. "That June night in 1975. And given what happened, I think you saw something—or *someone*—out in the storm. I think that someone was Sally. And I don't think she was all that keen on the idea of robbing the local manor."

Joanne's scrubbing slowed.

"I know she was still in the village after you all left the pub. She used the phone box to call my father. Did you hear he was arrested?" Another long pause. "By the time he got there, she was already dead. Five minutes after the call. I think that gave you just enough time to run into the manor to warn the others, which would explain how Mrs Winchester noticed that smell of lavender. I think you all fled... but not before one of you stopped Sally from telling people what she knew."

Joanne twisted the cloth so hard her knuckles turned red. Then white.

"Was the money worth it?" Ellie asked, her voice quieter now. "Did you spend it all? Or did something go wrong? Were you a first-time burglar or is this something you do every weekend?"

Joanne dunked the cloth back into the bowl with a sharp splash. The bowl tipped, and soapy water sloshed across the tiles. She let out a sharp breath and looked around, flustered. Ellie spotted the paper towel roll and passed it to her. Joanne took it without hesitation. Their eyes connected, just for a moment.

"Oh, good," Ellie said as she stepped back from the spreading puddle. "You can see me. I was starting to worry I was talking to myself."

Joanne mopped up the water, her continued silence more telling than anything she could have said.

"Thank you for mentioning Phil, by the way," Ellie added. "Last time, I mean. I don't think I would have got this far without your little slip-up. Loose lips sink ships, right?"

She froze, and this time Ellie had struck a different kind of nerve. Ellie wasn't supposed to know that, but it was what Terry had said last night. It was like she'd stumbled into a secret code word. A pact.

She almost pushed with more questions but Joanne wasn't going to say anything.

And neither was Phil.

Her suspect pool was shrinking and time was running out.

Ellie left Lovely Bubbly more frustrated than when she'd arrived. She considered heading for the garage, but Terry had made himself clear last night.

She trudged up South Street, thoughts spiralling, until a familiar voice called out. "Ellie!"

She looked up to see Auntie Penny waving from outside the pet shop. Duchess stood regally at her side, tail swaying. Next to them was her mother, Carolyn, glamorous even in jeans and trainers, a glossy shopping bag looped over one wrist, large black sunglasses shielding most of her face.

"The catalogue shoot is tomorrow," Carolyn said, adjusting her sunglasses. "We're picking up last-minute bits. And Duchess is scandalously low on her duck chews," she added, scratching the dog behind one ear.

"To tell you the truth, I'm quite nervous. I've practised the poses, but you never know which direction you should go in until you meet the photographer again—"

"Dad was arrested," Ellie said, bursting her mother's bubble so easily reinstated.

"I know," Carolyn replied, her expression hidden behind the oversized shades. "He called me. Yesterday."

"You were his one phone call?"

"I suppose I was. He wanted to know if I knew a decent solicitor. I only had the name of my divorce lawyer, but she passed him on to someone more criminally inclined."

"How did he sound?"

"He couldn't say much, but he hasn't given up," Carolyn said, offering a glimpse over her glasses. "He said your talk at The Burrows helped him see sense. It sounds like you put the fight back into him."

"As difficult as things can seem, the only way to face them is head-on." Ellie glanced up the street, watching as people continued to skirt around Meadowfield Books, a shop now tethered to a man who can't stop drowning people. "Reopening the shop taught me that. But keeping it open is a battle I'm not prepared for. Not with this fresh smudge on the family name. It's going to take a miracle."

"Or the truth," Penny suggested.

"The truth would be a miracle now," Ellie replied, glancing at the soap shop, where Joanne had resumed her scrubbing, her face turned away. "I'm being frozen out by a group of old thieves all hiding in plain sight."

"We popped into the bookshop earlier, just to check on you," Penny said gently. "Your gran mentioned getting everyone together for a proper meeting to see what we can do to help Peter."

"And I, for one, think it's a fantastic idea," Carolyn said. "Though I did insist it happens at my house at six. I need to be asleep by nine. Not *in* bed by nine," she added, almost hissing. "*Asleep.*"

"And you will be," Penny said, fanning her palms at Carolyn. "I got you some of that tea you like, remember? The one off the internet. From that woman in the Cotswolds who reads your tarot cards over FaceTime once a fortnight? You'll be asleep in two sips."

"I must look rested," Carolyn sighed. "I'm hoping to pass for forty-nine so they don't put me in something frumpy. Or, God forbid, *pastel.*"

Ellie gave a breathy laugh. "Well, I'm glad your priorities are straight."

"You can worry about two things at once, dear," Carolyn replied, brushing an invisible fleck from her sleeve. "I can't drop my life, dreams, and aspirations just because your father decided to come back at the worst possible time."

The words might've sounded cutting from anyone else, but there was no venom in them. In fact, there was a weariness there.

Carolyn placed a firm hand on her daughter's arm.

"Dig deeper," she said, the words delivered with the crisp assurance of a director. "Find your motivation.

Because I, for one, would very much like to see your father a free man again."

Her eyes welled with sudden tears, and she turned away.

"Oh, Carolyn, I have a tissue in my—"

"Penny, get the dog treats," she interrupted, already whisking herself away. "I need to go home and rest."

"Of course," Penny called after her. "Put your feet up. I left a sheet mask chilling in the fridge."

Carolyn walked off without another word, leaving Ellie to watch her go in stunned silence.

"Mum was crying," she murmured. "Over Dad." She shook her head. "She's called him the dullest man in Meadowfield more times than I can count." But then she remembered something her mother had said while having her roots retouched the other day. "They were seeing more of each other before he left."

Penny nodded, eyes twinkling. "It was sweet, actually. Your mother had this… glow about her."

"A glow?" Ellie repeated. It was the last thing she'd expected. Her parents had spent the majority of her childhood avoiding even having to speak.

"I never told you this," Penny said, dropping her voice to a whisper, "but when he disappeared last year, he took that glow with him. She'd never admit it, but she missed him."

"But what do they even have in common?"

Penny laughed softly and patted her cheek. "You."

"No, but—what else?"

Penny leaned in like she was about to share something scandalous. "Sometimes," she whispered, "when Carolyn is staring out the window and claims she's manifesting or visualising her next role... I know she's just watching the birds."

With a knowing nod, Penny turned and ducked into the pet shop, leaving Ellie standing in the middle of the street, more confused than ever.

* * *

Back in the empty bookshop, Maggie was pacing behind the counter, peering under shelves and lifting stray teacups.

"If you're looking for your glasses," Ellie said, closing the door behind herself, "they're around your neck."

Maggie didn't look up. "It's not the glasses," she muttered, crouching to peer behind the till. "And it's nothing. Honestly."

"Doesn't look like nothing."

Maggie straightened with a sigh, brushing her hands down her cardigan. "While you were out, you missed a visitor."

Ellie's heart gave a small hitch. "Who?"

"Sarah. The teacher." Maggie planted her hands on her hips, scanning the shop and still looking for whatever she'd lost. "She was following up on what she said yesterday, about coming to find you. I tried to keep her talking about the old profession from class sizes to the curriculum, but she was on a mission to get on with her day."

Ellie stepped closer. "We keep missing each other. Did she say why she came?"

"Better. She left a message." Maggie reached into her pocket and retrieved a yellow post-it note, the handwriting slightly smudged. "She wants you at Meadowfield Manor tonight at eight o'clock sharp. She's nearly got everyone on board, whatever that means."

Ellie took the note, staring at the time and address as her thoughts raced. "Interesting timing."

Maggie hummed, taking in the entire shop once again. "She left… and something's been bothering me ever since."

"What is it?"

"Benjamin's books," Maggie said, her tone flat. "That's what I can't find. They're gone."

A cold prickle ran down Ellie's spine. "Stolen?"

"They were both here on the counter," Maggie said, placing her hands on the empty space. "Nobody else came in but—" She paused and half turned. "Sarah asked if I could make her a latte, and I was more than happy to. I didn't think anything of it, but I had my back to her."

"She was in the back room at the launch too," Ellie remembered, wondering if Sarah had the audacity to steal something like that from right under Maggie's nose, turned or not. "I caught her peeking at the manuscript. Too curious not to, apparently. But stealing it?"

Maggie pushed the post-it note across the counter. "I suppose you'll find out tonight." She studied Ellie's face. "It could be a trap. Or a performance. Or both."

"I've got a few hours to decide how reckless I'm feeling," Ellie replied, tucking the note into her pocket. "In the meantime, I need to know how far the silent treatment has spread."

"How are you going to do that?"

Ellie paused at the door. "I need to find Tracey."

* * *

Next door in the cheese shop, Sylvia was mid-flirt with a man ordering an alarming quantity of Stilton, one hand on her hip and the other waving a sample cracker with theatrical flair.

When he left, red-faced and clutching his paper-wrapped haul like treasure, Sylvia gave Ellie a knowing smile.

"How goes the hunt?"

"Still chasing," Ellie said. "Tracey's pulling ahead. She knows something. Since the two of you are neighbours, I don't suppose you know where I'd find her this time of the afternoon?"

"Usually," Sylvia started, wiping her hands on a gingham tea towel, "she'd be flower arranging at the church right around now, but I've just come from the café. Tracey's in there at the corner table."

"Alone?"

Sylvia nodded. "But from how she was jumping, I'd wager she was waiting to meet someone."

Ellie thanked Sylvia for the tip-off and wasted no time jogging down to The Giggling Goat. She pressed a hand to the café door and hesitated. Through the glass, she spotted Tracey hunched at the back, cupping a mug of tea, eyes darting with every jingle of cutlery or scrape of a chair.

The bathroom door creaked open.

Terry emerged.

He loomed over Tracey, low-voiced and tense. Tracey flinched, shrinking into herself as he leaned closer. No one else seemed to notice, too busy with their pastries and oat milk lattes. But Ellie saw enough.

She stepped inside.

The doorbell clanged. Terry turned. His eyes landed on Ellie, and he didn't linger.

With a muttered curse, he brushed past her and barrelled out onto South Street.

Ellie took his place across from Tracey, who still hadn't moved. Her hands trembled around her mug.

"Loose lips sink ships," Ellie said quietly.

She shuddered. "I'm not supposed to talk to you,"

Tracey was the only one who might give something away, and she was brittle. Any wrong step might send her shattering. Ellie had to tread carefully.

"I can help you," Ellie said carefully, ducking to meet her downcast gaze. "I know you're scared, but if someone is threatening you—someone like Terry—hoping it'll all go away is the worst thing you can do."

Tracey stared into her tea, and Ellie couldn't see the locket. Had she taken it off, or was it hiding under her layers?

"Let's go somewhere else," Ellie urged. "Somewhere quiet."

Tracey didn't move. But Ellie saw the shift as something flashed behind her eyes. A truth, maybe. She stood. It looked like a retreat, a final decision not to speak after all. But as she brushed past Ellie's chair, she hesitated, her head tilted slightly to one side.

"The church," she murmured, her voice so faint it barely stirred the air. "There's a derelict coal outhouse at the back. Do you know it?"

"I… I think so?"

"Seven."

And then Tracey was gone. Out the café door and swallowed by the street.

Ellie let out a long breath.

Her second invitation that afternoon.

Sarah at the manor at eight.

Tracey at the church at seven.

And before either of them, the emergency meeting at her mother's.

She made her way to the counter, where Oliver was rearranging loaves in the display case like he had nothing better to do.

"What's going on, Oliver?" Ellie asked, leaning her elbows on the counter. She resisted the urge to bang her forehead against it. "They're going to charge Dad this afternoon if I can't pull something out of the bag."

"If only I knew," he said, poking a focaccia. "And didn't my mother tell you last night during your cosy little takeaway tea party—which, I might add, I was *not* invited to—that she thinks there's a chance they'll apply for an extension?"

Ellie straightened. "An extension? You mean they can keep him longer?"

"If they believe they can prove guilt with a bit more time, yes," Oliver said, far too casually. "They'll argue they've got reasonable grounds and just need another day to finish tying the noose."

Ellie's stomach churned. "Brilliant."

"Could mean they've got something up their sleeve," Oliver offered, scrunching a paper bag.

"Or it means they're desperate." Her voice was low, laced with frustration, and she noticed Oliver didn't meet her eye. "You don't think he did it, do you?"

He cleared his throat. "That picture is… convincing."

"That picture isn't what it appears to be," Ellie snapped, her palm hitting the counter with a dull thud. "And I'm going to prove it."

She peered out of the café as the sun retreated behind the clouds, suspicious grey clouds replacing the bright blue of the morning.

Her afternoon deadline had melted away.

Joanne wouldn't speak to her, and neither would Phil. Confronting Terry again seemed like a death wish.

But she had Tracey. And Sarah.

The two people who'd held her at arm's length yesterday had, of their own volition, asked to meet today.

Before then, the family meeting. An opportunity to pool ideas she couldn't let go to waste—and she knew exactly how to prepare.

Chapter 18
The Wrong Font

Ellie's mother's sitting room was stuffy, too many people in one small room after the weather's humid turn. The rain was hammering the windows in earnest now, turning the view outside into a watercolour blur of grey.

Auntie Penny finished passing out cups of tea while Carolyn continued to angle herself away from Maggie, who was squashed up next to her on the sofa. Oliver had an armchair to himself, too distracted by whatever was happening inside his phone.

"We can't do this alone," Ellie said, handing out the printed manuscript packets one by one. "Someone has been stealing the few physical copies that are floating around. Mrs Winchester's manor was broken into again, and Benjamin's were burned. This book must be important—but we're still struggling to see why."

She'd included the handwritten chapter titles she'd

noted down before the charred copy disappeared, apparently stolen by Sarah.

"Oh, it's just like a book club!" Auntie Penny beamed as she sandwiched herself in on Maggie's other side, pushing them closer together. "I do love a romance."

"Feels more like a script meeting," Carolyn added, sitting unnaturally upright like she expected someone to yell 'action' at any moment.

"I was thinking production meeting, actually," Ellie said, scanning the room. "Speaking of—Daniel?"

"Here. Sorry," came his voice from the hallway, followed by the slightly soggy entrance of him and a large presentation board. He was damp around the shoulders, hair frizzing in the humidity. "I was just taking my shoes off."

Ellie helped him manoeuvre the board into position at the front of the room. It wasn't fancy—lines, dates, scribbled arrows—but it looked like something. Like progress. Like proof she was doing something more than pacing and worrying and hoping someone else would step forward.

"She's spent all afternoon on this," Maggie said, and there was something in her voice—not just pride. Relief, maybe. "It's all there. Every detail."

"She always did throw herself into her homework," Carolyn added, squinting at the sequence. "Is it a storyboard?"

"A timeline," Ellie replied. "Of the night Benjamin died. There are gaps that don't make sense. Little things in the continuity. Five minutes here. Ten there. People who were 'just nipping to the loo' and then show up half an hour later face down in a pond." She turned to Oliver. "Any word from your mum yet? About confirming the ambulance call time?"

"No," he replied, edging forward like he had something more important to say. "But Joey wants to know what everyone wants from the Chinese."

Soon the room was buzzing with hot debate over crispy duck and Auntie Penny insisting that they should all order their own prawn toast instead of sharing. Ellie hovered at the edge, her notes loose in her lap, wondering why it suddenly felt like everything was drifting again.

"It's impressive," Daniel said, eyes back on the board.

"Leftover skill from my old job," Ellie replied. "I got used to whipping up visuals. It was like it didn't count until people could *see* the ideas." She offered a half-smile. "I'd call it a transferable skill, but it's not every day you're making a timeline to prove your dad isn't a murderer."

"On a fifty-year killing spree, no less!" Daniel's nan announced as she let herself in, soaked right through her floral housecoat, water dripping from the hem. "The door was open. What's all this?"

She helped herself to a copy of the manuscript and sank into the armchair as though she'd been invited.

"I think you need to kill more than two people to

count as a spree," Penny mumbled through a mouthful of a custard cream.

"Not that he killed anyone," Maggie confirmed loudly, wrestling for space on the cramped sofa, sending sharp looks in both directions.

"Nan," Daniel groaned. "I told you I'd be back later."

"I couldn't hear *Pointless* with all the shouting about prawn toast, could I?" she retorted, pushing her giant reading glasses higher on her nose. "Lemon chicken and egg fried rice for me. And if you don't *tell* them you want the free prawn crackers, they won't put them in the bag."

Daniel looked like he wasn't sure whether to laugh or quietly expire from embarrassment. He turned back to Ellie. "I could use your help with my classroom display boards. The other teachers are putting me to shame."

"I'd love to," she said, caught off guard by the softness in his voice.

"Really?"

"Yeah."

"Alright," he said. "Something to look forward to when all this is over."

"*If*," she said.

"No ifs. Look how proactive you're being."

She smiled faintly, though her mind was elsewhere now. "Speaking of 'if'… can I ask you something? About one of your colleagues."

As Oliver tried to shush the room so he could call to

order ahead, Ellie nudged Daniel through to the kitchen. They ducked into the back garden together, stepping into the sheeting rain.

The sky had gone completely grey, and the rain felt colder than when they'd ran across with the board, slicing rather than falling. They sprinted to the greenhouse at the bottom of the garden, threw open the door, and slipped inside with a squelch of shoes on wet tiles.

The air inside was thick and steamy, smelling of damp earth. Her father's bag still waited for him in the corner.

"I still can't believe he was living in here," Ellie said, wiping a sleeve across the misted glass. "When he gets out, he's not going to know what a real bed feels like."

"Something for him to look forward to," Daniel said. "You wanted to ask about my colleague? I'm guessing it's Sarah?"

Ellie nodded. "There's something off about her. She's helpful, but only to a point. Yesterday she admitted she lied about leaking the information about the manor, and today, I think she stole Benjamin's books from right under my gran's nose." She inhaled a breath, pushing her damp hair from her face. "You said she plays favourites?"

"That's just school politics," he said. "It doesn't mean she's a criminal."

"But she *was* involved," Ellie said, more certain now. "I just don't know how deep her involvement goes. But she's called a meeting tonight at the manor. She said it could help clear some things up."

Daniel was quiet for a long moment. "She's a good teacher. People trust her. But lately—"

A scream sliced through the rain.

They froze, exchanging glances.

Then came another cry. Raw and high-pitched. Panic, pure and unmistakable.

They were already moving. The greenhouse door slammed shut behind them, its echo lost in the roar of the downpour.

Rain hit hard and fast, soaking them through in seconds. They sprinted down the back alley, puddles exploding beneath their feet. Ellie's hair clung to her face, her breath sharp in her throat as adrenaline surged.

The screams took them to the church. Reverend Catherine stood motionless in the rain, her black robes plastered to her skin.

"He did it!" she cried, tears and rain becoming one. "He killed her—my daughter—he *killed* her!"

"Your daughter?" Ellie's voice caught.

Daniel was already on the phone. "Yes. St Mary's. Yes, now."

Ellie ran into the church. Spiced incense hung in the close air, barely masking the smell of sweet rot that came with old buildings.

At the front, near the baptismal font, Phil, the postman, knelt in a pool of holy water, his sleeves soaked.

Tracey was in his arms. Her cardigan was sodden, clinging to her frame. Her silver-streaked hair lay across his knee as she stared up at nothing.

"I found her," Phil said, hollow, as his eyes darted from the font to Ellie. "I didn't… I swear, I didn't…"

The font stood beside them, nearly empty. The water had poured out and pooled around them in a wide, silent ring.

And like her father before her, Ellie noticed the absence of a locket around the victim's neck.

The one that should never have been found.

Ellie's breath locked in her throat. She checked her phone for the time. Quarter to seven. Fifteen minutes before she was supposed to meet Tracey behind the church.

A third drowning.

And she'd been fifteen minutes too late.

"Loose lips sink ships," she said to Daniel when he joined her in the church. "Tracey knew what was going on. She was going to tell me the truth, but someone got to her first. She took the picture, she had the locket, and now… she's dead."

Chapter 19
Benjamin's Final Word

Rain hammered the church roof, a relentless percussion that only seemed louder in the silence beneath it. Blue police lights flashed through the stained glass, casting fractured colour across the white sheet covering Tracey. The water she'd drowned in was already drying on the flagstones.

Ellie sat beside Reverend Catherine at the end of the first pew, the exact spot where Ellie and her gran had talked to Tracey only a day ago

Another circle. Another ripple.

DS Cookson and PC Walsh talked under their breaths by the altar, occasionally glancing their way. Phil hadn't moved since they'd arrived, sitting hunched over in the last row, staring at the ceiling like he was looking for the answers in the beams.

Catherine dabbed at her nose with a crumpled tissue. She'd been silent for nearly twenty minutes, her shoulders rising and falling with breaths that seemed too shallow to sustain her. Her white collar was askew, and her usually neat bob clung damply to her head.

"That window," Christine said suddenly, her voice catching Ellie by surprise. She pointed at the tall stained glass above the altar as the rain streaked through the colours. "They put it in during the restoration in the 1860s, I think. A memorial to Canon Silas Godfrey and his wife. He was the vicar, and he saw the whole place was refurbished. These days, we can barely fundraise for the leaky roof." She frowned, distracted by a thought. "I don't know what the original designs would have been. Lost long before then. Fire, maybe. Or just forgotten."

Ellie followed her gaze. The figure in the centre was robed in deep reds and soft golds, framed by angels and lilies, bathed in the morning light.

"Tracey used to sit here and make up stories about that window for hours," Christine said, resting a palm on the space between them on the pew. "To her, the woman in the window was an angel who watched over the village. She didn't know it was a memorial. I never corrected her."

She tugged at her clerical collar, unfastening it with trembling fingers. She placed it on the wooden pew beside her, then folded her hands in her lap and turned away from it.

"The Ten Commandments," she said, her gaze drifting back to the window. "We're meant to build our lives on them. Not just preach them, but live them. Honour thy father and mother. Remember the Sabbath.

Thou shalt not kill, steal, covet..." Her voice thinned to a whisper. "Thou shalt not bear false witness." She gave a brittle laugh, barely more than a breath. "If you tell one lie in 1975, is that the sin? Or is it the choice to let the lie keep living, every day since?" Her fingers found the tissue again, working it into shreds. "People usually come to me with these sorts of questions. I'm not Catholic, but they confess anyway. Tracey used to say I should write to the local paper and offer to be their agony aunt—back when we still had a paper."

Ellie recognised the detour for what it was—the mind's way of circling around pain too sharp to touch directly. But she needed to know what Catherine was trying to say.

"You've been lying about something," Ellie prompted.

"You were right," Catherine said finally, as if reading her thoughts. "Tracey was among those who foolishly decided to break into Meadowfield Manor that night, and I found out about it. I decided to protect her in any way I could, forsaking everything else for my flesh and blood."

She twisted the tissue between her fingers until it tore in two.

"She was always so easily led. As a child, if you asked her to do something, she'd do it. No argument. I thought it was a blessing at first, but then school and all its influences… she was just always getting herself into trouble. Going along with the wrong people in the wrong directions."

"I think she still was," Ellie said, daring to glance at where Tracey's body lay. The sheet rose in small peaks and valleys, a landscape of what once was a person. "Your daughter was to do some confessing of her own tonight. She asked to meet me in the coal shed behind the church."

Catherine smiled at this, a distant expression that suggested she was seeing something else entirely.

"If I never knew where to find her," she said. "Tracey would be in there, playing with old bits of coal. Maybe I should have introduced her to more children younger. She had no cousins or neighbours her age, and she started school a year late because of whooping cough." She paused. "Would that have made a difference?"

Ellie considered if it would. "I think it's too late for those sorts of regrets."

"Yes, perhaps." Catherine sighed. "I found out about them breaking into the manor when Tracey brought Joanne home. Joanne was trying to hide from me, but she was shivering in the wardrobe. I could hear the rattling coat hangers. They were both soaking wet, so I insisted they sit by the fire to dry off."

The rain seemed to grow louder, as if trying to drown out her words.

"Neither of the girls would tell me where they'd been, what they'd been up to. Pub. That's all I got when I asked. *Pub*." She shook her head as though it still frustrated her. "I left them to make some cocoa, but I lingered in the hallway. I know I shouldn't have, but I was too curious to know what they'd say."

Ellie leaned in. "What did you hear?"

"I heard Tracey ask if they were going to be alright, and Joanne said they would. 'But you ran in saying you saw someone. That you saw her,' Tracey said. And Joanne replied, 'It's sorted.'"

Ellie could see the scene by the fire as clearly as if she'd been there. Two girls drying off, a secret hanging in the air after the most eventful night of their lives.

"After Joanne left, I pushed Tracey to tell me where she'd been," Catherine went on. "She told me about the people she'd met at the pub. About how they talked her into thinking it would be a good idea to go wandering around because they thought it was empty. She swore on the Bible she didn't steal anything, she was just... caught up in the storm. There was no harm done."

"Except to Sally," Ellie said, remembering how quickly the vicar had dismissed the connection during afternoon tea. "Did you connect what they were talking about to Sally?"

Catherine's fingers stilled on the shredded tissue. "News of Sally's drowning didn't reach me until the following morning, and I jumped through every mental loop to convince myself that wasn't what Joanne had been referring to. But the tone of her voice chilled me so much, I forbade Tracey from talking to her ever again."

Across the church, Angela caught Ellie's eye and

excused herself from her conversation. She made her way across the aisle, heels clicking against stone.

"What about here and now, Catherine?" Ellie asked, seizing the moment before Angela reached them. "Something tells me it wasn't in character for her to be wandering around the village with her phone out ready to take pictures as late as she was."

"Usually in bed with a Horlicks and fluffy socks by nine." Catherine nodded. "That's what I'd done. I didn't know she'd been out until morning when I saw that her shoes were by the door, and she'd brought back a bag of clothes. Said someone had left them on the doorstep to donate, which wasn't unusual, but it was more likely to be left here than at home. And she'd left the bag by the bin." She pressed her lips together. "She denied leaving the house at all, at first, but then when she came forward with the photograph, she admitted to going out for a walk, and I couldn't get more out of her than that."

"What kind of clothes?" Ellie asked, curious.

"I didn't look." Catherine flinched, sniffing hard. "I couldn't bring myself to touch it."

Angela cleared her throat as she reached them, rain still glistening on her coat. "Reverend, I need to go over a few things again, if you don't mind."

Catherine nodded, seeming almost relieved at the interruption.

"Can you tell me exactly what happened tonight?" Angela asked, flipping open her notebook.

"After the six o'clock news, Tracey was eager to go

for a walk," Catherine started, glancing at the white sheet out of the corner of her eye. Her gaze didn't linger. "When I offered to join her, she made sure to get her shoes on and go by the time it took for me to rinse out the teapot." Her voice had grown steadier, the truth coming out easily. "I followed her down into the village, but I lost her on South Street. She rounded the bend and I didn't know which way she went. I checked The Drowsy Duck, The Old Bell, and then I saw that the church door was open. When I got here, Phil was holding her head down in the water—"

"He claims the opposite," Angela cut in, consulting her notepad. "According to Phil, you saw him pulling her out of the water, and that he only walked in a few minutes before you."

"But he was following her?" Catherine's eyes cut across the church to where Phil sat. He hadn't moved, hadn't even seemed to blink since Ellie had arrived.

"He was delivering a parcel from Northash, Lancashire," Angela said, checking the pad. "Addressed to you, Catherine."

"Oh, that'll be my candles. I had them sent here so Tracey wouldn't see them. They were supposed to be her birthday presents." Her voice cracked on the last word, and she began to cry fresh tears again.

To Ellie's surprise, Angela placed a consoling hand on Catherine's shoulder before she excused herself, heading for the vestry in search of more tissues.

Angela turned to Ellie as the silence settled. "Are you alright?"

"I will be," Ellie said, though she wasn't entirely sure.

"Why were you here?" Angela probed.

"Meeting at my mother's. We were putting our heads together." Ellie swallowed, the moment slipping away. "We went outside for some quiet, and then I heard a scream. We ran over and saw Phil holding her on the floor."

Angela let out a long breath, frustration evident in the tight lines around her mouth. "A drowning. The rain. I'm getting déjà vu. The kind that gets under your skin and moves around too quick for you to scratch it."

"I think Tracey was the accomplice, Angela," Ellie said firmly. "You need to check the bag of clothes at her mother's house because I bet there's a flat cap in there. Someone talked her into taking that picture."

Angela studied her for a moment, then called PC Walsh over and instructed him to do exactly that.

"Are you going to let my father go now?" Ellie asked.

Angela hesitated before saying, "That's not my call alone to make."

As she marched off, Ellie crossed the church in the opposite direction to where Phil sat. He didn't acknowledge her approach, staring straight ahead. His hands were clasped and he seemed to be praying.

"Was she your friend?" Ellie asked.

He didn't reply, still giving her the silent treatment.

"Look, I know you're not supposed to talk to me, but—"

"I always felt like I had to keep an eye on her," Phil said suddenly, his voice rusty. "Neither of us walked away from the manor with anything, and if anyone was going to buckle, it was Tracey."

"A lost opportunity," Ellie said, relieved to hear his voice again, "but not an accidental one."

"It was almost a joke," he insisted. "Or something close to one. Once the idea that the manor was a sitting duck was out there, it just kept building, all of us adding to it. Terry said he'd drive and offered a crowbar. I slipped up that I knew there was a service door on the side they sometimes kept unlocked. It was only my first year delivering post."

He scrubbed a hand across his face, wincing as his nail grazed the cut on his lip. "By the time we were all at that door in the pouring rain, I'd convinced myself we were just checking to see if it was unlocked. When it wasn't, I was relieved. A silly game of chicken that had gone too far. But then Terry pulled out his crowbar and Sarah directed him to a window."

"Sarah was there?" Ellie asked, surprised.

"She kept joking she was there to make sure we didn't break anything, but she was like a tour guide." He glanced up. "She can tell you herself." He checked his watch. "I assume you're going to the meeting at the manor?"

"Tracey was supposed to be there too, I assume?" Ellie asked, the realisation sinking in. "Will it still go ahead?"

"I hope so," Phil said, glancing towards Tracey as

the crime scene photographers moved around her. The sheet had gone. "I don't know who killed her. Or Sally. Or Benjamin. But I think you were right, Ellie. It was one of us from that night."

Ellie hadn't expected the admission. Then again, nothing about this week had gone the way anyone could have predicted.

"I need to clear my head before whatever's waiting at the manor. For Tracey's sake."

"Before you go," Ellie said, remembering what Catherine had said about Tracey and Joanne that night. "What do you think of Joanne from the soap shop? She was more than happy to give your name to me. Why would she think you'd have revealed her involvement?"

He rolled his eyes. "Because she threatened me after the robbery. Joanne was fanning the flames at The Old Bell more than anyone. She was desperate to get her hands on some money so she could move out from under her controlling mother."

"She wanted to be a nurse," Ellie remembered.

"Something like that, but either way, she unravelled and said if I ever told anyone about her involvement, she'd kill me. I didn't believe her, mind you," he added quickly, "and I told her that if she ever brought my name up, I'd make sure I took her down with me. We've never needed to test each other on that until you came along asking questions." He sighed, looking off to the crime scene one last time. "I suppose we got too good at not talking about that night, we never learned to talk about it without cracking."

With that, he got up and left, heading for the church door as a commotion broke out by the crime scene.

One of the newly arrived forensic officers was crouched beside Tracey's body, holding something between gloved fingers. Angela hurried over, and Ellie strained to hear what they were saying.

"A black residue," the officer explained. "On the floor in a partial shoeprint."

Ellie's mind immediately went to the garage and she called out, "Is it oil?"

"It's dusty," the officer replied, rubbing a speck between her gloved fingers. The stuff disintegrated. "Chalky."

Ellie slipped out the side door into the dark. The rain had eased, leaving everything damp and gleaming. She followed the path round to the back of the church, phone light sweeping ahead.

The old coal shed sagged beyond the gravestones, roofless and crumbling. Ellie stepped inside. She only knew the place from childhood, once the best hiding spot in village-wide games of hide and seek. The stone walls were cracked and caked with moss, and there hadn't been a lump of coal stored here for as long as Ellie had been alive.

No chalky black residue.

But something caught the light.

She crouched. On a flat stone under the rim of an intact windowsill, sat a silver locket. She picked it up, thumb brushing the robin etched into its surface. The metal felt cold in her palm.

Sally's locket.

Someone had taken it from Sally's neck in 1975. Then it had turned up in Benjamin's pocket this week. And somehow, Tracey Harper had ended up wearing it, given to her by a 'friend', only to leave it behind in her old hiding place.

And now it was Ellie's turn. She slipped the locket into her coat pocket and stood.

If she could uncover who Tracey's mysterious 'friend' was, she might finally unpick the knot tying all three deaths together.

"There you are," Daniel said from behind her.

Ellie stepped out of the coal shed, the weight of her discovery pressing in her coat pocket. "I was—" She gestured vaguely at the darkened doorway, unsure how to explain what had drawn her in. "They found some chalky black residue at the scene. I thought it might be coal. Where've you been?"

"I thought you'd want space," he said, his cheeks flushing. "You looked like you had things handled with the vicar."

Ellie let out a breath that brushed the edge of a laugh. "I'm making it up as I go. And I'm not even sure she counts as a vicar anymore. But I do feel for her. She got pulled into something she never asked for, just like Tracey."

She reached into her pocket and drew out the locket, its long chain looped in her palm. The etched robin caught the glow of a nearby street lamp.

"Tracey left this in her old hiding place," Ellie

said, her hand tightening around the locket. "Tracey knew it mattered. Not straight away, but something shifted after I pointed out who it used to belong to. Maybe that's why she changed her mind about meeting me?"

Daniel leaned in, studying it closely without touching. "What's inside?"

"It's stuck," Ellie replied, testing the clasp. It wouldn't budge.

"My nan's got a tiny screwdriver kit," he said, holding out his hand. "I'm always fixing her wobbly glasses."

Ellie hesitated, then let the locket slip into his palm. If anyone could be trusted with it, it was him.

"We should head back to your mother's," Daniel said, his voice steady. "I popped in to let them know where we'd gone. Told them what happened to Tracey, but they're deep in something. Your mum thinks she's spotted a clue in Benjamin's book."

Ellie checked her watch. Quarter to eight. An hour since they'd found Tracey. The manor meeting loomed, and she couldn't shake the sense that whatever happened there, it would change everything.

"I can't be late again," she said, watching Daniel pocket the locket. "And sorry for missing drinks last night. Again."

"That's why they were 'maybe' drinks," Daniel said, wrapping his hand around hers as they took the church steps two at a time. "And you won't be late. I'm coming with you."

* * *

"I've solved it!" Carolyn declared as Ellie and Daniel stepped into the sitting room. Her hair was now in giant rollers, a pencil behind one ear, and she waved a page of the manuscript like a lottery ticket. "It was right there the whole time!"

Maggie, perched on the arm of the sofa, gave Ellie a small shake of the head. "We're *still* piecing it together," she said, steady as ever. "But your mother has made an… *interesting* observation."

"It's more than that," Carolyn insisted. "It's a breakthrough."

"It supports something Peter said," Maggie allowed. "But we need more."

"Back to front," Carolyn said, tapping the page for emphasis.

Ellie stepped further into the room. "What are you talking about?"

Carolyn paced the living room like she was back on stage. "The final line of the book, or rather, the final word—it's backwards."

"It's written backwards?"

"No, the word is 'backwards'," Carolyn corrected, clearing her throat. "'…love, like tides, doesn't care for logic, it just pulls you backwards.'" She lowered the page. "Any actor worth their salt checks the opening and closing lines of a script to see if the story comes full circle. The first and last impressions are important."

"Bookends," Maggie agreed.

Carolyn thrust the page towards Ellie, finger jabbing at the final sentence.

"The opening line mentions 'The final letter.' Then it ends with... this."

"The final letter... backwards," Ellic read aloud. "That doesn't make much sense."

"But if we're looking for a code," Oliver said from the window, checking the curtains, "it's the kind of place you'd hide one, right? The beginning and end."

"It would make sense," Maggie said, and Ellie noted, with a flicker of surprise, how smoothly they were all working together—for once.

"But what letter?" Ellie asked, scanning the text. "There are loads. The ex writes a dozen throughout the book."

"Check the final one?" Auntie Penny suggested, emerging from the kitchen with a tray of fresh mugs.

"But do we read it backwards by word or by letter?" Maggie clarified, already sounding annoyed. "Or perhaps through a mirror?"

As the others began flipping through pages, Ellie backed away and found Daniel at the kitchen island with tweezers, a pin, a miniature screwdriver.

"Did your mother crack the code?" he asked.

"I can't tell. They might be onto something or they might be delirious. How goes the operation?"

"Nearly there," he said, easing the pin along the seam. "It's rusted tight. Probably water damage."

The locket gave a faint click. Gently, he eased it open with the screwdriver's edge.

"Got it!"

Ellie moved closer. Inside lay a small overexposed photograph, blurred and browned with age. A little girl sat on an older man's lap, their faces soft with time, almost lost to it.

"That's it?" Daniel sighed. "A photo?"

"Sally and her grandfather. It's sweet," she said. "Were you expecting a confession?" She turned the tiny picture around and checked for writing, but it was blank. "You're supposed to keep pictures in lockets. The locket isn't the clue—it's about *where* Benjamin found it. One of them must know."

She checked the time on the oven.

"We only have five minutes," she said, snapping the locket shut and sliding it into her pocket. "Let's go and see what Sarah has planned."

Outside, the rain had officially passed. Stars pinpricked the sky above the rooftops. Beyond the pond, the manor's windows glowed like lanterns in the night.

Ellie tightened her grip on the locket in her pocket. This wasn't just about clearing her father's reputation or the bookshop's launch.

It was about Sally and Benjamin. And Tracey too. Three people who knew too much about a strange night in 1975.

"I just had a horrible thought," she said, her voice low as the gates of the manor loomed ahead. "Everyone who's had this locket has ended up dead."

Chapter 20
Fifty Year Reunion

Ellie had no idea why she'd been invited.

Standing on the doorstep of Meadowfield Manor with Daniel, she could see them through a window: Terry pacing like a caged animal, Phil staring into the fire as though it might answer back, Joanne hunched in a chair against the wall. Mrs Winchester was perched in the centre, unbothered as ever, a small glass with something dark in hand as if it were bridge night.

Ellie leaned close to Daniel. "Do you think this is the first time they've all been in the same room since 1975?"

"Minus Tracey," he said, his voice low.

Ellie glanced at him. "You said she and Sarah were close?"

He nodded. "They'd have lunch together in the church garden sometimes. I'd see them chatting here and there, and it wasn't just small talk."

Before she could respond, the heavy front door swung open. Jeffrey, the manor's butler, appeared with his usual immaculate timing and unreadable expression.

"This way, please."

They stepped into the entrance hall, the vastness of the manor swallowing them up. As Jeffrey led them towards the drawing room, Ellie caught movement through an open door off to the right. The downstairs powder room. Sarah Mills stood at the sink, patting her eyes with toilet paper, her pale grey cardigan soaked through.

She straightened, folded the paper neatly into the bin, and emerged, her smile tight. "Ah, Ellie. Good. You came. Daniel—I wasn't expecting you, but... well, I suppose that's alright." She glanced at Jeffrey as he lingered by the drawing room doors, then stepped closer. "Have you heard about Tracey?"

Ellie nodded, keeping her involvement at the church to herself for now.

"Phil told us," Sarah explained. "It's shaken everyone." She gestured to the drawing room. "Shall we try and piece together what everyone knows? For Tracey's sake. That's the point of all this—answers."

Ellie placed a hand on Sarah's arm before she strode off in that quick way she did. The cardigan was damp and cold. "In the spirit of answers, I need to ask you something."

Sarah pulled her arm away. "Yes?"

"You came into the bookshop earlier," Ellie said,

keeping her voice low, "and you took something when you left, didn't you?"

A flicker of resistance passed over Sarah's face, but it faded quickly. She let out a long breath. "I think you're referring to the manuscript."

"I think you know I am."

"Yes," Sarah said, folding her arms into a tight shrug. "I'll admit it. I took it. I told you, I was curious. After everything that's been said about clues and codes, it felt like the only way to know for sure. It's not as if copies are growing on trees."

She turned, already smoothing her hair as she swept into the drawing room.

Terry muttered under his breath, pacing back and forth. Phil hadn't moved from the fire. Joanne didn't even look up. Mrs Winchester raised her port in silent greeting.

As Ellie crossed the threshold, feeling annoyed and brave, she called, "Did you steal your aunt's copy of the manuscript too?"

"Ellie, please," Sarah replied, pleading.

"What was that?" Mrs Winchester's voice cut across the room. Her glass hovered inches from her lips. "I suppose we're skipping introductions and explanations about this rather unusual gathering and getting straight to the meat of things?"

Her sharp eyes skimmed the group without truly landing, though her nose gave an involuntary twitch in Joanne's direction—as though she could still smell the lavender.

"Why would Ellie ask you that, Sarah?" she repeated.

"Because…" Sarah looked around, cornered. "I took her gran's copy of Benjamin's book. I shouldn't have. I saw it on the counter and made a rash decision." She paused, her breathing shaky as she gathered herself. "Aunt Vivienne, I didn't take your copy. I didn't even know you had one. I just… I wanted to read it. That's all."

"Funny, though," Ellie said. "The only two copies known to be in the village—both stolen." Her eyes shifted to Phil. "And the rest? Burnt."

He hadn't moved, still staring into the fire.

Mrs Winchester, on the other hand, hadn't taken her eyes off Sarah.

"Well," Sarah muttered, brushing her still-damp fringe back with the edge of her knuckle. "This wasn't how I thought this would get going. I'll fetch your manuscript—"

"No need," Ellie said. "I made a copy. Well, *copies*, actually. My family are reading it right now." She exchanged glances with Daniel, hoping the clue-hunting operation hadn't stalled over food arguments. "If one of you was hoping to get rid of all the copies, you could say the book is out of the bag."

Sarah gave a small nod but didn't speak.

"So," Mrs Winchester said, placing her glass on the side table next to a large vase of water filled with lilies. "You said you had something to tell me, Sarah. And now you've invited strangers into my home. Please. Let's not drag out the suspense."

Sarah took a moment to gather herself. She clasped her hands in front of her like she was addressing a school assembly.

"It's about the truth," she said. "About clearing the air around what happened in 1975. Because the story's twisted now, and Benjamin's dead. And Tracey…"

"I think it's safe to say someone in this room drowned her," Phil muttered. His voice wasn't loud, but it filled the space. "You're all soaked. Where were you all this past hour?"

"It's raining," Terry scoffed. "And who says it has to be one of us?"

"Because this is about *that* night, Terry," Phil snapped, stepping forward. He pointed across the rug, eyes sharp now. "We sat in that pub while the storm thrashed outside, and for a reason I still can't understand, we decided to break in here. Sally *tried* to stop us. She was the only one with any sense."

Mrs Winchester raised her glass in a slow, sardonic toast. "Well, it's nice to put faces to the feet I saw from under my bed all those years ago. Sarah, I think I get the hint."

Sarah moved to her aunt's side, her voice gentler now. "I wanted to tell you for years. I almost did, more than once. I—I didn't want one awful night to ruin our relationship."

Mrs Winchester tilted her head, watching her closely.

"I'm the reason anyone thought this place would be vacant that night," Sarah confessed, staring at the rug, her gaze tracing the swirls. "I said something at the pub. An offhand comment and I've been sorry ever since."

Vivienne didn't speak, giving nothing away as she processed the revelation. A woman so civil and poised that even a betrayal of this size needed to be considered. When she spoke, her voice was even.

"So, that's why you've been so persistent with your visits over the years. All that tea and all those scones, and all the endless chatter about school inspectors and end-of-year plays—"

"No," Sarah said, the whites of her eyes flashing. "That's not fair. We were just kids. Stupid, thoughtless children who made a mistake. If I started to visit more often, it was because I was growing up. Because I realised how much you meant to me—how much family means."

The silence that followed was heavy, but it didn't feel finished.

"Silly children?" Vivienne's voice cracked like a whip. "You were in your twenties, Sarah. You stole from your own family—from *me*—tens of thousands of pounds in jewellery. If you needed money, you only had to—"

"Ask?" Sarah jumped in, sharp, like she'd been waiting for that line. "You'd all cut my father off. The no-good son with the horse-betting habit. And me—by extension—his no-good daughter who didn't know better. I knew I wasn't welcome to any of the Winchester fortune."

She looked at her aunt, not pleading, just tired.

"So yes, that night, maybe I let my imagination get the better of me. The thought of a holiday somewhere sunny and a car that didn't need to be rolled down a hill to start. Too much beer and rain, and I let those ideas sweep me away. We *all* did."

She looked around the room for someone to back her up. No one spoke.

"It wasn't supposed to be this serious," she said.

"You're making it sound like *The Famous Five Rob a Manor*," Vivienne muttered, her voice bone-dry.

"We didn't walk away with anything," Joanne said, almost too quietly to hear. Her voice cracked halfway through. "The jewellery was lost."

"It's true," Sarah said. "On the way out, we stuffed it all into one bag. Someone dropped it, and nobody ever owned up to it."

Terry snorted. "You've got a nice house now though, haven't you?" He fixed Sarah with a look. "Nicer than mine. Nicer than Phil's. Funny, that."

"I've climbed my way up," Sarah snapped. "My career didn't happen by accident, but we're talking about *one* night. One stupid, stupid night."

"And one of you made the worst decision of all," Ellie said.

It was the first time she'd spoken since Sarah had confessed. Her voice cut clean through the heat of the room. She stepped away from Daniel's side.

"Joanne," she said, her gaze steady. "You were outside, keeping watch. You saw Sally, and I'm going to guess it was in the phone box. You ran inside, told the others, and you all piled into Terry's orange Allegro."

She looked to Terry, waiting.

"Were you *all* in the car?" Ellie asked. "None of you stayed behind?"

Terry glanced at Sarah. She looked back. Something passed between them.

"What?" Ellie said.

"I didn't see her in the phone box," Joanne murmured, drawing Ellie's attention back to her. "She came to the manor to stop us. I tried to calm her down at the gates, but she was upset, crying about Terry going back to stealing again—how he promised he'd change."

"She had a saviour complex," Sarah said suddenly. The words sounded bitter. Ellie turned to her, surprised.

"What would you know?" Terry barked. "She didn't even like you. But yeah, I admit she was too good for me. I should have stayed in the pub with her, but I was too taken in by the thought of an easy job. I never wanted to believe it was one of us who..."

His voice trailed off. No one filled the silence.

"But maybe Phil's right," Terry continued, scratching his stubbly chin. "Because it can't be Peter, can it? He's still banged up, and now Tracey is dead."

Silence again. Dense. Waiting.

"Sorry to interrupt," Daniel said gently, raising a hand like he was still in the classroom. "I... put a pin in something earlier, and now seems the perfect time to bring it up." He cleared his throat. "W-where were you all the past hour? Phil pointed out that you're all soaked, yet none of you offered an alibi."

"I was working," Terry grunted. "Had to change a tyre in the rain. Didn't have room to back the car into the workshop."

"Who was it for?" Ellie asked. "Did you get a name?"

Terry shrugged. "Just some bloke. Paid in cash."

Phil muttered something under his breath.

"What was that?" Terry roared, spinning on him.

"Likely story!" Phil snapped, slamming his palm against the marble mantlepiece.

Mrs Winchester jumped, her glass sloshing dark port onto her trouser leg. She dabbed at it with a napkin, then tucked a cushion over the mark without comment.

"Terry Tall Tales," Phil pressed on, "that's what they used to call you at school. You once told me your dad was a seven-foot boxer in a travelling circus."

"So what?" he replied, uninterested. "I was a kid."

"You were a thief then, too," Joanne said, quietly but clearly. "And a bully. You stole my cousin's bike."

"Your cousin should have locked their bike up better." Terry straightened, darting a finger between Sarah and Joanne. "What about you two? Don't you have an alibi?"

"We were here," Sarah answered, cutting him off before Joanne could speak. "Together. We've been getting ready for you for about… an hour, Joanne?"

Joanne frowned, figuring something out. "Yeah. About that."

"Getting ready for what?" Phil asked.

"Do you think those chairs arranged themselves?" Sarah asked, gesturing to the circle they'd all refused to sit in, except for Mrs Winchester, still sipping port.

"You thought we would sit around in a circle like we're in an AA meeting, and one of us would stand up and confess?" Terry said, turning to the window. The rain had started again. "I've got nothing to get off my chest—except that when I find out which of you killed Sally, I hope you can outrun me."

"Outrun you?" Sarah replied dryly. "You're an old man now, Terry. None of us are running anywhere."

"Fifty years," Joanne said, more to herself than anyone else. "That night ruined everything. I just wanted to start my life… and if I could go back and trade it all in…" Her eyes darted around the room like something might pounce. "I don't feel safe," she said suddenly. "What if I'm next? Tracey wasn't even supposed to be there that night. She only came to the pub because of me. We hadn't been friends long. We bonded at a bus stop over our overbearing mothers." Tears rolled unchecked now. "What if we're being picked off, one by one, until only one person's left standing?"

"And then what?" Terry cried, throwing his hands out. "Single yourself out as the last one standing? Stop feeling sorry for yourself. Tracey didn't just die because she was connected. She must've known something about what happened to Sally."

"But it was one of *us*," Phil said, quieter now, like he was talking to the fire. "There was that window of time after we left the manor and before you pulled the car around. We split up to find the missing bag. For a couple of minutes at most, but it was raining, and dark, and… anything could have happened."

"One of you must've found Sally," Ellie said, looking at each of them in turn. "At the phone box, maybe. You wondered who she was calling, and you realised she wouldn't keep her mouth shut. Who would've heard her scream in that storm? You drowned her to cover your backs. And then you took this."

She reached into her pocket and drew out the locket. It swung in a circle at the end of the chain like it might point at one of them. She didn't need to explain what it was—they all seemed to recognise it.

"Benjamin found it—somehow, somewhere. That's how he knew. Which means someone stole the locket twice. Once from Sally. Then again from him. And then you gave it away. To Tracey. A friend." She let the word linger, her gaze moving slowly across the room. "In her eyes, I think that title could've applied to any of you."

She let the silence grow.

"Catherine's going to be devastated," Mrs Winchester said. She wasn't speaking to the room, just stating the truth. "Tracey was a sweet girl. Loyal to a fault."

"She was keeping secrets," Ellie said, taking them all in. "Loyal to someone in this room."

No one answered.

"Well," Mrs Winchester said, sounding more disappointed than angry, "*that* was the time to confess." She looked around the room as if none of them quite measured up. "I dread to ask—where do we go from here? I could telephone the police and report that my burglars have *finally* confessed and that I'd like to press charges. I've been friends with the Chief Constable for years, and I'm sure the media would adore a trial this unusual. £52,000 back in the mid-seventies went a lot further."

"Rate of inflation from then to now is about ten to one," Daniel said quietly. "I was teaching it last week in maths."

Mrs Winchester arched an eyebrow. "So, a half-a-million-pound five-decade-old jewel heist. I imagine it would make quite a bit of noise in *The Times*, if that's what you all want." She turned her attention back to the room. "But the alternative is this—and I'm talking to everyone *except* the person who knows they're guilty— if that person is found, I will personally see to it that the rest of you face no repercussions for what happened that night."

"But how?" Joanne asked, her voice hoarse. "I've told you everything I know."

"The book," Mrs Winchester said simply. "If Benjamin knew the answers, he wrote them somewhere in there."

"But we don't have it," Terry pointed out.

"Sarah?"

"I left it at school," she said. "After rehearsals. But Ellie, you said you had a copy?"

"On my phone," Ellie said, unsure how that would help seven people squint at a single screen.

"Wait here," Phil said suddenly. He turned to Daniel. "Could you give me a hand with something?"

Daniel looked at Ellie, hesitant to leave. She nodded. "Go on. I'll be fine."

Their footsteps faded down the hall.

In the silence, Sarah cleared her throat. "Ellie, I know you don't trust me right now. You've grown into a bright woman since you were that little bookworm in my classroom. But just trust that we're on the same side." She turned to her aunt. "And Aunt Vivienne… I really am sorry I caused all this."

"Sarah…" Vivienne sighed. "Save it until this is over. Then we can talk."

Phil and Daniel returned, dripping from the fresh rain, carrying a large cardboard box between them. Phil dropped it heavily onto the floor.

Ellie's eyes caught the marking on the side. *2/2.* "You kept it. Which means—"

"*I* burned Benjamin's books," Phil said, dropping his head. "I was supposed to deliver them. Instead, in a moment of madness, I did the last thing a postman should ever do—I stole mail."

"But you kept one box as a souvenir?" Terry said, shaking his head. "That's sick."

"No," Phil said, kneeling beside the box. "I could only carry one at a time. A group of dog walkers showed up. I panicked, and I drove off."

He ripped open the tape. Inside were glossy, untouched copies of The Last Love Letter. For the first time, Ellie saw the cover in full—a stormy Devon landscape, ink-washed and windswept. Plain and simple, and they wouldn't have caught her eye on a bookshelf. A little mismatched to a romance, but given the odd contents, it fit right in.

"And why," Mrs Winchester asked coolly, "would you want to destroy these in the first place? Seems an extreme act for someone with nothing to hide."

Phil shook his head as though he didn't know why either. "Tracey kept bringing up the rumour that Benjamin had hidden something in the book about that night. She was worried it'd come back to bite us, and it was like she was trying to convince me that destroying the books was the only option."

"Like someone had put her up to it?" Ellie asked.

Phil nodded, retreating into himself.

"You know destroying mail can land you in prison?" Mrs Winchester exclaimed as she turned the book over in her hands. "You tried to destroy the story, but what about the author? Did you kill him?"

"I didn't," Phil said quickly. "I swear."

"Did you steal my manuscript?" Mrs Winchester continued.

"No."

She looked to the others. "Terry? Joanne?"

"Not me," Terry grunted.

Joanne just shook her head.

Mrs Winchester exhaled and reached for the bell on the side table. She gave it a single sharp ring and announced, "Then I think we're going to be here for a while. Ah—Jeffrey, would you top up my drink and perhaps fetch some coffee for our guests? I think we're going to need it."

"I don't have to stay for this," Terry muttered.

"Then don't," Mrs Winchester said flatly.

He huffed and grabbed a copy, flipping it open. Sarah took two, passing one to Joanne, who flinched at the sound of the page turning.

Ellie spoke up, listing off what they already knew— about the chapter titles, the first and last lines, the strange standalone storm scene. The room grew quieter as they listened. Then, one by one, they broke off and began to read.

When they were settled, Daniel came over. "Are we staying?"

"You go," Ellie said, suppressing a yawn. "See if they've made any progress back at my mother's. Two rooms working on it are better than one."

His brows twitched. "Are you sure?"

"I'm not alone," she said, nodding to Jeffrey as he poured another measure of port for Mrs Winchester. "Besides, don't you want to go check on your nan? See what trouble she's causing?"

Daniel laughed. "I wouldn't be surprised if she's got your mother in a headlock."

"I don't want that to happen," she said. "Not unless I'm there to witness it. Though… my mother hasn't been so *herself* lately. Something about Dad's return has softened her. Turns out they were getting cosy before he left."

"Love changes people," he said.

"I didn't say anything about love."

He smiled and kissed her. "Don't turn your back on any of them."

She watched him go, then looked over at Terry. He'd claimed to have loved Sally. The firelight caught the edge of his jaw, hollowing out his cheeks and showing the lost years. Could he have done it? Drowned his girlfriend in a pond for a few glinting stones?

And if not Terry, which of the rest of them?

She took a book from the pile and dropped into an armchair facing the fire. Tucking her feet under, she slouched into the cushions. The sting of tired eyes made the cover blur.

She looked for a clue, even a magic eye trick, but nothing.

Inside, she saw the dedication for the first time:

To Sally. For what never was.

The fire popped in the grate as the soothing rain drizzled down the nearby window, and the soft sound of turning pages filled the room. Ellie sat up, blinking, digging her nails into her palm. She needed that coffee.

She turned the page and reread the first line: 'The

final letter of importance came on the tenth day of the tenth month…'

Fighting the fluttering, she read on.

* * *

The increasing heat was gentle at first, dancing behind her eyelids like the edge of sleep.

Cosy. Safe.

But why were her eyes closed?

Ellie jolted awake. The book slid in her lap. She noticed a full cup of coffee beside her—cold, no steam rising in the firelight.

She wasn't in her gran's cottage.

She was still in the grand drawing room at Meadowfield Manor.

The fire roared, casting an orange glow across the darkened room. Someone had drawn the curtains, not a sliver of moonlight making it through. The heat pulsed heavy against her cheeks.

She frowned at the book, still open to the second chapter. She hadn't even made it halfway through. She'd fallen asleep in a room full of people before the coffee turned up.

She turned in her chair, finger marking the page. "Hello?"

The book slipped from her hand and hit the hearthrug with a soft thud at what she saw.

In the centre of the room, the box of books was burning.

Not a flicker. Not a spark.

Ablaze.

Ellie stared. The flames licked up the cardboard sides, pages curling black at the edges, the room pulsing with heat and light. She couldn't seem to move.

Then, she remembered the lilies.

She grabbed the vase from Mrs Winchester's side table in the half-light and tipped the water across the box, flowers and all. The fire hissed and gave a reluctant shudder before collapsing into smouldering smoke.

But just before it died, in the second before the light extinguished, Ellie saw something.

A figure.

She blinked. Smoke suffocated the air, rolling like fog. The fireplace light flickered weakly, just enough to catch an outline at the far end of the room. Unfocused, like an old film projector with a dying bulb.

Still holding the vase, Ellie crossed to the window. She threw the velvet curtains wide, glancing back over her shoulder.

The figure moved.

She shoved open the window with one arm and fanned the smoke from her face with the other, coughing. The night air blew in, damp and refreshing.

"Who's there?" Ellie asked, backing into the open window, one hand behind her on the frame.

No answer.

Then, something flew through the smoke and dark. A marble bust smashed onto the floor in front of her, hard enough to make her hop back, the split face of a man skimming against the white tip of her shoe.

She looked up, eyes stinging.

A second object hurtled towards her—a crystal decanter. It crashed against the wall, glass exploding above her head as she ducked.

There was only one thing for it. She threw the vase.

It missed, exploding against the wooden floor with a hollow thunk, scattering glass in all directions.

The door burst open. Jeffrey appeared, pale and confused, a fire extinguisher clutched tight to his chest.

"I smelled smoke," he said, flicking on the light switch. The chandelier buzzed to life above them, illuminating the scorched box.

Another door slammed on the other side of the room.

"That decanter was two hundred years old!" he gasped, stepping inside and catching sight of the broken glass. "Miss Swan, what on—"

"Where does that door lead?" she interrupted, already moving, weaving past the smouldering box. Her heart thudded in her chest. The crystal knob slipped in her grip, her hands slick with sweat. She wiped them on her jeans and tried again. This time it gave.

She pushed through into a formal dining room. Empty. Grand and echoing, with doors in three directions.

"Where is everyone?" she called, spinning back. "And why was I left alone in the dark?"

Jeffrey gave the smouldering box a few cautionary blasts of the foamy extinguisher.

"Mrs Winchester noticed you'd nodded off," he said, measured as ever. "She assumed you must be exhausted from your investigation, and she suggested the others transfer to the library so you could rest."

"They're still there?"

He nodded. "As of ten minutes ago when I topped up their coffee."

"Can you take me?"

"Of course, Miss Swan. This way."

He led her down a long corridor of parquet flooring, dark oil portraits watching from the walls. The hush of the house rang in her ears, and the lingering scent of smoke clung thick in her nostrils, turning her stomach.

The library door creaked as Jeffrey eased it open.

Only Phil was there, standing beside an armchair, not reading—just holding the book as if he'd forgotten what it was for.

"Where is everyone?" she asked.

Phil shrugged. "I don't know."

Footsteps echoed from separate directions. A door opened, and Terry appeared, then Sarah from the other side, each stepping in as if nothing were amiss.

"Where were you?" Ellie demanded.

"Toilet," Terry said, thumbing over his shoulder. "Is that not allowed?"

"I was showing Joanne out," Sarah added. "She has a headache and wanted to catch the late-night chemist."

She gave Ellie a once-over. "I was thinking—we should move this to The Old Bell. Give Jeffrey a break from us loitering. You're welcome to join us."

Ellie blinked. Her mind hadn't caught up—it felt like waking three chapters ahead of where she'd left off, all from one careless nap.

"Which one of you just tried to kill me?" she asked.

None of them offered an explanation.

"What happened?" Sarah asked at last.

"I woke up to a box of burning books before someone tried throwing marble and glass at my head."

"What's in the coffee, Jeff?" Terry said, half-laughing. "I'm voting pub too. I need a pint."

They started gathering books like this was any other night, like it was really a book club. Like Ellie hadn't just accused them of attempted murder.

"Oh, Ellie—before I forget," Sarah said, rummaging in an oversized bag Ellie hadn't seen earlier. "I ran back to the car while I walked Joanne to the gate. Grabbed these." She handed over the manuscript and the half-burnt book. "Pass on my apology to your gran. I should have just asked."

"I thought you left them at the school?" Ellie recalled.

"My car was parked at the school," she said, looping the bag back around her arm. "If you change your mind about the drink, we might be at the pub for a while."

The group drifted out. Sarah, Terry, with Phil

323

trailing behind, like the night hadn't warped at the edges.

Ellie stood in the quiet, clutching the books to her chest. The size of the house seemed to compress around her.

"Shall I telephone for the police, Miss?" Jeffrey asked, hovering nearby.

"I'll do it," Ellie said, steadying herself. "I should get back to my family."

She turned to go.

"Miss," Jeffrey said again. "Before you go… just one thing. Those chairs in the drawing room—"

She turned back.

"I arranged them," he said. "Before anyone arrived."

Then, with his usual quiet dignity, he bowed and disappeared into the depths of the manor.

Ellie wandered back towards the drawing room, footsteps slow. It wasn't until she reached the door and saw the circle of chairs arranged around the books— neat, deliberate, like petals around a flower—that she realised what the butler had meant.

Chapter 21
Locked In

Ellie paused at the edge of the green.

Across the road, the four of them filed into The Old Bell—Terry, Sarah, Phil, Joanne. They weren't speaking, but they didn't need to. She wondered how many secret meetings there'd been over the years. Had they ever all been in the same room again before now? Or had they stuck to chance encounters, doorstep chats, and polite nods between post deliveries and soap purchases?

Or maybe they'd done the opposite and denied it. Not just to each other, but to themselves. When the postman dropped off a letter at Lovely Bubbly, it wasn't anything more than that. Not a visit between two people bound by a night they never talked about.

But they must have known.

Even if they'd tried to forget, even if they'd buried it… they must have known one of them was behind Sally's drowning.

Ellie's fingers tightened around the locket in her pocket.

If she'd stayed asleep a minute longer by the fire, she might've been the next to go. Another unsolved tragedy for the latest holder of the robin locket.

She watched the pub door close behind them, then turned and made her way to her mother's cottage.

The moment she stepped inside, everything else peeled away.

Her father was standing in the hallway in a pair of borrowed pyjamas, blowing on a mug of tea, hair damp from the shower. The pyjamas were ridiculous—bright pink, patterned with enormous cartoon cats grinning like they knew something—and somehow, it made her chest ache.

He looked up.

They didn't speak at first. He set the tea on the hallway table, and they folded into each other like they'd been waiting for the moment.

"Nice pyjamas," she said.

"You can thank your Auntie Penny," he replied, the smile just strong enough to be a lie. They both laughed anyway.

"They didn't go too hard on you, did they?"

"Not my worst interrogation," he said. His voice was dry, but his eyes were heavy. "And I think I've got an alibi this time. Apparently, it's difficult to drown someone at the church from inside a cell." He shook his head. "I still can't believe it. Another murder."

"And almost another," Ellie said, brushing ash from the sleeve of her coat. She still smelled of smoke.

They moved into the sitting room. The scent of Chinese takeaway lingered thick in the air—sweet and spicy, and the leftovers had long since turned cold. Daniel's nan was asleep in one of the armchairs, a cruise brochure open across her chest, the manuscript nowhere in sight. Penny was nodding off in the other chair, head lolling gently as she read.

Oliver lay sprawled across the carpet, half-reading, half-texting. Joey, if Ellie had to guess.

Only Carolyn was upright, surrounded by highlighters and sticky notes. She was muttering quietly to herself, lips moving around the words like she was back in a production, learning lines two days late. The sight hit Ellie unexpectedly. Familiar. Comforting. A memory of sneaking downstairs for water and finding her mother still up, still working.

Still there.

"Where's Gran?" Ellie asked.

"Kitchen," Carolyn said without looking up from her page. "With *her.*"

Just from the tone, Ellie knew exactly who 'her' meant.

"The ex and the mistress under one roof," Oliver said. "It's like Diana and Camilla all over again."

"I was never a mistress!" Carolyn said, far too quickly.

"And Angela and I were… separating," Peter added, voice soft, like he wasn't quite sure if it still mattered.

"She got here just before you, Ellie. Said she had something."

"I've got something for her too," Ellie said, lingering behind the sofa, too restless to sit. "Has anyone here ever almost been hit with a whisky decanter?"

"Yes!" Carolyn said at once.

"On a film set. Made of sugar glass," Penny clarified around a yawn. "And I think the script said it was brandy. Is anyone else reading the same line over and over and occasionally seeing double, or is that just me?"

"Did someone hit you, Sparrow?" her father asked.

"They tried."

That got their attention, and she told them everything—waking alone, the fire, the smoke, the figure in the corner, the marble bust, the shattering glass. And the same playing-dumb routine in the aftermath.

"Well, that explains why you look like milk left out in the sun," Carolyn said. "Near-death will do that to a person."

"Enough cups of tea," Penny declared, clapping her hands once and startling Daniel's nan awake. "Let's go to the pub. We all need a stiff drink."

"It's turning into one of those nights," Ellie said, rubbing at her temples. "But the pub's full of suspects at the moment, and I'd rather not mix cider with suspicion. I don't know where to look next."

"Hello? Whichever direction gets you out of this

village," Oliver suggested loudly. "Who's to say they won't try again? Pack a bag."

"Raid the biscuit tin and vanish, you mean?" Peter said, with a sad smile. "I had a lot of time to think in that cell, and I realised something for certain—running away made things worse. If I'd stayed and faced whatever Benjamin had found, maybe we could've cleared the air and worked together." He paused. "Maybe he'd still be here."

"Or maybe you'd both be dead," Carolyn said, not unkindly. "Don't do that to yourself, Pete."

"*Pete*, is it?" Ellie couldn't help herself, smirking faintly. Then frowned. "Where's Daniel?"

"He went back to the church," Penny said, drawing the curtain back and peering out as if she might see him on the path. "Something about black residue. Poor Tracey. She always said hello to me when I was out with Duchess. Never really knew her, but you recognise people, don't you, in a village like this? We're all Meadowlings. Another one gone."

Ellie felt the ache of it too now. That strange weight of injustice. And stranger still—she'd been circling Tracey as a suspect for days.

"Maybe this is too big," she wondered aloud. "Dad's out. That's what I wanted. Maybe I need to know when to let go. If I hadn't pushed the bookshop open so quickly… if I'd just waited… maybe none of this would've happened. You're not the only one who can blame yourself."

"Listen to yourself," Daniel's nan snapped, startling

them all. She was wide awake, looking right at Ellie. "Feeling sorry for yourself won't get you anywhere. You lot think life's meant to be fair. It's not. Not unless you *make* it fair."

Before Ellie could answer, footsteps padded in from the hallway.

Maggie appeared, carrying a plastic bag straining from its fabric contents. Angela hovered behind her in the hallway.

Carolyn turned her whole torso away, but her eyes locked on Angela like she might pocket the family silver.

"Ah, Ellie, you're back," Maggie said, relief in her voice. "I was starting to worry."

"And rightly so!" Penny boomed. "Someone tried to *kill* her!"

Maggie's expression crumpled. Angela stepped into the room, filling the doorway.

"They didn't," Ellie said quickly. "Which is the main thing. I'll explain. But is that bag what I think it is?"

"The clothes Tracey took home after the photograph," Maggie said. "You were right. Flat cap and all."

Angela gave a slow nod. "And you were also right to question the… gaps. Phone records show that Peter called for the ambulance at four minutes past midnight, long before the photo was taken."

The win of the concrete evidence settled on Ellie slowly, like warmth returning to a frozen hand.

"Here, put this on," Ellie said, tossing the coat to Oliver.

"Ooo, dress-up," he said, wriggling it over his arms. "Is this the only colour it comes in?"

"That is evidence," Angela warned from the doorway.

Oliver sniffed. "Nothing in the pockets."

He tugged at the sleeves. "It's tiny. And there's something on it."

Ellie stepped forward, pressing the flat cap onto his head. Her fingers caught on something rough.

"Here too," she said, brushing the fabric. "Black. Chalky. Smells like fire." Just like what they'd found at the church. "Dad, put your coat and hat on."

Peter blinked up from the sofa. "Oh. I... can't remember the last time I had my hat."

"Happy to reunite you with the raggy old thing," Angela said, pulling a sealed evidence bag from her pocket and tossing it to him.

Peter caught it, gave her a wary look, and opened it. He perched the cap on his head and stood beside Oliver.

"It's close enough," Ellie concluded.

"Close enough to fool the whole village," Maggie agreed.

Ellie should've felt vindicated. Her gut instinct had been right. The timeline, the photo, and the shape of the man in the frame. But her father was already free, and all it confirmed was that Tracey had been the accomplice.

Someone else had dressed up as Peter Cookson that night.

"I need to go," Angela said, already gathering her things. "Peter—stay out of trouble."

"Don't you owe him an apology?" Maggie asked. "For treating him like a murderer?"

"I was doing my job," Angela replied without pause, heading for the door.

"Hmm," Carolyn muttered, flipping back through the manuscript. She underlined something firmly. "Temper, temper." She flicked her highlighter again. "And another ten. 'Ten cows in the field' this time, which makes it… how many, Penny?"

Penny perked up, consulting her notes. "Ten, actually."

"I'm on the final chapter," Carolyn boasted. "As an actor, you learn to read fast and still spot the details."

Ellie leaned against the doorframe, eyes drifting to the book in Carolyn's lap. She'd noticed it too. Ten chapters. The word 'ten' scattered like crumbs throughout.

There was a soft knock at the door. The letterbox rattled. Through the flap, Ellie saw a pair of glasses and Daniel's flushed face squinting in.

She opened the door. His cheeks were pink like he'd just sprinted there.

"I thought you'd be at the manor," he said, catching his breath as he stepped inside. "Jeffrey was sweeping up the bits of a two-hundred-year-old decanter he's devastated was smashed. Said someone threw it at you?"

"I didn't see who," Ellie said, glancing at her fingers. The black smudge from handling the flat cap was still there. "You went to the church?"

"I did." He frowned, spotting the black stain. "I had a hunch and thought—what would *you* do? So, I followed up." He brushed his fingertips against the residue. "Where's that from?"

"Tracey's Peter Cookson cosplay."

Back in the sitting room, her father was sinking into the cushions, coat and hat now folded neatly beside him. He looked like he might drift off at any moment, but he was still fighting to stay upright.

Oliver still had the tiny coat and flat cap on. He'd taken to collecting cups and takeaway containers around the sitting room like he was the world's most theatrical barman.

"Right," he said, dropping into a thick accent and twirling an imaginary towel over his shoulder. "What'll it be, lads? A pint of mild and a knuckle sandwich?" He dropped the *Peaky Blinders* act to check himself in the mirror. "Should I start wearing flat caps?" he asked, turning his head left and right. "Or is it too... 'man who spends too much time outdoors'? No offence, Dad."

"What was that, son?" Peter said, his head turning slowly. "I wasn't listening."

"And we're back to normal," Oliver said.

Daniel, however, was staring at Oliver like he'd sprouted antlers.

"You look like someone who might sweep chimneys," Daniel said slowly.

Oliver turned back to the mirror and tilted the cap. "Yeah, maybe."

Then he stopped. His expression dropped, and he ripped the coat off like it had started smoking.

"Oh no. No, *no*. I just realised the last person to wear this was fake drowning a dead man." He shook out his arms, flapped his hands like he'd touched something cursed. "Demon out. *Demon out!*" He wafted the coat as if banishing spirits. "Anyone got sage?"

"Second drawer down in the kitchen," Penny called. "But save some for the shoot tomorrow."

"The shoot!" Carolyn touched the rollers in her hair, as if remembering they were still there. "I'm supposed to be in bed."

She glanced at the clock. Then at Peter.

"Ten more minutes," she said, easing back into her chair.

Penny gave Ellie a small wave and then, catching her eye, mouthed 'the glow.' She discreetly pointed at Carolyn, whose face Ellie couldn't see—but she could see her parents, seated either side of the sofa, their toes almost touching in the middle.

But Daniel was still staring at the coat. That same frown hadn't left his face.

He picked it up again, turned it inside out, and ran a finger along the seam of the inner collar.

"I knew it," he said, checking the hat too. "I know

who wore these before they ended up in Tracey's photograph."

Ellie's stomach twisted. "Who?"

Daniel held up the coat, fingers dusted with black. "And this residue—it's coal." He looked right at her. "This is Milo Perry's coat."

"Oh, not another new name to learn," Carolyn groaned, setting the book aside. With a dramatic swing of her legs, the moment of toe-touching intimacy vanished. Peter straightened too.

"I don't think I can cope with another late-in-the-day suspect," Carolyn went on. "Really, I only just learned Joanne and Tracey were different people when one of them died."

"But they live *here*," Oliver said, half amused, half stunned. "Don't you… pay attention?"

"I have a very busy schedule," Carolyn said, re-fixing a sagging roller with flair. "Though, for the record—rest in peace, of course."

"Of course," Oliver echoed solemnly before inhaling and turning to Ellie. "Half-sister, were we switched at birth, and is it too late for a mother swap?"

"I'll draw up the paperwork tomorrow," Ellie said, though her smile faded quickly. "But tonight, we need to focus. I know it's late—and I'm grateful for all of you still trying—but we can't give up."

"Peter is out, dear," Carolyn said gently. "That's what we wanted, wasn't it?"

Ellie nodded, but her mind wandered to the church.

To Tracey, limp in Phil's arms. To Catherine, tugging off her white vicar's collar with shaking hands. She couldn't let it end like that.

"Life isn't fair until we make it fair, right?" Ellie said, glancing at Daniel's nan—now fast asleep again, mouth open, head tilted back. Ellie was jealous, but not ready to follow. "Daniel, who is Milo Carr?"

"A student in Year 5. He's playing Bert."

"*Wait.*" Oliver raised a hand, taking back the coat. "Two things. First, I can't believe you're letting those children massacre *Mary Poppins*. Your ten-year-old Julie Andrews has very big shoes to fill. And second, are you saying I fit into a child's coat?" He held it up in the mirror. "And I'm not even on a diet."

"Can we be serious for thirty seconds?" Ellie rubbed her forehead. Her head throbbed.

"If you can laugh at it, you can deal with it," Oliver said, throwing the coat back at Daniel.

"Oh, that's very wise," Peter said. "Which philosopher said that?"

"Joan Rivers."

Peter nodded, though Ellie wasn't sure he knew who that was.

"Oh—before I forget," he said, sitting up straighter. "One of the officers let something slip during my last interview. About Benjamin's original statement. About the locket."

Ellie pulled it from her pocket, the chain catching on her sleeve. Peter stilled.

"There it is," he said. "Can I see it?"

She handed it over. He turned it gently in his palms, as if afraid it might fall apart.

"It looks exactly as I remember," he said. "And yet I never actually held it. Why would I? But it played such a big part in my life." He popped the clasp, revealing the tiny picture inside. "Benjamin said he found it at his cottage while packing to move."

"It was at his cottage?" Ellie asked.

"Wedged in the back of an old chest of drawers," Peter said, closing the locket with a tight pinch. "They took a statement but never followed up on anything. The officer said he'd worked the case in '75 and assumed Sally hadn't worn it that night. That it wasn't as important as they thought."

"But it was enough to start all this," Ellie said, her mind reeling. "Enough for Benjamin to dig everything up again."

She turned to Daniel. "You're sure this is the missing chimney sweep costume?"

"Last seen on Friday." He turned out the lapel and pointed to a stitched logo. "Milo's been wearing his dad's coat all week while we waited for this one to turn up."

"You might want to buy a new one," Ellie said. "This one's been used to almost frame someone for murder."

"To a ten-year-old," Daniel shrugged, "that might make it cooler."

"Ten, ten, *ten*," Carolyn muttered, snatching up her battered manuscript again. "He alludes to ten *ten* times."

"Over ten chapters," Ellie added, her eyes drifting to the pub's glow across the green.

Penny was at the window again, watching the night sky like it might change.

"Benjamin said it was a numbers game," Peter repeated what he'd said in The Burrows. "A simple one."

"But why ten?" Carolyn asked. "Why not eight? Or twelve?"

Ellie didn't answer.

Her mind was drifting. The coat, the locket, the photograph—they didn't point in every direction.

They pointed in one.

"*Amour Amici,*" Oliver said in a vaguely Italian accent. "Or is it French?"

"I think it's both," Ellie replied.

"I know *amour* means love," Carolyn announced, suppressing a smile. "I was in a French film called *L'Amour en Silence*—translates to *Love in Silence.*"

"How ever would we have figured that out?" Maggie muttered, sweeping in with a tray of fresh tea.

"What was it about?" Oliver asked, genuinely intrigued.

"A deaf woman falls in love with a mute man after they meet at a sign language school."

"So romantic," Penny sighed.

"I'm guessing you weren't the mute man?" Oliver teased.

"She wasn't the deaf lady either," Maggie added under her breath, tapping Peter's thigh. He shifted obligingly and she wedged herself between him and Carolyn—a familiar territorial manoeuvre Ellie had seen since childhood.

"I was the neighbour," Carolyn said, still proud. "She had a rich interior life that didn't quite make it to the script—but it was there, you know. Behind the eyes."

"On the DVD," Ellie said. "They cut your scenes and left them in the extras with the green screen still in the windows."

"Well, we didn't *actually* film in France, did we?" Carolyn said, leaning towards Oliver like she was about to spill a trade secret. "Leeds. But you'd never know."

"As fascinating as this is—" Ellie began.

"We *must* focus on the book," Maggie interrupted, reaching for her copy on the cluttered coffee table and rocking back into place, squashing Peter and Carolyn to either edge of the sofa. "So, *Amour Amici*? Half Italian, half French. It means love and friends?"

"I took it to mean falling in love with a friend," Ellie said. "Or love from friendship?"

"Is that a clue?" Oliver asked.

"Why go to the trouble of such a strange title?" Maggie mused. "And you're only on Chapter Four, Oliver?"

"You know I'm not a fast reader. I'm trying to really

absorb it. *Amour Amici,*" he repeated, trying a more French flourish. "*Amour Amici.*"

He squinted at the chapter header. "Ten."

"Where?" Carolyn snapped upright. "Because if it's the thing about the ten seagulls and the pasty, I caught that one hours ago."

"Okay!" Oliver raised his hands. "I don't like your tone right now. I didn't realise this was a race, diva."

"It is *literally* a race," Ellie said, her voice rising. "A race against the next drowning."

"I *do* need to be in bed within the next ten minutes," Carolyn said, fluffing her hair.

"These nighties," Oliver asked, shuffling closer across the fluffy rug. "What's the art direction?"

"Tasteful," she replied, lighting up. "Classy, you know?"

"And now I remember why we're all rarely in the same room at the same time," Ellie said, more to herself. Cupping her hands to her mouth, she called, "Guys—please. Focus."

"The other chapters all have ten letters," Daniel said calmly, finally looking up from the manuscript he'd been quietly reading. "Ignoring the spaces and the one apostrophe… I've double-checked."

"That might explain why they're so odd," Maggie said. "He was forcing each title to fit a pattern. Vaguely romantic, always ten letters."

"We tried reading that final letter backwards," Penny added. "Word by word, letter by letter. Through a mirror. Upside down. Nothing."

Ellie dug into her bag, flipped past the stack of threatening letters and found her notes. She laid them out:

1. Tender Kiss
2. Love Unveil
3. Heartswell
4. Amour Amici
5. Forever Him
6. Lovers Path
7. Beloved Ada
8. Forever Her
9. Love's Drama
10. Heartsouls

"Ten mentions of ten," Ellie repeated. "Ten chapters, ten letters in each title… and Benjamin left them off the early manuscript. Maybe to keep them secret. Or maybe he hadn't thought of them yet."

Her fingers grazed the locket in her pocket as her eyes landed on the stolen *Mary Poppins* jacket resting over the back of the sofa.

She already had a name in her mind.

Mentally, she counted the letters in their name.

"Tenth letter," she said, her mind spinning back to the first line. "'The final letter of importance came on the tenth—'"

"In other words…" Maggie said slowly, picking up the thread, "… the tenth letter is important?"

"Do the final letters of each chapter title spell something?" Ellie called out.

"Oh! I made a note of those," Peter said, rifling through his pages. "They struck me as odd."

He mumbled to himself, running down the line.

"S… L… L… I… M… H… A… R… A… S."

"Sllimharas," Ellie said, trying it aloud.

"Sounds delicious. I'll order two," Oliver said without missing a beat.

"Could be an anagram?" Maggie suggested, scribbling on her pad.

"Or coordinates," Peter said, his pen scratching at his tatty hair. "Or maybe each letter represents—"

"No," Ellie interrupted softly. She knew what she was looking for now. "Mother, you were right."

"I *told* you!" Carolyn chirped. "Right about what?"

"Bookends," Ellie said. "The first words of the book are 'the final letter'. And the last word is 'backwards.'"

"Read that word backwards," Maggie said, flapping her finger at Peter's notes. "That's what Benjamin meant. *The final letter… backwards.* It's a puzzle. And being a typical accountant, he couldn't make it straightforward."

"I *knew* I noticed something," Carolyn muttered, satisfied, mostly to herself.

Abandoning her notepad, Ellie slipped out of the room. The locket was clenched so tightly in her hand she could feel its edges digging into her palm. Cold and sharp, like a warning.

"Ellie?" her father called, hurrying after her. "What is it?"

She stopped in the hallway, her jaw set as she stared across at the glow of the pub. "You said Sally went to The Old Bell that night," she said, her voice tight. "To ride out the storm. With her boyfriend… and someone she didn't like from work?"

Peter nodded, squinting back into his past. "Sally would talk about her sometimes. If Sally did anything wrong at work, she'd amplify it, and she was always reporting back to Benjamin as if Sally was difficult to work with. I know there was a brief period where Sally and Benjamin tried to patch things up, but this woman seemed intent on driving a wedge between them." He paused. And then, as if it had just come to him, said, "She was that old schoolteacher of yours. Benjamin's first fiancée, when he was in that rock band."

"Benjamin Brown was *not* in a rock band," Carolyn said, appearing from nowhere like a spectre in a glistening sheet face mask. She drifted towards the stairs, hair still in rollers. "He was in a *folk* band."

"Well, it all sounded like noise to me," Peter grumbled. "Same difference."

"And that's how rumours start," Carolyn replied. "He said, she said—"

"By the seashore?" Peter finished.

Carolyn let out a giggle. A real one. Ellie couldn't remember the last time she'd heard it.

"It's funny," Carolyn said, lingering at the bottom step, adjusting a roller in the reflection of a picture frame. "Benjamin actually played the fiddle and used to sing sea shanties. His band kept the crew entertained during night shifts. Shame what happened to him. He could've been a real musician."

"Or," Ellie said, "he could have still become an accountant."

"Peter," Carolyn called back as she ascended the stairs, "if you're staying, sleep in the guest room. I'll padlock the greenhouse if I have to."

She climbed a few steps, then stopped. "Penny! Can you do me a tiny, little favour?"

A beat. "Yes?"

"Make up the guest bedroom."

Carolyn continued upstairs. Ellie watched her father watching her mother for only a split second, relieved to catch Daniel's eye at the far end of the hall. Her father slipped back into the sitting room. Whatever that had been, Ellie was glad to be out of it.

"This might be the strangest night of my life," she whispered. "I don't know what's scarier—waking up to a box of burning books, or my previously highly estranged parents flirting."

She looked down at the locket, still in her hand.

She opened the door. Across the green, the lights of The Old Bell burned bright.

She knew what she needed to do.

"Are you sure it's her?" Daniel asked behind her.

"Benjamin was sure."

"But are *you*?"

Ellie stepped outside, unsure how to answer. Instead, she held out her hand.

"Do you finally want to come for that drink we keep missing? Just the two of us."

"Now?" he asked, but he took her hand anyway. "Where?"

"There's only one choice tonight," Ellie said, starting across the village green. "The Old Bell—back to where it all started."

She didn't look back, Daniel's hand firm in hers.

"Let's go find out how sure I am."

Chapter 22
The Long Way Around

The moment Ellie and Daniel stepped into The Old Bell, the thud of darts meeting cork rang out, followed by a jubilant cry.

"Bullseye!" Sylvia cried, her dart still quivering in the board. A hulking man beside her muttered something into his pint. "Just a little something I picked up in my university days," she said, smugly wiping her hands on a pub napkin. Her lips and mouth were stained the colour of red wine.

"Sylvia?"

"Ellie!" She turned to them, voice louder than usual. "What can I get you? We were just raising a toast or two to Tracey. It's affected us all so deeply—such a terrible, terrible shame."

"Sylvia—"

"How's the case going? Anything I can do to help?" Sylvia leaned against the bar now, steadying herself with one elbow. Still upright. Just. "Are you being followed again?"

"You could tell me if you've seen—"

"The thieves?" Sylvia cut in with a whisper that still carried. She tilted her head towards the far corner of the pub. "Last I saw, back there. Plotting something, no doubt."

She took a sip of something sharp, then added, more quietly, "Oh—and I did have a thought. I heard there was black residue found at the scene?"

She was teetering between tipsy and theatrical, but trying for composure.

"Remember what I said about my digital radio being stolen?"

"It's not oil," Ellie said. "It's coal."

"Coal?" Sylvia frowned. "From a fireplace?"

"From a prop cupboard," Daniel said, ducking to glance under the bar's polished arch through to the pub's back room. "I can see them. They're a few drinks in. They're… reading."

"Keeping up appearances," Ellie said. "Or at least one of them is. The rest have Mrs Winchester's pardon dangling like a party favour. Not exactly the prize they wanted when this all began back in 1975."

"I'm feeling a bit left out of the loop, and that makes me itchy," Sylvia said, hooking an arm around Daniel's shoulder and throwing a wink Ellie's way. "Daniel, be a gentleman. Catch me up to speed."

Ellie didn't need a second hint.

She crossed the room, her shoes muffled by the

pub's faded carpet. At the corner table, three of them sat beneath a battered wall sconce: Terry, Phil, and Joanne. Pints half-drunk, a copy of *The Last Love Letter* each, open to pages that no one seemed fully reading.

Sarah Mills looked up from the book. "Ah. You decided to join us."

The others barely glanced up. Not hostile. Just weary. Ellie pulled out the empty chair, but she decided to stay standing.

"Can you all remind me of your alibis again?" Ellie asked, her voice steady. "For when Tracey died. Terry, you were…"

"At the garage."

"And the two of you were at the manor, getting ready?" She turned to Sarah and Joanne.

Joanne gave a shallow nod, glancing at Sarah.

"Arranging chairs," Sarah said. "Like I told the police."

"But you were wet," Phil cut in. "Both of you were soaking when I arrived."

"We ran down to the gates to open them," Sarah replied.

"They opened automatically the first time I visited," Ellie said, the memory landing fast and cold. "Jeffrey did it from the house."

"They're not always reliable," Sarah replied as fast.

"Neither are alibis," Ellie said. "I know you didn't arrange any chairs."

"You *know*, do you?" Sarah's voice was soft, but her gaze was hard as glass.

Ellie felt her face warm, but she didn't look away.

"Sarah, how long were you in a relationship with Benjamin?"

"Three years."

"Long enough to live together."

"No. Not before marriage. My mother wouldn't have liked that."

"But you visited his house?"

"Yes."

"Half of the week?"

Sarah hesitated, breaking the tension with a light laugh. "I suppose? What's the point of this?"

"That you had space there," Ellie said, revealing her point. "Somewhere to put things?"

"A whole chest of drawers, actually."

"Ah. *There* it is." Ellie reached into her pocket. "That's where you hid this."

She tossed the locket onto the table. It clinked against the pint glasses, sharp as a bell.

"Did you panic when you realised it was gone?" Ellie said, looking at Sarah and only Sarah. "It was wedged at the back of the drawers. Annoying when that happens, isn't it? You put something in to keep it safe, and by magic, it falls down the back, never to be seen again. Except, this one came back after all this time. Benjamin found his sister's missing locket when he was packing to leave, finally ready to let go of the past. A past you used to be part of, Sarah. I'm going to assume you're the only person around this table who had access to Benjamin Brown's house in 1975?"

Phil and Joanne looked stunned.

"I'll admit I nicked a telly off him in '97," Terry offered, "but no, I didn't leave a locket in some drawers. And the telly was crap."

"But you *could* have," Sarah snapped, her voice too loud for their quiet corner of the pub. "Really, Ellie? That's a long leap without a bridge."

"Do you want my workings, Miss Mills?" Ellie asked, the quick-fire reply raising an eyebrow from her old primary school teacher. "Turn to the contents page of Benjamin's manuscript and read the final letter of each chapter backwards, or in a list like this, bottom to top."

"No way," Terry muttered, a grin flickering. "There. It. Is."

"Sarah Mills," Phil said flatly, staring at her.

"You're in it," Ellie said. "Chapter Seven. A woman called Ada walks into a pub—just like this one—on a stormy night. She tempts a woman named Margaret into ransacking an old flour *mill* farmhouse full of heirlooms. Sound familiar?"

Sarah didn't blink. That teacher's mask of hers didn't so much as twitch.

"It proves Benjamin thought what you're thinking," Sarah said coolly. "Not the same as proof. I've given the police my alibi, as has Joanne. Haven't you?"

Joanne didn't answer. She was staring at the manuscript's table of contents, eyes scanning the words over and over. Down and then up. Her lips moved silently over the letters.

And Ellie could see it—Sarah's story fitting into the spaces Benjamin had left behind. Not just one secret. Layers. Threads knotted and rewoven.

"You kept the jewellery," Ellie said to Sarah, quiet now. "You knew that house well enough to hide it. Not that anyone would guess from looking at you in your sensible cardigans. Maybe the studs in your ears are real diamonds. Tiny ones, of course. You couldn't risk attention—couldn't risk anyone wondering."

Sarah said nothing.

"But say you needed money," Ellie continued. "For something important. A *bribe*, maybe?"

Joanne winced.

She didn't say a word, but she didn't need to.

She was already cowering.

"Sarah paid off your shop's debts, didn't she?" Ellie said. "That's why you stopped speaking to me. Why the clearance stickers vanished overnight."

"A friend can't help another friend out?" Sarah replied, her tone gentler now, calculated. "It proves *nothing*." Her eyes skimmed the table. She was no longer speaking to Ellie—she was performing.

"It's almost like you rehearsed this," Ellie said. "How are rehearsals going, by the way? Without your Bert costume? Don't worry—it turned up. I'm guessing you told Tracey to throw it away, but she didn't quite manage it. That coat must've been tight, but from a distance…"

"What are you on about?" Terry demanded. "Who's Bert?"

"Ellie's right," Joanne said quietly, eyes fixed on the locket. "You did give me money yesterday."

"Joanne——" Sarah warned.

"I was grateful." Joanne's face twisted as she half-turned away from facing Sarah. "Too grateful to realise it came with strings until you told that story about us being together when Tracey died." She met Ellie's eyes, shaking her head. "I wasn't with Sarah. I was in my shop, paying off various different debts, all of which will have phone records. My clothes were wet because I'd run from South Street in the rain. Sarah was already at the manor when I arrived."

"And when I got there," Terry added, arms crossed.

"Me too," Phil said. "You were alone when I arrived, Sarah. I told you about Tracey, and you looked like you look now, with that cold, detached look glazing over your eyes." He gulped, joining Joanne in turning away. "You were soaked because you'd been out in the rain."

"I told you—to open the gate," Sarah replied quickly.

"But alone?" Ellie pressed. "You're saying now that Joanne wasn't with you?"

"I thought it would look suspicious if I said I was alone," Sarah admitted, placing both palms on the table. "I panicked. I improvised."

"But that was the truth?" Ellie asked.

"I'm telling the truth," Sarah said. "*Now* I am."

"No wonder Tracey was scurrying about doing your dirty work," Ellie said, a lump rising in her throat. "You lie so easily. Was the stolen manuscript in the school or the car? Did you reveal the location as a joke—or were you the tour guide for a robbery?"

She mirrored Sarah's hands on the table and leaned closer. "Did you ever tell Tracey the truth about anything?"

Ellie stared directly into Sarah's eyes. Sarah, in turn, looked straight through her. Phil had been right. That glazed detachment wasn't just a look—it was armour.

"Tracey didn't know you drowned Sally, did she?" Ellie pressed on, her voice low. "I don't think she would have been able to keep that secret for anyone. But you kept her close. Just like you sent my father those anonymous letters over the years, just in case he saw something he shouldn't have in the rain."

Sarah's jaw clenched.

"You *are* a good liar," Terry said, sounding the steadiest Ellie had heard him. "I've always thought that. And I know liars." He gave a thin smile. "You're right, Phil. I am Terry Ten Tales. I've got a mouth on me, so I know when someone's spinning a story. I saw it fifty years ago, right here. She *led* us all into that manor job. Said it was just a laugh, just a look around. But she knew where *everything* was. Every drawer, every hiding place. She'd cased the whole place."

"And we were just the sorry idiots who got sucked in?" Phil asked. "Just a bit of fun, we thought."

"But it wasn't fun for long," Ellie said, pushing away from the table, her palms sweaty again. "You drowned her, Sarah. You knew the woman you worked with, who you were always nitpicking, wouldn't keep your secrets. Your boyfriend's sister, who you were trying to push away from her. To what end?"

"Because you were always jealous of her," Terry muttered darkly.

Sarah snorted. "Please."

"No, it's true," Terry continued. "I spent so long discounting anyone who wasn't Peter Cookson that I didn't pay attention to the fact Sally used to come home from teacher training, crying about some way you'd humiliated her. I'd tell her, if that were two blokes in a garage, I'd think the one doing the humiliating was jealous of the other lad's work, and wanted to make himself look better."

Sarah didn't try to defend herself.

"You took her locket," Ellie continued, picking it up from the table again. "Then my father found her, and that was good enough. A messy but convenient explanation for people to believe. You let the village settle. You nudged a few people, reminded them what would happen if they started talking, and got on with your life like nothing happened."

Still nothing. But Sarah's expression was tightening, the crack starting to show.

"Then Benjamin figured it out," Ellie said. "You heard about it—of course you did. That's Meadowfield. My father heard, and he ran. But you stayed. You let Benjamin live until the night of the book launch."

Sarah's eyes withdrew to slits, and her mask slipped.

"Because I didn't think the idiot could actually

figure it out," Sarah said in a cold, flat voice. "He never had the nerve. But then, by a stroke of luck, all my nagging of Tracey about those books paid off, and they went missing. And the fool had to give himself away— he couldn't stop looking right directly at me as he toasted to his book. And I saw the sparkle in his eye. The knowing." Almost as an afterthought, she said, "I had to do *something*."

Ellie held her breath.

Phil leaned forward, voice low. "That sounded like a confession."

"It did," Joanne agreed.

"You waited for Benjamin to leave the pub," Ellie said, her voice sharp like wire. "You followed him to the pond. I bet he was often drawn there, never more so than after a few too many whiskys. You did to him what you did to his sister. And you took the locket again and left him, knowing my father would find him. Because of course he would. *You* were watching."

Sarah said nothing. Her hands clenched into a ball on the table, nails biting into her skin, leaving faint crescents.

"You slipped that note under my dad's glass," Ellie said. "It led him to a crime scene just in time to look guilty. Everyone saw him confront Benjamin. A broad daylight motive, and all you needed was for someone to witness him near the pond with another body."

Joanne looked away. Terry hadn't moved a muscle. If he was breathing, Ellie couldn't see it.

"But he didn't behave like you needed him to," Ellie

went on. "He made an anonymous phone call. Then he ran. Cowardly, yes—but not useful for you. So, you improvised. You walked to the school around the corner and raided the play's props cupboard for something close enough to pass. A chimney sweep's coat and cap. From a distance in the middle of the night, good enough. Then you told Tracey to meet you, and… what? You told her to stand at the corner and take a photo of whoever and whatever she saw at the pond?"

Ellie stepped closer.

"You were seen arguing on the green afterwards," Ellie said, calling Sarah's bluff. "Perhaps Tracey didn't like what you were up to. Or she didn't want to take the clothes you needed to get rid of. Was giving her the locket your way of smoothing things while also incriminating her?"

Sarah shifted in her seat, now staring into her lap.

"Tracey didn't realise that it was Sally's locket until I told her," Ellie said, dropping to meet Sarah's eyes. "But maybe that was enough to make her notice how strange your requests actually were." Ellie's voice dropped. "She trusted you. The teacher. The deputy head. Mrs Winchester's niece." Her final words jammed in her throat. "She thought you were her friend."

"Do you know what it's like?" Sarah said, her voice trembling with fury. "To be born into wealth but never able to touch it? Because your father can't stop betting on horses, and even though he dies before your seventeenth birthday, your own family still freezes you out?"

"I don't want your sob story," Terry said, calm and low.

Then—without warning—he swept the table aside. Glasses smashed, books flew. Ellie jumped back. In two strides, he was on Sarah.

"Don't say I didn't warn you," he growled. "I'm going to kill you!"

Sarah bolted, knocking over chairs, slamming into a couple trying to exit. Terry staggered after her, fury outweighing speed.

"I can't believe it was really her," Joanne breathed, stunned. "All this time... I thought you had the jewellery," she said to Phil.

But Ellie was already moving, tearing through the pub.

"Ellie? What's going on?" Sylvia called from the bar.

Ellie didn't stop. Further down the street in the car park outside The Drowsy Duck, a crowd had gathered around scuffling and screaming. People watched, but nobody intervened.

"Go on, get him!" someone yelled.

"I think that's a woman!" another voice cut through. "Give over, yeah? She's half his size!"

But Terry wasn't listening. He'd got hold of Sarah, dragging her by the arms through the cars and towards the pond.

Ellie reached them just as he forced her under. His face was raw with tears and hot rage.

"You took the only good thing I ever had," he said

to the bubbles crashing into the surface around Sarah's head. "I knew she'd leave me one day—but *you* took that from her too."

Sylvia charged, out of breath. "I wish I had my baton," she hissed, then snatched up a tree branch and cracked it against Terry's back.

Nothing.

Daniel and Ellie pulled at him, but he was too driven after a lifetime of wondering, too strong from years of working with his hands.

"Terry," Ellie said, levelling with him, risking getting within swinging distance so that he could see her. "If your love for Sally was real, you know she wouldn't want this. Let Sarah live with what she's done. Not you."

Terry froze. Then—slowly—he let go.

Sarah collapsed onto the bank, coughing, choking. A few murmured relief. Others watched, grim and silent, the truth sinking in.

"Sally told me you were trouble," Terry spat, chest rising and falling, still on the edge. "Even before you invited yourself to that storm lock-in."

"And I only invited myself because I knew *you'd* be there," Sarah rasped, struggling to push herself up. "Her lovesick grease-monkey with a bad boy reputation. She thought she could change you. Benjamin too. She was just too *good* for her own good. I knew if the stars ever aligned for me to get my hands on my slice of Winchester, you were the man to talk to." She coughed more water into the grass, peering up at him with bloodshot eyes. "Maybe all of this really is *your* fault."

Terry lunged. The crowd gasped.

Sarah scrambled away, slipping in the mud.

Daniel stepped between them—trembling, arms out—but enough.

Sylvia leaned on Ellie, catching her breath.

"How much wine have you had?" Ellie asked.

"Glasses or bottles?"

"What's the difference at this point?" Ellie said, watching Sarah struggle to sit up. "You don't happen to have handcuffs in that magical handbag, do you?"

"No, but—" Sylvia brightened. "Five metres of rope and a working knowledge of at least fifteen knots."

"I think it's time," Ellie said. "Citizen's arrest."

"Say no more." Sylvia pulled the rope from her bag, handed the bag off to Ellie, and, without hesitation, straddled Sarah and tied her hands behind her like she was a turkey ready for Christmas.

They pulled Sarah to her feet and turned her to face the crowd outside The Drowsy Duck. Phones were raised, flashes lighting up the dark. The flowers she'd laid the day after murdering him were at her feet, wilting and trampled, the card staring up at them:

I wish things had ended differently. I really do.
Your Sarah

"This was always how it was going to end for you," Ellie said, holding Sarah's tied hands steady as she struggled against Sylvia's grip. "Soak it in—your new reputation."

* * *

The air in Meadowfield had cooled. The crowd had thinned, the drama dissolved into murmurs and the distant rumble of a wheelie bin trundling over cobbles. By the gate of The Old Bell, DS Angela Cookson stood with her coat pulled tight against the night as Ellie approached.

Angela didn't speak straight away. She simply handed Ellie a paper cup of tea.

"No idea where Sylvia got it," she said. "Might be from the pub. Might be from her handbag."

Ellie accepted it gratefully.

"Do you know why she was carrying so much rope?" Angela asked, taking a sharp sip of her greyish tea.

"No," Ellie replied, testing her own. Tasteless and hot, but better than nothing. "And honestly, I find it's best not to ask. She has no filter and she *will* tell you, at length."

She took another sip. "I assume you've enough to charge Sarah?"

"Some," Angela replied dryly. "We can build cases for three murders, one attempted, historical theft, money laundering, witness intimidation, obstruction, coercion, and I'm fairly certain attempted fraud." She glanced sideways at Ellie. "And thanks to you, a confession in a crowded pub. Or was it thanks to Mr Brown's book?"

"He might've started us off," Ellie said, nodding towards the school across the green, tucked beside the church. "But in the end, it was Bert. The missing chimney sweep costume made me realise that only one person had access to every corner of the case. Cracking Benjamin's code was just the icing."

"I'd say I wish he'd chosen a more straightforward way to say it, but someone cut him off before his locket statement ever reached me. I only read it in full this afternoon. He *named* Sarah. Handed us a murderer, and nobody followed it up."

They stood in silence for a moment as the village stirred around them, neighbours drawn out by the siren call of scandal.

"Oliver said your mum and Peter are a… *thing*?"

"I don't know if I'd call it a 'thing'. But there's a… glow."

"Doomed," Angela said. "Probably. But good luck to them. She was welcome to him back then."

She smiled faintly and checked her watch. "Well done, by the way. I don't say that lightly."

Ellie looked down into her tea. "I fell headfirst into it."

"From where I was standing, it looked like you were charging."

Angela turned to go, then paused.

"Your dad's cleared. Officially. We'll issue a statement tomorrow. An apology for how he was treated in both cases. I'd recommend opening an inquiry into the '75 investigation, but none of the lead officers are still with us. Terry's uncle died years ago."

"Maybe there comes a point when it's enough," Ellie said, watching the police car ease away, Sarah stoic in the back seat. "From where I'm standing, the case is closed. We know what happened."

"They got in Sarah's way," Angela said quietly. "That's all. A quiet, easy life—interrupted."

She turned and crossed the street to rejoin her colleagues, gathered by the cluster of police cars.

Across the green, Daniel sat on the war memorial, leaning against the moss-covered cross like he didn't quite know where he was.

"Sarah really did it," he said as Ellie approached. "All that time. Our teacher. My deputy head. A *murderer*."

Ellie nodded. She was too tired for shock.

"I worked beside her," he said. "I trusted her."

"She was writing threats to my dad the whole time," Ellie said. "Using details she'd picked up in the classroom when we were kids. I've been tangled up in that old case my entire life, and I never even knew."

"A cold case no more," Daniel said, rising. "Thanks to you."

"You helped. Everyone did, in the end," she said, resting her head on his shoulder. "Let's see what's left at my mother's."

In the sitting room at the cottage, Auntie Penny was crouched over Daniel's nan, gently tucking a blanket across her knees with the precision of a nurse attending royalty.

"What are you doing that for?" snapped Daniel's nan, eyes flying open.

"You were asleep!"

"I was no such thing! Daniel, I'm ready to go home now."

"You live next door, Nan," he said, gently but firmly. "I'm staying here with Ellie for a bit."

She grumbled but didn't argue. At the door, she paused beside Carolyn's tray of immaculately arranged chocolates, slipped a generous handful into her coat pocket, and said, "I suppose the two of you should come for breakfast tomorrow. I'm making poached eggs."

She glanced at Ellie. "Do you like white or brown bread?"

"Oh. Erm. Either is fine."

"Well, I only have white," she said, and swept out.

"She only makes poached eggs on special occasions," Daniel said, nudging her arm with his. "She likes you."

"Don't push it."

Penny yawned her way into the hallway. "Where did you two sneak off to?" she asked. "Up to mischief, no doubt."

"Putting an end to some," Ellie replied, the confrontation in the pub on the tip of her tongue. "Go to bed, Auntie Penny. My mother will keep you busy with the shoot tomorrow. I'll explain in the morning."

"Fine," she yawned, already halfway up the stairs. "But I want full details by elevenses."

The house fell quiet. Ellie and Daniel stood among the wreckage of mugs, metal food trays, and the lingering scent of his nan's housecoat. Manuscripts, timelines, and scribbled notes lay strewn everywhere, remnants of the puzzle that had finally made sense, back to front.

"Now what?" Daniel asked.

Ellie took in the chaos. "Like you said, case closed. Let's tidy up because if my mother sees this place before her photoshoot tomorrow, we'll have another murder spree on our hands."

Daniel picked up a cushion and lobbed it onto the sofa. "Let's save some lives."

Ellie began gathering the manuscripts, dog-eared and tea-stained. But very useful in the end.

"All in a day's work," she said.

Chapter 23
Mrs Winchester's Final Word

A week later, Ellie and Maggie sat behind the counter of the bookshop, the bell above the door giving the occasional jingle as customers drifted in and out. A pot of tea cooled between them; neither of them had converted into full-time coffee drinkers yet. Maggie's glasses were perched on her nose as she leaned in to squint at the article on Ellie's laptop.

Sarah's full confession, printed in black and white. No denials, but lots of justifications.

At the end, the journalist added a small paragraph to state that Sarah had been paid for the interview and, at her request, a donation had been made to a memorial bench fund set up by the locals.

"A genuine move for atonement?" Sylvia asked, chewing thoughtfully on a wedge of cheese. She'd invited herself to lunch again under the loose guise of market research. Ellie had begun to notice the extra hole on her belt making an appearance, but the free samples were too delicious to turn down. "I'm not buying it. I'm not even renting it."

"Or a ruthless attempt at some positive spin before the trial," Maggie suggested as she added some shavings to a small cracker.

Ellie didn't say her thought aloud: that it wasn't about atonement or spin. It was one last way of leaving her mark on the lives she'd already taken.

"It didn't sit right with me," Maggie said, reaching for the tea. "We're raising funds for the bench, but I don't want anything of hers near it. It's not meant to be an ostentatious display piece. The reprint of Benjamin's book will see us right."

"So what did you do with the money she sent?" Ellie asked, though she already had an inkling.

"I asked Catherine if Tracey had any favourite charities. She said she used to volunteer at the food bank. I sent it there. Quietly. In Tracey's name."

"Oh, that poor woman," Sylvia exclaimed. "Since she passed, I've heard nothing but kind things. Sarah really got her wrapped around her finger. I heard Catherine's retired."

"I heard that in the café," Maggie said.

"Post office for me," Ellie added.

"I couldn't imagine her staying on," Sylvia said, lowering her voice. "Not after carrying that knowledge for so long. Unlike *some* around here, I won't speculate about what she *did* or *didn't* know, but it was generous of her to deliver that final sermon. Asking for forgiveness after admitting she kept Tracey's involvement secret all these years." She paused, then added, "I'd better get back to the shop. And don't forget to rate the cheeses on the little scorecards. I'm collecting feedback. This is market research, not a picnic."

"We'll see you at the garden party later," Maggie called.

"Wouldn't miss it," Sylvia said, already halfway out the door. The bell gave a chirp as she vanished into the bright afternoon.

Ellie stood and looked out across the shop. It was mild for once. Not frantic, not silent, but a hum of browsers, with a few cheerful voices upstairs in the snug.

It was the first day of June. The clouds had disappeared, and it hadn't rained since the day Tracey died.

"We're doing well," Maggie said, surveying the bookshop. "Busier than it ever was when I ran it. And even if it's not heaving, just look how happy people are."

She nodded towards a school-age girl curled over a book while her parents browsed historical autobiographies. The child's face lit up.

"New worlds to explore," Maggie said, inhaling as though she could smell every story within every book. "Exciting new people to meet, places you've never been to visit, and you can find it all here in our shop. That's why we're here!" She gave a nod, glancing at Ellie out of the corner of her eye. "And if you're using the shop as some sort of barometer to gauge whether your father's reputation has tarnished our establishment by association, let me assure you that after Mrs Winchester's garden party this afternoon, it won't matter. Speaking of which, we need to write a sign for the door. Not that there'll be many people on the streets."

"Are you sure enough people will turn up?"

A smile tickled her lips. "Mrs Winchester let the rumour slip that she'd put together a very select guest list—then proceeded to have an invitation delivered to every household in Meadowfield. Everyone feels like a VIP. Do you remember the last time a Winchester threw a party at that manor?"

"I have no memory of that happening."

"Exactly! Because it hasn't happened since at least the eighties. Everyone will be there. And after today, no one will have any doubts about who was behind those drownings." She caught sight of someone outside and lit up. "Oh—look at him!"

Peter stepped into the shop with a fresh, neat haircut and soft new clothes. He looked like a different man. Lighter. Rested. Still nervous, perhaps—but unburdened.

"Give us a twirl," Maggie said.

Ellie watched him, astonished by the change. It was amazing what a week of good food and undisturbed sleep could do.

"While I was getting my hair cut," Peter began, tugging at his cuff as though he could still feel the itchy hairs, "I had time to think. I want to get back to work. Maybe find a little place of my own to live. I could take up gardening again—or try something new. It'll be small, mind you. Rented. But it's time I had a little nest of my own."

"Whatever you decide, we're behind you," Maggie assured him. "And until you've got the keys to that nest, your old room's waiting. It's nice, having the house full again."

"Two readers and a birdwatcher—you'd never know anyone was home most nights," Maggie added, sticking a hastily made sign on the door before unlocking it. "Right. Let's get this over with."

Peter crammed his flat cap on.

"Oh, Peter!" Maggie sighed.

"What?"

"Your new haircut looks lovely."

"I'll need a hat if I'm out gardening, won't I?" he said, adjusting it just so. "It's not like it's a big fancy party. I heard she only sent out a few invites."

"Who told you that?" Maggie asked, arching a brow.

"Quite a few people," Peter said earnestly.

Maggie cast Ellie a pointed 'I told you so' look as they stepped out into the sunshine.

* * *

The lawn was sprawling, yet somehow still felt packed. Meadowfield had turned out in full force, and Mrs Winchester had planned the affair with military precision. Waiters floated among the guests like dragonflies, each tending to a small flock, bearing champagne flutes and canapés Ellie couldn't even identify.

From a patch of shade, Mrs Winchester observed the crowd from her throne-like wicker chair, sunglasses perched, expression one of quiet amusement and satisfaction.

"Well, this is a sight I never thought I'd see again," she said as Ellie approached. "I've heard stories about my grandfather Cecil throwing grand parties here in the twenties. Though I thought better of hiring flapper girls to come and dance." A wry smile tugged at her lips.

"If you're expecting a big speech or some grand, dramatic turning point—there won't be one," she added, her gaze drifting over the crowd with a hostess' shrewd calm. "But it's already happening. I pre-invited twenty of the most indiscreet women I know to an exclusive afternoon tea earlier this week. I gave them a few carefully chosen talking points: 'Did you hear Peter Cookson was falsely accused not once but twice? And that it was our very own wayward niece all along?' Then I told them not to repeat it, if they could help it."

She picked up a hand fan and began to waft herself with slow, easy elegance. "By the end of the hour, I suspect that's all anyone will be whispering about."

Peter chuckled, a touch nervously. "I don't know how I'll ever repay you."

"I owe *you*," Vivienne corrected. "My niece tried to frame you. And if I'm honest, I think I was the root of her resentment. She never asked for anything—not that she needed to, after robbing us—but she did want *this*. I never stopped to consider that she might have seen me as… flaunting it, especially after her father's downfall."

The fan paused mid-air.

"Jeffrey told me she once bragged in an interview. Spoke about her little system of how she'd take a piece of jewellery to sell in every new town she visited, each with a colourful backstory involving her old Aunt Viv." She sighed and said, "She never left a trace and tracked their value like stocks over the years, selling one or two pieces here and there. I hear the police found over a hundred thousand pounds in cash hidden in her house."

"She thinks she won," Maggie said with a sigh. "And I suppose… for a while, she did."

"Depends how you measure your life," Vivienne went on. "She never married. Never had another go after Benjamin. Perhaps killing your fiancé's sister puts you off romance. She advanced in her career, kept a pristine house, played her part, but she was still hiding. Even from me. It must have been exhausting always looking over her shoulder."

She lifted her glass.

"Anyway. Enjoy the food. The jazz band starts in

fifteen minutes, and the fireworks will send everyone home satisfied, satiated, and set right."

"What's next?" Maggie asked. "Fire-breathers? Parade of elephants?"

Vivienne grinned. "They weren't available on short notice. But I'm taking notes for next time." She lifted her glass again but paused. "And if any of you ever need anything, you only need to ask."

Peter hesitated, then blurted, "There is something, actually. This estate is beautiful and clearly well looked after. And if there's ever an opening in the garden… I'd love to be considered."

"Do you know your stuff?"

He turned and pointed without hesitation. "That's red campion. Over there, oxeye daisy. Those silver birches need cutting back, but not until autumn. And those drains." He nodded off to the manor's roof. "This garden must use a fortune in water. You could cut the bill in half with a proper run-off collection system."

"The water bill is astronomical," Vivienne admitted. "Have you got all your fingers?"

Peter held up his hands.

"Your own teeth?"

"Mostly."

Vivienne laughed. "Peter, I'm pulling your leg. Speak to Jeffrey. He'll put you through your paces, but he'll find the right spot for you."

"Sharp eye," Ellie said. "He noticed Sarah, didn't he?"

"He tried to warn me, back in the late seventies,"

Vivienne admitted with a sigh. "I was talking about a piece of jewellery that had gone missing, and she chimed in—'the one with the emeralds?'—just a beat too quickly. It slipped right by me. Jeffrey caught it. The theft kept me up at night, and he told me... and I told him never to say such things again."

She turned to Peter, took his hand, and gave it a firm shake.

"Welcome to the big house," she said. "Now go enjoy your party. You've got until the first trumpet for people to come over and say very sympathetic things."

"Thank you," Ellie said softly. "You might have just changed his life."

Vivienne paused. "I never believed he did it. Maybe you can't always tell when someone's lying, but you can usually tell when they're telling the truth. Or maybe I just want to believe that. Because my most regular visitor all these years was a murderer... and I rather enjoyed her company. I have to believe at least some of it was real."

She turned to Ellie.

"And you, Miss Swan. You put an end to it."

"I had a little help from Benjamin."

"Yes," Vivienne said. "He tried to do the right thing, in the wrong way. He wanted to stir the pot. I doubt he imagined his rather dull romance novel would set fire to the whole village."

She leaned in. "Personally, I'm more of a Mills & Boon fan. Do you stock those?"

"Of course. Dependable sellers."

"Put me together a selection," she said, settling into her chair. "I'll send Jeffrey round."

* * *

The following Saturday, the shop was full again.

After a week of steady footfall and flyer-fuelled curiosity, Ellie and Maggie were hosting their first official book launch: *The Last Love Letter – Expanded*. Benjamin's final novel, reissued with additions that turned it into something far more.

The new edition included forewords from the surviving members of the manor robbery—Terry, Joanne, and Phil—each giving their own unvarnished account of what happened that stormy night in 1975. Ellie had contributed a short piece on Benjamin's use of hidden words and backwards letters, his subtle breadcrumb trail that, in the end, cracked the code to his thinking.

And at the back of the book, among the extras, were scanned pages in looping, hurried handwriting. They weren't Benjamin's.

They were Sally's.

An early concept for a love story. A seaside setting in Devon. A quiet heartbreak of a love left behind. Her story. Her voice. Her fingerprints, in the margins.

Benjamin hadn't written a tribute to her.

He'd written with her and for her.

"They're getting grilled," Sylvia said, peering over her reading glasses at the signing table. "Compared to what Sarah did, what they were involved in barely registers."

"They wanted to be here to tell the truth for Tracey," Ellie said. "They came to us with the idea. And thanks for the help with the lawyer."

"No problem," she said in a naughty whisper. "It's technically not legal, but a small run of a locally published book when the copyright holder is dead… I'd say you could make enough for a memorial bench in that legal grey area. Now, I should get back to my shop. When this place is busy, so am I."

She swept out with a wave, leaving behind the last trickle of guests.

Joanne stood first, rolling her shoulders. Phil rose next, then Terry. None of them spoke to each other, and when they left the signing table, they didn't speak to Ellie or Maggie either. It wasn't another vow of silence, just the sense that everything that needed saying had already been said.

Ellie had heard that Phil was let go before he could retire, his career ending four months shy of its fiftieth anniversary. Terry's garage had seen a suspicious number of vans, as if his secret shop was being emptied. And Lovely Bubbly had already closed. When someone in the café asked Joanne why while Ellie queued for lunch, she shrugged and said, "I don't care about soap or my mother's shop enough to keep working into my retirement like she did," and that was that.

They were each off on their own path—tarnished, perhaps, but oddly freer for it.

Ellie and Maggie began clearing the signing table, stacking books, folding the cloth, and restoring the shop to its everyday rhythm.

"So," Maggie said, balancing a teetering pile, "your Auntie Penny gave me an idea in the middle of all the chaos. I put a pin in it."

"Go on," Ellie said, brushing crumbs into her hand from the counter.

"Why don't we start a book club?"

Ellie nodded, letting the thought settle. "Have you ever run one before?"

"Never," Maggie admitted. "But I'm sure we'll figure it out."

Ellie smiled and reached for a pen. "Why not?" she said, and scribbled on the notepad by the till with the gold pen Daniel had given her on opening day. To the bottom of the to-do list, she added: 'Start a book club.'

Outside, the sun burned down on South Street. A new season stirred the air. Her father was home. The long-held secret had been pulled from the depths of her family, and the past had been reckoned with.

And though she'd never look at the pond the same way again, the bookshop felt exactly as it should be: full of pages yet to be turned.

Thank you for reading, and don't forget to RATE/REVIEW!

* * *

Ellie and Meadowfield return late summer 2025
PRE-ORDER NOW

Sign up to **AgathaFrost.com** to never miss a release!

Thank you for reading!

DON'T FORGET TO RATE AND REVIEW ON AMAZON

Reviews are more important than ever, so show your support for the series by rating and reviewing the book on Amazon! Reviews are **CRUCIAL** for the longevity of any series, and they're the best way to let authors know you want more! They help us reach more people! I appreciate any feedback, no matter how long or short. It's a great way of letting other cozy mystery fans know what you thought about the book.

Being an independent author means this is my livelihood, and *every review* really does make a **huge difference**. Reviews are the best way to support me so I can continue doing what I love, which is bringing you, the readers, more fun cozy adventures!

WANT TO BE KEPT UP TO DATE WITH AGATHA FROST RELEASES? *SIGN UP THE FREE NEWSLETTER!*

www.AgathaFrost.com

You can also follow **Agatha Frost** across social media. Search 'Agatha Frost' on:

Facebook
Twitter
Goodreads
Instagram

Also by Agatha Frost

Meadowfield Bookshop (NEW)

Join Ellie and Granny Maggie in their Meadowfield bookshop for page-turning murder mysteries…

Peridale Café

There's always a cup of peppermint and liquorice tea with a helping of murder in the Peridale Café…

1. **Pancakes and Corpses**

Claire's Candles

Head to Northash to join Claire as she solves mysteries from her candle shop…

12. **Peach Blossom Peril**

11. **Spiced Orange Suspicion**

10. **Double Espresso Deception**

9. **Frosted Plum Fears**

8. **Wildflower Worries**

7. **Candy Cane Conspiracies**

6. **Toffee Apple Torment**

5. **Fresh Linen Fraud**

4. **Rose Petal Revenge**

3. **Coconut Milk Casualty**

2. **Black Cherry Betrayal**

1. **Vanilla Bean Vengeance**

Printed in Great Britain
by Amazon